I071344Ø

LAST RITES OF THE CAPACITANCE

Christopher Michael Carter

Supposed Crimes LLC • Matthews, North Carolina

This book is a work of fiction. Names, characters, places, and incidents are products of the author's imagination or are used fictitiously. Any resemblance to actual events or locales or persons, living or dead, is entirely coincidental.

All Rights Reserved
Copyright © 2017 Christopher Michael Carter

Published in the United States.

ISBN: 978-1-944591-34-2

www.supposedcrimes.com

This book is typeset in Goudy Old Style.

*"This is Dr. Angelique Puck of the Capacitance to base on a distress call.
My crew...they're all dead. S.O.S."*

The footage & journal entries herein are all that is left of the ship, the *Capacitance*...

Stem-Cam: *camera located at the nose of the spacecraft looking out.*
Deep space. Far beyond the outskirts of the Milky Way Galaxy. Dark. Silent. Empty, yet full. Uninviting, yet welcoming at the same time. No planets, no moons, no sun, and no satellites. A sea of black with distant stars appearing as pinpricks through a thick velvet cover. Moving ever so slowly into the void.

Stern-Cam: *camera located in between the rockets at the very rear looking out.*
The rockets, on either side of this camera, haven't been used in some time. Frost is evident. Some breaks away, floating outward, only to be replaced by more in time. Stars slowly become smaller at a snail's pace, while more darkness stays right behind.

Security Feed—Inside, Various: *every room on the Capacitance comes equipped with security cameras positioned to view the entire room.*
A slideshow of footage from all throughout the ship reveals a cold emptiness not unlike the space beyond its walls. Beyond electronic hums, sound is sparse, and silence is stark.

Room after room—vacant, silent.

Every room is made up to each crew member's lifestyle and liking: homey. And void of life.

The cockpit is empty as well. The control panel lights up and blinks by its lonesome while the window above it reveals the darkness beyond.

Labs are empty and darkened. Except for DocLab 7: sterile, lit, and occupied. A lone woman sits amongst beakers, blood samples, and microscopes. She works as though it's another day at the office, going through reports and making notes; an office floating around in outer space.

> *Capacitance* crew login 7575 profile:
> Dr. Angelique Puck
> Experimental Medical Scientist, Pharmaceutical Researcher & Engineer
> African-American
> Female
> 6'
> 180lbs

//

> Ship Journal
> Dr. Angelique Puck: Login: 7575
> Subject: **They're All Dead**

There were eight of us: Toni, Miguel, Harper, Stanton, Lou Ann, Chloe, Saxon, and myself, Angelique. I've been out here for a while. I'm starting this journal now because it's all I have. The others, my crew, they're all *dead*. We came out to space on a routine medical mission to find a cure for a growing epidemic. What we found was worse than what we were trying to cure. This isn't my first rodeo. It certainly never occurred to me this would happen to me. One never does, I suppose. They hear and see stories of tragedy and never once think it could happen to them, and when it does, the surprise is one of shock and awe. My usually exploratory nature has led me from attempting to secure the survival of millions of others to explore my very own survival.

My crew was comprised of hardworking talents in their various fields...

Toni and Miguel were a married couple, scientists I'd known prior to this mission as well as friends of mine. Lou Ann was always cold and was often known for her annoying questioning: her job, as she was assigned by corporate. She was a reporter of sorts, and regardless of personality clashes, she was fairly good at it. Harper was our captain, and Stanton was the pilot; they'd known each other for a while and had a great rapport. Both were "old world" men, hardworking and weathered. They were kind yet different with Harper the strong solid type and Stanton far more relaxed.

Chloe was special. She had everything we needed; she was young, eager to learn, bright beyond words, and gorgeous to boot. Chloe had a wonderful future ahead of her as a pharmaceutical researcher and probably more.

Saxon was a former soldier, strong-willed, and he stuck by his beliefs even if it ruffled the rest of our feathers. He was aboard for security purposes, though the others and I had felt it was pointless to have him there as it was a simple medical mission and we wouldn't be encountering anybody or anything, let alone anything *hostile*.

We were wrong.

We all took our training for the mission separately as our schedules wouldn't permit all of us to do it at once. I assume the others had the same cluster of testing I had: physical, mental, and technical. The ship we were to, and *did*, take is the *Capacitance*: a large spacecraft with plenty of resources for a crew of our size. I can't really go into all the details of its working parts, as I'm not a mechanic in any way.

Something that always bothered me about science fiction stories growing up was they'd have a biochemist or something onboard and, because they were *scientists*, all of a sudden they knew all the ins and outs of a spaceship. I found out early on this couldn't be further than the truth. I am an experimental medical scientist and wouldn't know how to change a blast pod if I tried. Luckily, from what I *do* know of the *Capacitance*, the bulk of the controls, beyond what Stanton used to steer, are digital and often operated by voice command, which I'm using to record this journal, my survival log, if one could call it that.

I am the last member of the *Capacitance* and not embarrassed to say I didn't think, in a situation like this, that I would be the one to be so. I made the trip with seven other individuals well-trained in their fields, and through unexpected mishap and tragedy, I ended up shipwrecked: a woman alone on an island, figuratively speaking, of course. Each member was granted so many resources so we'd all make it through our trek with no trouble. Everything was rationed—food, water, even air—with everyone having an adequate personal amount.

Once I realized I was the last one, I began my plan of using each set sparingly. I shut off each system, and when the one I would be using at the time would finally run out and falter, the ship would seamlessly switch to the next. I understand that could sound bad from a certain point of view, as if it's disrespectful to the dead, but the decision was purely survival-based. I didn't know how long I'd be out here and needed to take precautions.

The *Capacitance* is currently dead in the water with no way to fly it. The problems we ran into randomly took out a lot of our controls. I say *randomly* because I still have lights, air, and door controls, but our drive systems are down along with our communicators, so getting messages to Earth has been hard. I keep trying even though I have no clue if any of them are getting through.

I can honestly say that Stanton and Harper made this look easy. I'm not trained as a pilot and am no navigator, but I'm working with this system the best I can to survive and get through the universe to find my way home. I know I'm beyond our galaxy quite a ways, but I don't know my coordinates. All I see from the window is black. I won't lie—I'm lost.

Each struggle we'd run into on our mission, along with

redirections, would push us in a furthering wayward direction. There are no roads (or signs for that matter), no junctions, and no freeways up in space, no rest stops to ask for directions, and after what I've now seen, I'm not sure I'd stop to ask if there was one. I've been lost in the woods before, and while it's similar, it's quite different at the same time. Our navigation systems are down or else I'd find a way back to the Milky Way in no time. There's really no north star to follow when up here. Actually, while up within said galaxy, we can rarely ever see the stars: kind of bittersweet, really.

We spend all that time on the ground, wanting to be up among the stars, but when we get there, we can't see them through the solar rays. Of course, they don't tell us when we're children that the stars we gaze at and wish upon are long dead. Beyond the outskirts, where I happen to be, there are plenty of stars in the distance. These days, my excitement to see them has dwindled as when I do see them, I often see them crawling toward me. Ugh...my skin crawls thinking about it, so I try my best not to. Sometimes I can put the image out of my head and appreciate them for what they are, but other times, it's not so simple.

Other than trying to get back home, I'm doing as I've always done, diving headfirst into my work as my options are limited in my current predicament. It's taking longer to pinpoint answers without a team, but I'm still determined. I have breath in my body and the will to continue, so it's onward and upward, regardless. The diseases aren't holding off because of tragedy, so I shouldn't either.

I've found myself with plenty of time to think and reflect on life. Not having many friends is actually kind of a relief for me as I'm not really as worried as I would be had I had a large group of loved ones awaiting my return. Two of my closest friends I did have died on this very mission. When this mission started, I had a girlfriend, Serena. We were in a relationship for three years. She was afraid and hated that I had to go on this mission, and now I understand why. We came to find a cure, and what we found was death. I reiterate this once more to make it clear this was nowhere near what we were trained for or expecting.

This was an exploration I fought tooth and nail for. A simple routine expedition hit with horror and ending in tragedy and loneliness, not really what I had planned when I signed the paperwork and assembled my team. Loneliness is one of the first ailments humans tried to cure with the advent of social media and interactive artificial intelligence. Both things ended up becoming society standards as common as our very rights we fight to protect. My team wanted to dig deeper and eliminate problems from within, the diseases that haunt and torment so many, which led us here. Now I'm out here all alone with my work and this journal as my only companions. If I indeed survive this, I'm curious of the psychological consequences that'll occur.

I found it interesting that no one else had used this log. They all preferred keeping notes in handheld devices among other things if they, indeed, kept notes, but this journal was vacant when I decided I should start documenting what had taken place and so here I am. I don't know who will find this or when, but I'm going to keep updating—the last rites of the *Capacitance*, if you will.

First entry completed. Time to get back to *work*. Unfortunately, there's not a whole lot more for me to do. I can't get the ship moving. I can't contact base. I'm lost. I'm scared. I'm...I'm so far from home. But I have to keep going. I *have* to.

//

NEWS REPORT - NMC CONFERENCE
Streaming from the logs of the *Capacitance*.

Mounted on the wall of the ship's break room area, a screen lights up with a series of cataloged news footage. Dr. Puck stands on a stage while her name and title scrolls across the bottom of the screen. After the scrolling, the title "NMC COFERENCE" stays. Angelique is well-dressed for the event in a black dress with her hair up. She speaks to her audience, a who's who of those in the scientific community.

"Hello, all. I am Dr. Angelique Puck. As you know, different sections of my team have previously come up with new treatments and cures for various forms of Cancer and Lupus, but we've been facing another growing epidemic."

A holographic screen is revealed behind her with MULTIPLE SCLEROSIS in large letters floating about.

"Numerous diagnoses and cases of Multiple Sclerosis had ravaged the world and there was still no cure."

Angelique clicks a remote in her hand, changing the holographic image to Earth with sporadic spots of the world highlighted in bold red.

"The percentage of MS patients had gone up 65% in a year's time and continued to grow."

New Slide: a close-up of nerves appear behind her.

"Our nerves are covered in myelin, a protective coating. Think of it as the rubber or plastic sheathing over the wires in your computers. We have the same protection over the wires in our personal computers: our *brains*."

She works the remote again, changing the background to an inner look at nerve endings.

"Multiple Sclerosis is a neurological debilitating disease that dissolves the myelin, leaving the nerves raw and exposed, susceptible to a multitude of problems. With the myelin gone, so is the protection."

She changes the imagery to a plethora of medicines: needles, pill bottles, and bags of fluid. The holographic visuals seem to float as the words and images prior.

"We'd tried with medications over the years but nothing would stick for longer periods of time—no treatment had longevity."

Dr. Puck clicks the remote again and looks behind her at the image of myelin dissolving. The nerve's outer sheath decays, exposing the frayed nerve beneath.

"My team and I had attempted repairing the nerve's protective sheath only to find the disease would eat it away. But then..."

Angelique steps forward before changing the hologram to the solar system. It's beautiful and bright; an image full of wonder.

"...we found alien life."

A slight commotion raises in the audience.

She nods, chuckling.

"When this was announced, everyone panicked and expected creatures like they'd seen in the movies and read about in books." Talking with her hands, she holds her finger up. "Without taking into consideration that even the smallest living molecule not of the Earth would be considered an alien life form."

She stops, looking out into the crowd of listeners taking such information in, and then clicks the remote. The holographic background becomes a close-up of what appear to be tiny cells beneath a microscope. The tiny "mites" are black and chrome in appearance with no set form and move around freely.

"The microscopic beings we had found had great potential."

Another click and an image appears of Dr. Puck and her crew working diligently in the lab, everyone in protective gear.

"Through hours upon hours of testing, we found that with applying excess pressure, the cells would fuse together forming one cohesive organism."

Click: the same cells seen prior now fused together, appearing as one.

"We added more of them, and as we hypothesized, they melded together."

She changes the next image to a clear stirrer coated with the organism made by the bonded cells.

"We found that the organism would graft itself around an item in a sort of shell. We had been searching for something with this capability for years, and we had finally found it. It was *perfect*."

Angelique smiles and walks across the stage. Various news reports scroll across the bottom of the screen. She presses on her remote more, showing images of bionic limbs.

"For years, the multi-billion dollar medical and surgical industries were coming up with artificial replacement limbs, organs, bones, joints, and skin grafts, but nobody was coming up with synthetic wiring for our very human computers, and that's what set us apart from them. We didn't have the resources to make it happen, and now we do."

Click: she turns, revealing the holographic close-up view of the tiny space mites, now coated around previously exposed nerves.

"Finally, using our newfound gifts we'd found amongst the stars, we'd successfully made synthetic myelin."

The crowd applauds; however, there are still some with trepidation.

She nods and holds up her finger again. "There are still issues that come with the disease, but the trouble is nothing like it was. MS patients have undergone surgical procedures implanting what we'd simply dubbed the Nu-Myelin Cell, or simply, NMC."

The image becomes an even closer view of these grafted microscopic aliens: one cohesive cell coating the nerve.

"It doesn't repair any damage the disease has already done, but it stints any of the same and future problems. It can't eat at it like it does our natural myelin. The NMC is far stronger. Upon early detection, patients can get this surgery. It isn't cheap but it is beneficial. The percentage has dropped significantly."

Click: the view of the world on the holographic screen shows much less red marked spots throughout.

"As the origin of the illness is still unknown, it doesn't eliminate there being more. We'd found enough on that galactic trip to last a while." The holograph fades and the house lights come on. "We'd stored enough NMC to take care of at least two decades of new MS patients. Thank you."

Applause from the audience. Photographers start firing away immediately with bright camera flashes. Reporters chomp at the bit for answers to their rapid-fire questions. One fires at her right away. "Dr. Puck, what are you and your team doing about the growing outbreak of RNS?"

Uncharacteristically, Angelique freezes and takes a breath before workers off to the side point at their watch. She turns back to her crowd. "I'm sorry. I don't have time for questions today. Thank you all very much for coming out."

The audience applauds more, and Dr. Puck smiles and waves briefly as she's painted with the flash of multiple cameras before she exits stage right while reporters ask questions regardless. The streaming halts, and the screen cuts to black before moving on to the next clip.

//

THE RNS REPORT
From the *Capacitance* logs.

Rabid Neural Stasis (RNS) is an infectious, debilitating and dangerous disease for both the victim and those around them. RNS renders one catatonic and otherwise paralyzed until their personal space is crossed and, much like a human Venus Flytrap, they lash out. The rest of the body will remain in its stasis while the head will lunge to bite, though they have been known to pull the rest of the body while lunging. The bite is found to be infectious, spreading the virus. Once infected, there's no definitive time frame in how rapidly it will take

shape. The first footage of Rabid
Neural Stasis went viral years ago.

RNS VIRAL FOOTAGE:

The video is shaky at best and appears to have been taken by a cellphone. A young man is sitting up in a chair with his head tilted slightly to the side. His eyes remain open without blinking, blankly staring out into the world. His body, incredibly still, appears frozen with an arthritic strain to his hands. The voyeur walks closer.

"This is my cousin, Dave. We used to hang out all the time before he got sick. Hey, Dave, how you feelin', man?" The one behind the camera, a young male perhaps around Dave's age, attempts to get some kind of reaction. He's closer. Dave's mouth foams. "Hey, *hey*, what's goin' on? Aunt Clara!"

A woman rushes to the confined man's side. The boy steps closer to help his aunt. Still catatonic, Dave's mouth continues to foam while his mother and cousin stifle their panic. She tilts his head forward so he doesn't choke on the thick oncoming saliva. Dave's already-open eyes widen as he turns his head and LUNGES, biting into his mother's arm.

"Oh shit!" the boy with the camera yells. Clara screams while Dave's head violently shakes and teeth snap in a rabid state with foam and blood running down his chin. The chunk of meat taken from his mother falls from his jaws. His eyes, no longer calm and lifeless, are bulged and ravenous with his bloody teeth clicking.

"Aunt Clara, you okay?"

Clara, with tears in her eyes, is more focused on her crazed son than the large hole in her arm or the large amount of blood coming from it.

"Your arm..."

She looks down, sad and scared like her nephew, as the blood flows. Dave's teeth snap loudly off camera.

End of video.

THE RNS REPORT Cont.
From the *Capacitance* logs.

In time, the body will return to their near-comatose state until the next incident. The bitten will feel ill with flu-like symptoms along with weakness and sudden memory loss and soon will lose all function. Again, there is no definite time for such transformation as every incident is different. A number of nursing homes have been repurposed to RNS Care Centers in hopes to rehabilitate the patients. Rehabilitation of victims of Rabid Neural Stasis have proven futile and such centers are now for common and hospice care. Nurses and caregivers have become infected themselves, and some have lost their lives. Now heavy precautions are taken. Footage from a Care Center in North Carolina revealed how careful they've become.

SECURTY FOOTAGE, NC RNS CARE CENTER:

The room is very large. Almost all furniture has been removed. More than a dozen RNS patients sit in chairs, perfectly-spaced apart throughout the room in a grid pattern while the caretakers walk along the outside of the square, keeping an eye out. The patients are fed through IVs running along to the sides where the bags are kept. Everything is very still while the nurses remain cautious. When they step too close to one of the chaired "spaces", the patient's head whips in that direction with snapping teeth. Losing too many workers already, the caretakers stay at a distance. The room itself appears cold and sterile, lifeless. Light classical music plays overhead while the patients remain largely quiet beyond the occasional biting and clicking of teeth or gurgling of foam. The nurses have casual conversation while looking over the patients.

THE RNS REPORT Cont.
From the *Capacitance* logs.

Reports of Rabid Neural Stasis are spiking at alarming rates. Though this isn't what we expected it to look like, there are some who are calling this an actual "Zombie Apocalypse." It starts in the blood stream, attacking the immune system before moving on to the nervous system. To date there is no cause found with no original case to stem from. There is no treatment and no cure, and if this epidemic continues, there won't be anyone left to find one.
END OF REPORT

//

Ship Journal
Dr. Angelique Puck: Login: 7575
Subject: **Modern Day Plague**

I know a lot of people say that it's important to enjoy the fruits of your labor and to stop and smell the roses, but for someone in my profession, it's a bit hard to. It's bittersweet knowing how many are still sick and dying in the world no matter how many have been helped or saved. I've always found it hard to celebrate my current accomplishments when there's so much more to do. We'd taken care of a few virus baddies such as the aforementioned Lupus and its rare forms and other various ailments, but there was still a ways to go before arriving at what one would deem a healthy society.

As stated previously, due to our research and methods, the percentage of patients with Multiple Sclerosis has dwindled greatly. The first case of MS was said to have been recorded in the 1800s, of course not named until long after. Many methods were experimented with over many years, and we were always getting closer to handling this disease, but not close enough. We didn't get to space until the 1960s and didn't go to space for medical purposes for another hundred years. After we'd found the tiny organisms we used in the Nu-Myelin Cell (NMC) for Multiple Sclerosis and later with the white blood cell treatment they'd dubbed The Bouncer for certain cancers, we'd thought to set our sights on another modern day plague: Rabid Neural Stasis.

RNS has been around awhile but only in the last decade has it really raised its ugly head and become more noticeable. The number of the infected has only escalated and continues to do so. Those bitten either become infected or bleed to death, *sadly there's no middle ground*, while RNS+ patients/victims will either be taken care of to the best of the caregiver's abilities or die from lack of nourishment. Like Multiple Sclerosis, nobody knows where it came from. It almost seems like an evolution of previous diseases as if they, themselves, are living organisms. Maybe they grow and become something else and the things we *currently* try to fight are simply in a cocoon stage, then hatch and become something much worse. If so, our treatments and medicines have only stalled the inevitable evolution. Perhaps we've underestimated diseases and they are a lot more like human beings: growing, evolving, and RNS is the next step, the killing step...

Rabid Neural Stasis came in like a prowler in the night, infiltrated our society and slowly grew and gradually picked up pace in its spreading. The illness is relentless, and as there is no cure, there's also no treatment. Doctors have done what they can but hit a wall pretty early on. In order to get blood samples from patients, they have to be put under with tranquilizers at a distance.

The thought of RNS continuing is terrifying: a world of crippled, deranged people dying and uncontrollably biting at anyone who dares come close enough to attempt to save them. I'd researched and planned a long time for this mission; all of my focus went into finding the end of this thing. This was going to be the BIG one, the one to cure RNS once and for all. Though I was already proud of my work thus far, this was to be an accomplishment I would proudly relish in. It was and remains my hope and prayer that we find the answer up here among the stars like the diseases before it.

I would take a break after finding this cure, but I know I'd end up right back to work on the next disease. I don't have a list; I just pour myself into each one I work on until it's done. There are plenty of ailments to fight on Earth, so I'll always have work to do and I'll never be short on goals. The day time travel becomes possible, I'd love to go back and find a cure for my parents before having to lose them...

//

Stem-Cam:
Blackness peppered with twinkling stars. The view drifts aimlessly closer with almost no speed; a ship anchored out in the middle of a black ocean. There's no weather to speak of and no land in sight. The surroundings are thick, heavy yet simultaneously weightless. Depending on one's mood, it can either look wide open and endless or closing in and suffocating.

Angelique's Room-Cam:
Dr. Puck's quarters are nice and clean. A twin size bed with an end table, a small table with a chair across the room, a dresser, a desk, and a closet. Still in her one-piece suit, she lies in her bed, stretching before reaching over to her bedside table to pick up the book sitting on it beside a photograph. Angelique randomly thumbs through the book before picking a page and reading it. She's done, closes the book, and places it back. She stands up, sighs, and walks to the door of her room. Pressing the button to the side, the metal door slides to the side within the walls, opening. She exits.

//

Ship Journal
Dr. Angelique Puck: Login: 7575
Subject: **Support System Down**

I had amazing parents. We had the same problems as any other family unit, but I loved them, treasured them. They were my greatest support system. They always backed my exploratory mind, even when I was a child studying plants and insects in the backyard. I'm sure they thought I'd grow up to be an entomologist. I studied everything, as inquisitive as I was, everything from bugs to plants to weather patterns. I never really thought if it was hard for them to have such a weird kid; I was the type of child that would watch the weather channel for fun. But they were great and always encouraged my inquisitive nature even when I struggled in school.

My grades were horrible in middle school as I was always distracted by my own thoughts, theories, and studies. I had no real interest at all in things like schoolwork. I didn't want to learn about what already *was*; I wanted to learn something new to the world, something up around the bend. I had spent so much of my youth yearning for the future that I would hardly ever take time to enjoy or take in the present. My parents had eventually sat me down and told me the only way I'd ever become an actual scientist, a *real* scientist, is if I did well in school.

They explained it the best way they could've, using something I loved and wanted. They explained the importance of learning from the world's history in order to grow to learn something new, to discover something to later be placed in the same books. After so long of being bullheaded, I finally understood what they were saying. My grades increased by the time I had went to high school.

I made sure to be the smartest I could be, desperately wanting to make a difference in the world. To make the difference I sought I would need power, and my parents and teachers instilled it in me that knowledge was power, so naturally I wanted more of it. My parents also reminded me that it wasn't only holding said power that would make a difference but remembering to be a good person at heart. They'd ask me, "What good is having all the knowledge in the world if you don't know how to treat people?" The advice always stuck with me.

At college, I put in all the time and effort I could humanly give and graduated with flying colors, and I was ready for the world of big girl beakers and Bunsen burners. My parents were so proud they were crying at graduation. I stood up there at graduation as a proud gay, black woman who never fell into a stereotype and worked hard for my dreams, shooting for the stars, always having my proud parents' support. Not many could say that; I'd been pretty blessed.

It wasn't long after I graduated when mom and dad both got

sick. They started coming down with something after getting back from a cruise. We all assumed it was food poisoning of sorts, but neither the doctors nor I could figure out what it actually was. The cold symptoms faded, but they started forgetting things, showing signs of Alzheimer's. Mom and Dad soon became immobile, stationed in their bed. They wouldn't, couldn't speak or move. When I'd change their bedding, their mouths would foam, and in seconds they were trying to bite me.

I'd never seen them like that. It was as if my parents had become rabid. It was scary and heartbreaking at the same time. Two of the strongest, kindest, smartest people I've ever known turned into these...*things*. I had workers from the hospital come in and help me strap their heads down to keep them from biting. I couldn't get them to eat so I had them fed through IVs. That kind of nourishment can only go so far.

We continued to search with no answers to be found. At the same time, my parents were falling deeper into illness, an old professor of mine and I were still pushing for a project that would seek medical answers out of orbit. To my surprise, our trip got the green light, but after thinking long and hard about it, I couldn't in good conscience leave my parents here without me for an undisclosed amount of time.

I passed on the trip, and my professor continued on with the team we had put together. There were no hard feelings, and I stayed behind to look after my ailing folks. It was depressing and fast the way they were depleting. My childhood heroes and mentors were dying, and I had to come to terms with it. I spoke to them often, read to them, but it was clear to me nothing was getting through. With the way their biting tendencies were, I couldn't even hug or hold them. **I-could-not-hold-my-own-parents.** I would later find out this was happening to many more.

Sadly, my parents both passed away months apart. They faded before my eyes in between moments of cold stillness and ravenous jolting. I was happy to spend their last moments with them despite seeing them in their condition. I would've missed that time with them completely had I gone on the expedition. I love them and miss them dearly. It took a long time before I could bring myself to think they were in a better, painless place. I hope they can see or know I was with them throughout. I lost the people I loved most in this world to what would later be named RNS and ever since then, despite being swamped with work, I'd privately been doing my own research on the side. They were my support system and losing them was the biggest blow I could've received. RNS took my parents, and I'm going to keep going until I make sure it doesn't take anyone else.

//

NEWS REPORT - PROTESTING THE OFFICE
Streaming from the logs of the *Capacitance*.

The viewing monitor for the ship continues to replay cataloged news reports with the screen filled with protesters outside of a medical facility. A mix of people with the same agenda, some in everyday clothes and some in suits, waving signs. A news anchor steps up front and center. He's well-suited with a microphone in hand, while the chaos ensues behind him and various news reports scroll across the bottom of the screen.

"I'm standing here at the offices of Dr. Angelique Puck, where things have gotten a *bit* out of hand. Dr. Puck and her medical team have recently announced their new treatment for Multiple Sclerosis involving surgically implanting alien life forms in the nervous systems of patients, and as you can *see*, the people aren't taking to it very well."

Protesters continue with shouting through megaphones, rallied around the facility. One of the many aggressively steps forward, picking up a rock and hurling it through one of the building's front windows. It shatters and the group cheers.

"I'd love to get a word with Dr. Puck or one of her teammates, but with all this, I highly doubt anyone will step outside, so that'll be an interview for another time. Back to you."

The screen cuts to black.

//

Ship Journal
Dr. Angelique Puck: Login: 7575
Subject: **A Long Road**

The road to even a *tolerable* world health is littered with disease and turmoil. As one could imagine, not everyone was on board with our surgically implanting ill patients with living organisms from outer space. I can't legally go into specifics on the case, but things got a bit hairy and lawyers were brought in. Various companies tried to pull the plug on me and my research, and despite having the support of patients we'd helped, the complaints kept on coming.

The interesting and more frustrating thing about the complaints was they weren't from people with the illness or even family members of patients; they had an opinion and a right to voice it, so they did. That's how the double-edged sword of living in a free country works, however; citizens express their right to voice their opinion and the people who are busy trying to make a difference in the world have to deal with it even when it interrupts their work...but I digress... We explained how everything had been well examined before used on anyone, but it wasn't enough. We were hit with fines for not going through codes of conduct and obeying standards.

Insurance won't cover experimental treatments regardless of the success rates, and it's a specialty procedure so it's not widely available to surgical groups or pharmaceutical companies. With that said, there wasn't much money to be made in the Nu-Myelin Cell and others we'd developed. It *is* expensive, but it's not something you'd have to get over time, like treatment. So, as these companies weren't making money like they would in standard treatments, they aimed to put a halt to our work.

While my team and I fought diligently to rid the world of illness one disease at a time, these greedy pigs were only worried about their pockets getting sick. Sadly, that's the state of the world, but I kept fighting. Patients had rallied and signed petitions and had gotten their own lawyers to join in the fight. We made our case with promising turnarounds in the health of several MS patients among others and proved what we were doing was right. We still had to pay the fine though, which ultimately set our research budget back.

The legal troubles weren't the only ones to arise. Since I was spearheading such missions to space to find these answers, I was held accountable for most of the flak. Once they found out the person who wanted to implant them with alien life forms was queer as well, shit really hit the fan. I was attacked and accused of having a "liberal lesbian agenda" infecting people how I saw fit; an accusation I still scratch my head over. Enough of the hate died down over time when more and more success cases came to light. No apology was given for my mistreatment, of course, but it didn't matter as long as people were finding relief.

I pleaded my case time and time again about how all I wanted to do was help find cures and rid the world of such horrid diseases, but it didn't matter to religious groups who protested our experiments and picketed our offices. They claimed what we were doing was against God's will. Such protesters also claimed this is "God's green Earth" and we didn't need to bring in any Godless creatures to fix what he made in his image. Despite not feeling a need to defend myself, my argument was always the same, "If God didn't want us to learn to save ourselves, why would he build us with such inquisitive minds?" Furthermore, why would he give us the tools to become more?

Even though people were saved, we were still berated for implanting innocent people with space particles. Naysayers claimed we should have experimented on inmates—like *that* would've been more humane. When asked how we thought we could do what we were doing, I gave them the same answer the military gives to answer for casualties of war. "They signed up."

With legal cases and religious protesters, it was getting harder to be a help to the world. I'm finding more and more, especially in this ill-fated mission, that no good deed goes unpunished. I always found comfort in knowing people in the past who'd left such extraordinary marks on the world were all met with the same friction from the ignorant. I've heard it all, from people saying "What if it takes over their body and they kill someone?" to "This will start an alien invasion!"

The thought of something being *out there* terrifies people. The thought of that something being inside of them, regardless of the cause, terrifies them even more. In the end, it all came down to money. When the companies trying to put us under had agreed to make a healthy donation to the protesting churches with their winnings, everything seemed to calm down. Of course, they didn't "win" but part of the fine we had to pay did go to them, regrettably.

Due to the increased amount of panic and fear surrounding the growing RNS epidemic, my request to find the cure went to the front burner seemingly overnight. Our budget was approved without *much* guff in the process. There are always going to be people who don't believe in the cause and will protest at any given chance, but they aren't the ones writing the checks for such missions, and they *also* aren't the ones going through the pain and sickness we're trying to stop. Well-seasoned in being protested against, I pushed forward, not paying them any mind but looking to a healthier and less panicked future.

I was determined. If there were still cures to find on Earth, we would have found them by now, so I kept my eyes on the skies. We pushed forward in interstellar medical science with the goal of stopping at nothing until everything this side of a hangnail was cured. The world is full of naysayers, but if what you're trying to accomplish is right and just, everything will work out in the end. I hope someday to live in a world free of debilitating diseases and untimely deaths, a world where children aren't orphaned and parents don't have their children taken from them. I suppose I could wish upon a star while I'm up here...but I'm a scientist.

//

NEWS REPORT - DIFFERENCE OF OPINION
Streaming from the logs of the *Capacitance*.

A news anchor sits behind a desk for the nightly news, white and well-dressed. "Well, creator of the Nu-Myelin Cell is back at it again as Dr. Angelique Puck and her team of experimental medical scientists are set for another mission into orbit to find the cure for a disease that is said to make AIDS look like the common cold, Rabid Neural Stasis. But not *everyone* is behind her on this." He turns to his side, revealing a guest. "Today with me, I have astrophysicist Carl Plympton." The news anchor and his guest, black and equally well-dressed, are sitting together at the desk. "Carl, thank you for coming."

"Thank you for having me." The scientist smiles and nods.

"Now, you've spoken out against these missions into space for cures, and I'm curious, can you elaborate on your stance?" the anchorman asks.

The guest nods. "Yeah, finding cures randomly floating around in space is—is just ludicrous." He shakes his head but remains smiling and doesn't become irate. "And using space particles as treatments is just as much so."

"They've had proven success with Multiple Sclerosis, and this RNS is supposed to be a pretty nasty virus, so why not take that chance?" the newsman presses.

"Well, honestly, I can't speak much on the severity of diseases, but I feel I can speak on the nature of what's beyond our atmosphere. I'm all for exploration, but finding medicine out there sounds so science fiction, even for *me*."

The two share a laugh together.

"No, in all honesty, it just doesn't sound safe. You're trying to cure Earthbound ailments by essentially fusing them with something of unknown origins: a living dust mite, if you will, floating around in space." Carl talks with his hands, exaggerating movements. "Imagine being out on a road trip or being out on your boat and reaching out, grabbing something, anything, and deciding to implant it into sick people on a whim. It—it doesn't sound smart."

"So, do you not believe the patients who have come forward in Dr. Puck's defense? Do you think they're paid off or what?" the anchor asks, leaning forward.

"I don't think they're paid off. I'm sure they're feeling as fine as they say. But what's the longevity to that treatment? What happens if those things die inside you? Will it eventually infect the person it was originally helping? It seems to me like there wasn't much in the way of risk assessment. And *now*, they're going out there again to try to fix this RNS, which is way worse than MS. What if whatever they bring back is put into these patients and it allows them movement but doesn't fix the rabid outbursts? Now you have the same thing but *mobile*. It's a hell of a gamble." Carl shakes his head.

"Yes, it is." The anchor turns his plastic smile to the camera. "Well, that's all the time we have for today. Back to you."

The screen cuts to black before moving on to the next file.

//

Ship Journal
Dr. Angelique Puck: Login: 7575
Subject: **Nightmares & Insects**

I'm waking up when the horizontal break of my eyelids reveals a bright yellow light. My eyes blink and my head shakes as I lift my head in a groggy state to find...a large *creature* standing in my quarters with the bright yellow light emitting from it. *It's found me.* I jolt up and scoot back against the wall as it approaches my bed. It appears to be shielded with a bright chrome armor and, for lack of a better description, star-shaped with five pointed, razor-sharp limbs. It's hulking, lingering over me, coming closer. I shut my eyes tightly, wincing so hard it hurts my face when I *wake up* to find I'm alone, no creatures big or small, just me—*alone*.

Nightmares like this are common for me now, as well as the feeling of insects crawling all over my body and in my hair, as shiny as the large thing coming toward me in my dream. I try to brush them off, step on them, and even get away from them, but they're too fast and there are too many of them. They bite me and infect me with something... Beyond the horror it is, it makes me think of what the people of Earth are going through right now with RNS, which gives me pause and makes me wonder if Rabid Neural Stasis is of alien origin, but I digress...

I can take all the showers I want, clean all that my heart

desires, and I *still* feel them, I *sense* them. After what we'd gone through, I find myself seeing things often. I know in my heart of hearts they're not really there, but creatures of various sizes show up in my mind's eye. It doesn't help matters that I work with microscopic organisms all the time. Then I start seeing things around the ship; tiny things crawling all over the floors, walls, and ceilings as if the *Capacitance* has taken on an infestation of spiders. I can envision these things reaching Earth... A young couple out camping and watching the night sky when they see shooting stars. They lose count after the first several in the barrage of the falling lights. It's so beautiful and awe inspiring to see it all around the couple. They look up in wonderment until they're covered in these things, devoured as the wildlife around them watches and scurries...and that would only be the start.

One night I was sitting in the Captain's seat, sending out a distress call, when I could've sworn I saw something *outside* looking *in*. I couldn't believe it. There's something *out there* staring at me. My heart skipped a beat, and I froze. I shut my eyes tightly, clenching my shaky fists, before reopening my eyes to see nothing—more darkness. I felt better after sleeping, but sometimes with nightmares such as these, it's not always the case. It's scary out here. There's nowhere to run, nowhere to hide, and no one to help me if I were to face the things these nightmares are made of alone. But as scary as it most definitely is, it's just as gorgeous. Space can be beautiful, not so much some of the things found *in* it. I suppose that goes for a lot of *humanity* as well.

//

A View from My Window

Bridge-Cam: *while most of the rooms contain one camera, the bridge contains two, this one is located center ceiling seeing all in the room.*
The bridge stays lit. It's clean, sterile. The door opens, and Angelique walks in as she's done dozens of times before and heads for what was Stanton's seat at the helm. She has her choice of seats, of course, but usually gravitates towards Harper's, the center chair, or Stanton's. In the clothing rotation, she's wearing her white and silver zip up one-piece.

Control Panel-Cam: *sitting in the center of various controls facing out.* Sitting back, she decompresses; her eyes look out and pull up above the camera. Angelique sighs and looks out of the window in wonder before staring directly into the camera within the front control panel.

"Looking out of the window of the cockpit, I finally take time to smell the roses. I've been so consumed with my work for so long that I've forgotten how beautiful and peaceful it is up here. The view is stunning. In the far distance I can see stars but still no planets, still no sun." She shakes her head. "Even looking out into the blackness is fantastic as it leads me to think, *'What's out there?'*"

Stem-Cam:
Deep space. Stars congregate in clusters, in their own cosmic cliques here and there in the darkness. The occasional asteroid and miscellaneous stray space rock the size of gravel pass by, faster than the ship. Debris floats freely at random, but the distant stars stay stationary. Layers of darkness would have one wonder—is it the debris floating over the black background or is it black weightless clouds hovering over the true colorful universe beneath? Space: it often looks thick and tangible, perhaps it is in its own invisible way. Perhaps things aren't drifting at all, but drudging through the thickened blackness slowing one's very movement.

Bridge-Cam:
Angelique sits in the pilot's chair, looking out of the large window spanning from left to right across the front of the bridge. She has a front row seat to a widescreen view of the universe. Asteroids and random bits float around. They're brown, gray, and with no set shape. The rocks only go so far out before being swallowed by the black.

"On Earth, dust, leaves, and various other particles blow around in the wind while out in space large chunks of rock float aimlessly into the void." She sits up, pressing her hands on the window, looking at the stones. More drift by the ship almost as fast as they disappear into the darkness. "I wonder what these pieces have come from. It makes me wonder how many planets used to be in our solar system, that maybe more planets from millions of years ago have cracked and broke apart, drifting through space. Perhaps our nine planets are the survivors in a galaxy which used to be littered with planets, or maybe more planets had more moons."

Stem-Cam:
While the stars sit still in their clusters and some by their lonesome, the asteroids float this way and that. It all seems so random yet all the pieces move forward beyond the spaceship as if being thrown from somewhere far behind.

"I'd like to do a study on currents out here, but it's not my department or my specialty. Space is a vacuum, and as you surely know, there's no gravity and everything's weightless. When I see patches of rocks flying through, however, there's a certain flow to them. There must be some kind of current out here in the void. It would really be something if the particles up here weren't moving but they were completely still and it's the layers of space itself moving."

Stern-Cam:
Through the frost, rocks of various sizes emerge from the darkness as small stones at the bottom of a riverbed. If asteroids themselves could think, they'd surely be wondering about the large metallic item lingering and loitering, blocking the flow and current the doctor ponders about. Out this far, the *Capacitance* is the alien object, the stranger in the house of the universe.

Control Panel-Cam:
Dr. Puck's hand brings up a hologram from the dashboard of such a spacecraft; a standard Milky Way map. The gorgeous spiral galaxy, bright in color, with red tracking lines going every which way for separate routes. The hologram spins slowly.

"When you look at a map of the solar system, everything looks so easy: the routs, the ins and outs, all so easy. When you're out here, though, it's a bit harder, well, a *lot* harder to navigate. It's the same as looking at a maze from overhead and then actually walking through it. I guess a lot like when you see a constellation from Earth and you come up here and you can't find them anywhere." Her finger selects Saturn, singling it out and expanding the planet's view. "Seeing the colossal rings of Saturn was something else. The way our lights hit them, they were gorgeous." She closes the hologram as it pulls down, disappearing into the control panel.

Top-Cam: *on top of the* Capacitance, *oscillating on a rod, seeing the overhead exterior.*
The ship floats, dead in the water and surrounded by black. Frost is growing on the *Capacitance's* exterior at a fast rate, faster than the ship's movement anyway. The asteroids pass it as if casually strolling by. Stars watch from their perches in this grand universe. If there's anyone or anything else out here watching the stalled and stationary ship, they're shrouded in darkness and not meant for humanity to see.

Stem-Cam:
Beyond the loose rock or distant star, there's nothing in the future distance for the *Capacitance*: the great black yonder. The moment stars seem to get closer, larger, they fall into the distance again, as if they're the eyes of predators in the wild, watching from the thick wilderness. Shifting faint twinkling lights, asteroids disappearing almost as soon as they emerge and layers of black; one would think the *Capacitance* has been going in circles rather than being anchored. With surroundings such as these, it would be tough to even tell if there was movement at all.

Bridge-Cam:
Angelique watches out of the window: desolation. Her cheeks rest in her palms like a child mesmerized. Her mind races.

"I'm constantly torn. My feelings go back and forth between being enamored with the stark beauty of the universe and the fear and loneliness that settles in me. I've found myself crying in bed more times than I care to count. Nothing makes me feel smaller than being up here. Sometimes it feels good to feel small. We've been beyond the Milky Way for some time now. No sight of a single planet or the sun now. The year we developed an efficient-enough fuel to make the trip, it was made, and we continued to push the boundaries of where human beings were 'meant to go.'"

She sits back in the seat and sighs. "At times I feel one with the helpful microorganisms we found up here. There doesn't appear to be a food chain in space; the natural order seems completely different out of atmosphere. Watching this ever-expanding universe from the window, it seems as random as we've ever thought. What I would call currents flow in different directions. After all this time up here, I'm still forever curious about what's out there beyond the wall of black."

Angelique Puck looks around the empty bridge of the ship. "The *Capacitance* is a smooth ride with very little bumps and shakes, if any. We were caught in an asteroid field months ago and managed to weave in, out, and around with no trouble." She runs her hands along the very seat she sits in. "Stanton was a good pilot, which is a lot more than I can say for myself. I'm winging it, or at least, I will be when everything comes back online."

Top-Cam:
The *Capacitance* looks peaceful. Its exterior has minor dings but, for the most part, looks fine with its lights illuminating its gunmetal color. The random frost patterns throughout shimmers under the light. The ship floats and drifts slowly and will stay its course and pace until she gets the thrusters back online.

"On our journey, sometimes it didn't feel like we're moving at all. People who are plagued with motion sickness would actually do quite well with space travel."

Stem-Cam:
The continued blackness of space, as serene as it is terrifying. Imagine walking into a pitch black room with no ends, no walls; you keep going with your arms held out expecting to, at some point, touch *something*.

"We used to take meditation moments and float around aimlessly alone, one by one, thinking to ourselves. Quiet time in a place where there is no sound. I miss that feeling. I probably need to do it again soon, but with my recent run-ins with trouble, I wouldn't trust it. It does feel good, though. You get suited up, not that they're the most comfortable suits, and drift out like floating on your back in the water, thinking to yourself. Sometimes I'd open my eyes and sometimes not. It's odd; I've always had a problem with heights, but up here, not so much. I guess it's because I can't see the bottom or the top—just a blank void. Where's there to fall?"

Control Panel-Cam:

Angelique sits up in the pilot's chair, looking at the camera, explaining. She talks with her hands most of the time.

"The suits are uncomfortable at first, and then after a while you get used to them. It happens the same way with every trip. It's like these." Angelique motions to her standard issue suit.

Bridge-Cam:

She stands and leans to the window, pressing herself against it, trying to get as close as she can while looking out into the void. Random asteroid pieces float by. She watches it all with wonder.

"The *Capacitance* continues to float through space, and I stand still watching it all go by me. The sheer awesomeness of this view could easily make me forget that I have a load of deceased crew members in the cargo bay. My colleagues were a lot like me, taking advantage of such a view over time." Her fingers touch the glass where the stars rest in the distance, outlining the clusters. "It's gorgeous and captivating, a moving painting I can't find myself to look away from. Before leaving the solar system, the planets were stationary like villages across a great land. Comets blow around like tumbleweeds through a small western town. It's peaceful. There's no bickering, no bigotry to be found in space and no war. No wonder people are always trying to move up here. Of course, that all will more than likely change once actual galactic migration is possible. The solar rays up here are strong, visible like the ones coming in a window at home, only with more girth and substance; however, the sun's long behind me."

Stern-Cam:

Darkness beyond the frost. Rocks still hurl through space while the lit stars remain stationary. The asteroids seem as though God himself is throwing them. Weightless: a world of buoyancy and unknowing. A whole universe hovering in an open void, an open plain in which astronauts try to take their steeds out at far as they can go...but should they? A question Angelique and her various crews over the years haven't thought to ask.

"If God created all *this*, I often wonder what else he created. What's beyond all this? Will we ever see it? I don't ask questions like 'Why are we here?' as I tend to ask questions like 'Where are we going?' It's human nature to be curious just as it is to be adventurous. We're all searching, and we're often searching in the dark and stumble upon new discoveries, whether they are on a grand scale or in our personal lives."

Stem-Cam:
More of the deep black she's been seeing over time. Nothing changes.

"I wonder how far out lies the planet with inquiring minds like ours, yearning for what's out here in our neck of the universe. Like in humanity's early years, when people from different lands wanted to know what was beyond their oceans, I believe there are planets where people are feeling the same in a galactic sense. I've always found it arrogant of people to think we were the only ones in the universe. If God created the universe, the galaxies within and, more in depth, our very own Earth, why wouldn't he create more? Why would we believe he created the Earth and leave it at that? How can people believe in one and not the other? I wonder if there are planets out there looking for ours. Perhaps our solar system is bigger than we know and the forefathers of science merely marked down what they knew and we've been going off of that since. The universe is full of mystery, more than we know."

Bridge-Cam:
Angelique sits on the control panel with her arms crossed, watching in amazement from the window.

"For a place where everything is weightless, everything seems pretty heavy, sturdy. Cinema doesn't do the sights justice. It's live art, calming and beautifully orchestrated. The hum from the lights in here goes well with the scenery; however, it is nice to turn them off and enjoy the silence with my surroundings. I *do* wish someone was here to share this view with me..."

//

Ship Journal
Dr. Angelique Puck: Login: 7575
Subject: **Living Comparisons**

Before my parents passed on, the crew that went up returned with so-so results. They didn't really know what they were looking for, but then again, you never really know when you're exploring. We had convinced our financiers to fund another mission, and this time, with my parents gone, I went up with them. I had been told the suits had advanced over time and, upon first trying it on, it was restricting, but then I got used to it. Most embarrassing, to say the least, were the MAGs (maximum absorbency garments) we had to wear. Yeah, *space diapers.*

My training prepared me for what space travel would *feel* like, but it didn't prepare me for the breathtaking imagery. My first trip to space was inspiring and frightening. I was in shock and awe of the galaxy. Despite having dreamed of that moment, it was overwhelming. The sight of the galaxy in real life and not in some old photos or textbooks was and *still is* beyond my wildest dreams.

Please forgive me for glossing over such *exciting* adventures as sitting around waiting for phone calls, standing in long clearance lines, mental and physical exams, and lots and LOTS of paperwork. I wouldn't want to excite you too much...

On Earth these days, everyone is required to have some sort of social media personality. Consider it our license and registration for citizenship; if you're not on social media, you're not considered registered. If one goes off radar for a certain amount of time, they're called, paid a visit, and fined. It becomes effective immediately upon birth as the parents/guardians are required to update the baby's social media account until they're old enough to do so themselves. Personally, I've been handling my own since seven years old.

When citizens pass away, their accounts become logged in memorials. The Internet, once a luxury, is mandatory now. No bill for service as the pay is lumped in with taxes. Coming up for this mission, we all received passes to put ours on hold until we return. What started so long ago as a way for people to communicate with one another had turned into a barcode we all pay taxes on. One of the nice things about being up in space is there's no mandatory status update required as we're well out of reach of any actual range. Of course, if I make it back home, I'll have to get used to updating every inane minutia of the day.

Living on the ship was quite different from back home. Back on Earth, if you were tired of something, you could walk away for a little bit. Up here there's nowhere to go. It's like camp...in an office floating literally in the middle of nowhere. I didn't get homesick like I thought I would. I missed my parents like crazy but knew they were proud of me, and I prayed and talked to them often. After a few months aboard the ship, it felt like home. When you're used to a home cooked meal, the space paste takes a bit to get used to. The sleep pods are also a different feeling from a warm bed but with what we were supplied to rest helped. I'd never felt more rested than after waking up in them. Things change over time: technology, mindsets, and limitations. On the *Capacitance*, like the last couple of ships I'd been on, we have beds as opposed to the pods. We were determined to find something up here, and all the hard work, patience, and prayer paid off.

We'd found what had appeared to be a cloud of debris in our navigation path. The captain had said it was nothing and to keep going. However, I pleaded with him to stop so I could investigate. Like the child analyzing bugs and plants in the backyard decades earlier, my curiosity and inquisitiveness drove me to go outside and take a look. Sure enough, the cloud turned out to be comprised of what would become the Nu-Myelin Cell.

I continued with three more treks to the stars after that amazing exploration. Each crew was different and every time *felt* different, but every time we made the trip out of the atmosphere was met with great results. We were constantly finding things to use for health needs. They might not have all been as big as the NMC, but they were helpful nonetheless.

Living with different kinds of people for lengthy periods of time was interesting. Imagine living in a hi-tech medical apartment with up to nine roommates. You spend the first chunk of time not trying to step on anyone's toes only to eventually loosen up and even play pranks on one another.

Problems on Earth aren't the same in space, mentalities such as bigotry and greed. Just as racism is always a staple of Earth, so is homophobia. Bigotry starts at home and is carried on—an earthbound ailment of humanity. I wonder if there is bigotry on planets beyond the black. If they'd all come up here, they'd realize how small we all are and how insignificant such bickering is. On Earth, we can feel big; out here, there's no chance. Out here, in my current situation, it's about survival.

When I'm in space, I dream of Earth, and when I'm on Earth, I dream of space. Nothing feels like this, being in a shuttle blasting through the universe. My job's amazing; I get paid for doing the same thing I did as a child only on a larger scale. Sure, I see my share of sick patients and sad stories but, all in all, I'm happy with what I do. I can say that I'm contributing, helping, and not merely watching the world go by me on a daily basis as so many do. I would say my worst days among the stars are better than my best days on the ground, but that was before this mission...but I'll get to *that* later, I'm—I'm just...not ready yet. My *usual* disappointing days in the great unknown are when we don't find anything, but the days we do find something useful I'm as happy as a clam.

I've had captains who are polite and cordial, and I've had captains who are socially tough as nails and well, frankly, jerks. Maybe being up here so many times left them cold and detached from humanity, I don't know. It's a lot like dealing with different professors. Despite getting along with almost everyone, I don't really have a big circle I run with on Earth, but I do get video messages from old classmates, colleagues, and professors, which is nice. I've tried not to let others get to me on these missions, but I'm human, and despite trying to stay strong and focused, I *do* have feelings as well. I occasionally think of things like owning a pet, but if I'm not working in the lab, I'm up here, so I wouldn't be able to really take care of it. Yes, the differences of living on Earth and space are aplenty, but I'm grateful to be here even in this state I find myself now.

I grew up a child with my head in the stars, and now the rest of me is here, too, for better or worse.

//

"*Capacitance* to base, come in... This is the *Capacitance* sending out a distress call. SOS... Come in. This is Dr. Angelique Puck of the *Capacitance*. Is anyone out there?"

A Quick Tour

Control Panel-Cam:
Angelique sits down in the pilot's chair, looking into the camera in the control panel. She has an apparatus on her head, not too large but noticeable. A metal halo circles the top of her head with a black lens off to her right side.

"Well, still no word from the space station. Our personal direct line, Extension 201, is who we normally call for assistance, but even *they're* unresponsive at the moment. I've sent out distress signals and various other messages, but we must still be too far out of range." She looks out of the window to her side still showing deep space up close and personal. "While waiting on a reply, I figured I'll take you all on a quick tour, which is why I have this on." She motions to her headgear. "All of our suits come equipped with cameras so it can catch what we're doing when we go out on our walks. I took this one out of the extra suits."

She stands up and motions around her. "We are aboard the *Capacitance*, a simple freighter ship modified and transformed into a craft specifically for experimental intergalactic missions. I can't tell you the size of it exactly, but it's big enough to house eight people and then some, have living quarters, labs, and cargo space."

Angelique's Head-Cam: *seeing what she sees.*
She looks around the bridge of this ship before turning to the window. The asteroids are coming as heavy as they once were, but stars are still in the distance, stationary. Below the window is the control panel full of lights, switches, and gauges. She narrates what she sees.

"Starting off here on the bridge, there's the window, the control panel, and the pilot's seat along with plenty of other crew seating. Each seat has a cooling and heating switch for your liking." She kneels down closer to the seats, showing the red and blue gauges on the sides below the armrests. Her view pans up to mechanisms coming down from the ceiling. "There are three viewing scopes capable of different lengths and zooms."

Angelique's head and view, moves all around the cockpit, showing its insides: floor, walls, ceiling. "This room, like the entire interior of the ship, is titanium, aircraft aluminum, and fiberglass from what I'd overheard; of course, *surely* there's more to it. There's really no special detail to it all other than charts, dry erase boards, and gauges."

Despite it being an advanced piece of equipment, this ship, it's not covered in overly detailed unnecessary pieces. Charts and gauges cover the blank walls. She looks up to a tunnel shaped opening containing a slide-down ladder. "Up above me is a hatch we call the Stargazer, I've usually used for stargazing though its use is more that of utility and maintenance."

Top-Cam:
The clear dome above the bridge is lit from below when Angelique appears under it, looking out into the starry sky.

"Above the surface is a clear bubble domed top so one could see without a use of a suit, hence the name. Though, the dome opens like a door."

Angelique's Head-Cam:
She approaches the door to the bridge and punches the large switch beside it as it slides to the side in between the walls, like the door to her room. Despite the size and sturdiness of it all, the doors are quite silent in their movements; however, like all the doors, there's a beep before opening.

"Past the first door is a long corridor separating the bridge from the rest of the ship." She walks through, and the long tube-like hallway is lit completely around with long florescent bulbs and the walkway is a chrome strip. There are no windows, simply a lit tube. Angelique walks through with her magnetic boots audible. She's opening the next door now, same thing as before. The next room is the break room. It looks about like any other office break room found on Earth. There's a screen mounted on the wall, playing an ongoing news feed, mostly cataloged.

She narrates... "I'm entering the kitchen and dining area. Here we have our table, cabinets, counters—everything you need for a breakfast nook in space." She moves to the next door, opening it, revealing a hallway of rooms cased in glass. Only one room is lit, and they all seem to have suits hung up inside alongside white lab coats. "Here's where the magic happens; no, not the *bedrooms*, the labs. To my left and right are various labs for testing, pharmaceutical, and various other examinations. All our suits are kept in these labs. That's mine there." She stops at the lit lab, looking in. The table is full, exactly as she left it.

"We'll keep going..." Another door, as there are many, leading to another hallway of doors. "Down this hall are all the bedrooms, the living quarters." Every door to the left and right down this hall is shut, and her view focuses on end of the hall where a door stands after a turn. "Down past the sleep hall is a door which takes us down to the cargo bay but...due to its contents at the moment I...I don't really feel like making the trip down there." Her view won't break from the inevitable end of the hall. Fear is evident in her voice. "I—I'm afraid to say that I'm not the best for a tour of any ship, but...I can show you what I've been doing. Let's go back to the lab..."

//

Testing

"I'm going to suit up and go outside to see what I can find..."

Angelique-Cam:
Standing on the exterior of the ship, Angelique looks around, seeing the metal ship below and the black space above and to her sides.

"We're out pretty far. No planets in sight."

The *Capacitance* rests among the blackness of the universe. The view is open, and the ship is only lit by its lights. Beyond the ship is the same view she's been seeing for some time now: black with muted twinkling. Her head scans the ship of various shades of gunmetal gray. The lights on her helmet and the one in her hand show her where the ship's lights won't. The black around the *Capacitance* is captivating and looks like it could swallow her up at any moment.

"Outside now; lovely weather out here... Having this voice recorder for the journal helps, now I just have to find debris. It's pitch black out; I'm hoping my light can catch them." Angelique steps forward in big childlike steps. "The magnetic strips on my boots keep me firmly planted to the *Capacitance* as I walk along the exterior of the ship. It tends to make movements more exaggerated, but it's better than not having them. My light's not catching anything. It only goes so far before it stops completely."

Her light appears to be eaten by the darkness. It's as if the black swallows the light only to digest it and release it into the universe as stars. She turns around from the front of the spacecraft, and the view to the rear isn't much different.

"I'm going to check the south end of the ship. The awe and wonder of being up here seems to fade when you're working. It's so black out here, it makes one wonder if they'd ever know if they're in a black hole or not. Black holes swallow light and everything with no release, and as I think about my current situation, it makes me wonder..." She walks slowly in the "night sky" with the ship beneath her. Angelique's surrounded by the encompassing darkness of space; she's the only living person for light-years but tries not to think about it. "I'm nervous making this walk; I've never been out here alone, not like this anyway." She nervously looks all around her, nothing but black to her sides and above her. Angelique checks the cable attached to her suit. "If my boots give out, I'll only have this cord to keep me tethered to the ship. *Stay focused, Angelique. Don't think about that.*"

She continues walking, hiking over the length of the ship. Something shimmers in the distance when her light is thrown in its direction. "I see something! There's something towards the back of the ship. I'm making the move, and I have the same bag we've been using to gather them; not very hi-tech but it gets the job done." Tethered to her suit is the bag, a butterfly net of thick, double-layered, strengthened plastic with a mesh inside on the end of a rod. The cloud of debris still shimmers from her light, but when the light moves from it, all appears as black as their surroundings.

"I hope the cloud doesn't disperse by the time I get there. I feel like I'm walking a tightrope and surrounded by darkness. Some would say I'm very devoted to my cause, others would say I'm a nutjob." She moves as speedily as she can as her cameras stay well-focused on the cloud ahead while occasionally looking down at the ship beneath her feet. She's nearing the rockets on the south end. "I'm getting closer to them now. It could be debris from the ship's rockets, but it *could* be what I'm looking for. The gamble of the business."

Contact. She approaches the shining cloud and grabs her gathering device. Angelique shines her light into the cluster, and they resemble a cross between lightning bugs and frenetic static. Carefully, she scoops the bag around them, collecting a large chunk of the galactic debris before letting out a sigh of relief.

"Okay, I've scooped the cluster up into my bag, and I'm going to try to get more."
She tries but doesn't get much more as the things making up such a cluster have scattered. She tries to catch some in her gloves, shining the light on them, but they blow away like dust in the wind. "Okay, I think I've got all I can get for now." Dr. Puck looks around with no sight of any shimmering mites or debris. Alone in the dark again, she sighs.

"Let's see what the universe has given us..."

DocLab 7-Cam:
Dr. Angelique Puck appears slightly exhausted as she hangs her spacesuit up on the hook next to the door of her lab, beside another. Like all over the ship, the sound throughout is stark besides the hum of the lights and various electronics.

"It seems to take forever to get this suit on and off alone sometimes. No word from home on anything, so I suppose I'll keep working." Angelique brings out the now-closed bag of space debris, carrying it over to a glass casing across the room. "It'll take a moment to retrieve them properly from the bag. When placing the bag in the casing, they tend to vacate themselves. Whatever doesn't, I'll shake out."

She turns and motions toward the table. "This is the room I mainly work in. On the table here are some of the samples we've taken from outside throughout the mission. They resemble the molecules used for the NMC but are different." As per usual, Angelique talks with her hands, explaining to the security camera and her journal. Regardless of their being inanimate objects, they're the closest thing she has to friends or coworkers at the moment.

"My proposal to cure the RNS crisis was a tricky one. Since it's been known to first attack the immune system and we'd had success with micro synthetic internal parts, I suggested a synthetic immune system. It sounded crazy and nobody was on board at first, of course. The plan was to find these *exact* types of cells and form a system, put the patient under and replace it. I know, it doesn't sound crazy; it sounds stupid and dangerous. The big question was 'How do we bring them back from that?' Cryogenics were discussed, but it's remained our big mystery. If we had the entire synthetic system built, we'd have to move fast to switch. *Because the disease moves on to the nervous system, I do wonder if a synthetic nervous system would need to be made or if the disease would halt at the new immune system.* This was all in theory, but that goes without saying."

She moves things around on the table in front of her, arranging. "Our next step was to infuse these cells in with the patient's current immune and nervous system and see if there would be any change *that* way. Of course, none of this could really be tested until we got back to Earth, something I'm not sure is in the cards anymore." She shakes her head, looking unsure. "One of the many technological advancements I've come to rely heavily on is this tool, an advanced microscope. It allows me to see things on a deeper molecular level than a standard issue microscope. I've since had all of my original ones replaced with these, the latest and greatest." She presents her tool before peering through the lens. "I can see these cells are compatible with one another; one step closer to success. These cells were found in the same kind of cluster as the previous ones we'd used to treat Multiple Sclerosis. They have similar grafting abilities but appear to be of a different species."

Dr. Puck sits back, thinking to herself before returning to looking through the lens. "To the naked eye they look like a speck of dust, but under the lens, they're quite lively with a silver body and clear exterior." Wheeling her chair over to a fridge, she opens it revealing bags of blood hung up. She grabs one, shuts the door, and wheels back to the table. "We had brought along with us bags of blood containing the RNS virus. I'm going to use this new batch of synthetic sheathing on some of the blood."

She uses a syringe and takes some of the blood from the bag and places it on the glass. She looks into the microscope and waits. "It's mixing now... The new cells look to be taking hold of the virus and... it dissipated. *Damn.*" Angelique sits back, disappointed. Her mouth scrunches, and her brow furrows in thought. "Along the way to success, failure is eminent. I know in the wake of what's happened on this mission, I should be focusing on getting home but 'the show must go on' as they say. If I'm up here, I might as well continue trying to find cures."

"I'm going to check one of the samples I just found outside." Angelique retrieves the particles and continues looking. "I've got them under glass and under the microscope. C'mon... c'mon... show me what I wanna see... *damn it.* It's just frost from the rockets..." She sits back, disappointed yet again. "Better luck next time I suppose. The frost *does* make me curious about something though... I'm going to try mixing the newer cells with cryogenics and see how they mix." She does so, mixing space mites with cryo from the steaming case. The sample is on the glass beneath the lens. Dr. Puck inspects. "...Okay, they freeze, but they're not entirely still. The cells continue to move about, graft, and coat despite the cold. It's good to know, but *what does it mean?*"

She pushes herself away from the table and moves for more items only to return. "Next up—to add cryogenics to the mix of RNS+ blood and new synthetic cells..." Angelique mixes the items mentioned and stands. "If I can get it all to freeze together but have the cells still work, I may have something. Time will tell; I'll have to leave this for now. I'm gonna get back to the bridge."

//

NEWS REPORT - A PUBLICITY STUNT
Streaming from the logs of the *Capacitance*.

The ship's screen reveals an angry mob of protesters. Everybody piles in to get in front of the camera and not one with a camera-ready smile.

The newsman on the scene, yet off camera, asks, "In the wake of the epidemic, a medical team is going to *space* to find a cure for RNS. How do you all, *the people*, feel about it?"

People bottleneck to get to the microphone. Everyone has something to say.
A woman up front swiftly answers, "It's a waste of tax payers' money! I mean, do they really need to go to *space*!? How do we even know what they're doing!?"

A man steps forward, "They could've sent up an empty ship and went on vacation somewhere! I don't trust them! They're not trying to help! It's all a publicity stunt!"

"Yeah!" Others agree as the commotion becomes audibly cluttered and indistinct.

The newsman steps in front of the camera as wide-eyed as other journalists and anchors across the country upon hearing such accusations from the people. "Well, there you have it, a word from the people. Back to you."

//

Ship Journal
Dr. Angelique Puck: Login: 7575
Subject: **Stationary**

After doing a routine check on everyone's rooms, I'm back on the bridge. The rooms all look like they had before: sterile and empty. I make another distress call, another SOS. No reply is given. Who knows if my messages are even getting out. I check the video messages, and they're empty, too. There's nothing but cataloged videos. It's hitting me again how alone I am up here. It's far from a vacation or a getaway; I'm floating alone in the outreaches of the universe in a ship with deceased colleagues. I suppose I could've used any of the organisms we've found on this mission to test them on one of the crew members to see if it'd make a difference, but it's too late now. Hindsight is always 20/20. Though, thinking about it, I highly doubt synthetic cells could help the dead.

I'm disappointed there have been no results, but that's the life of a scientist. For now I remain on the bridge, as stationary as the ship I'm in, thinking to myself and taking in the view of the wide open plains of the universe...

//

Angelique Room-Cam:
Angelique lies in her bed crying, sobbing into her pillow. On occasion things get too much even for a strong willed, intelligent woman. To her knowledge, she's the only one stranded out in the universe. She is a lone camel, trekking through a black desert and searching for some kind of society, some kind of stability. She has to put it out of her head how she's had to watch her team die followed by bagging them up and moving them to another space or room on the same ship she tries to live and survive on. The amount of pressure on her shoulders is immense, and she feels it all too often. Not trained for survival in a situation such as this, Angelique tries to survive, get the ship back to base with all the bodies on board as well as the urge to continue her work and do what she came up here to do—cure Rabid Neural Stasis. This is but a moment; a moment she's taking to allow herself to fall apart, and soon she will pull herself back together and get back to work the only way she knows how. Not being able to walk away, take a break, or let it all go, Dr. Puck cries into her pillow with stressful sobs, releasing the pent up tension. It's but a moment...

//

Ship Journal
Dr. Angelique Puck: Login: 7575
Subject: **Shipping Out**

It was a Tuesday morning, the day before shipping out, and I was more than ready. My palms sweat even in the shower. With my cereal and morning coffee digested, I was set. The house was cold and empty without my parents there anymore. I sat down and had a good cry. I prayed and talked to my parents, holding our family photo. I took it out of the frame and decided to bring it with me. I said goodbye to the house, knowing I wouldn't be back for some time as I would be going to mine and Serena's place after work and leaving from there.

We had been talking about this mission for two years. Roughly seven hundred days of convincing the suits that the cures for what ails all too many are up in the stars. That's a long time to plead your case before getting an answer. I had to point out my previous success with such missions time and time again. As I previously stated, once the RNS situation became hotter, they stopped denying, stopped questioning, and gave in. I didn't get total say in my crew despite it technically being my mission. I passed my physical and mental and packed my things. When I got to base, I met my crew. I was ecstatic to finally get to do this. I've made this trip before, but there was something about this one. I could feel it; we were going to make a bigger difference than ever, the opportunity to save the human race.

Sadly, we live in a time in which NASA doesn't fund these kinds of trips, and we usually have to go through independent financiers and alternate companies we'd have to convince to pay for such expeditions. We had all been given lists of dos and don'ts. The financiers of the mission told us what they wanted found and what they didn't want, regardless of my telling them it doesn't work like that. The head of such financiers was a man named Nelson. Now, for the most part, I always loved people in corporate; I understood them, and they understood me, but Nelson was a totally different beast altogether.

He held power over this corporation for a short time at that point and loved to flex his power, using his money as his weapon. We were met with a laundry list of things we needed to sign off on before they'd give us the budget for the mission. Along the list of things was Saxon, a soldier we were obligated to take aboard with us. I had a bad feeling about this guy from the beginning, especially after hearing him talk amongst his employers about working with minorities the likes of "niggers, spics, and dykes." I had a crew of myself, a couple of veteran cosmonauts in Harper & Stanton, a couple of fellow medical science techs Toni & Miguel, a pharmaceutical researcher in Chloe, and now the wrench in our spokes, Saxon—a boy and his gun.

Security Feed—Nelson's Office:
Angelique sits across a large desk from Nelson: he's white, in his forties, and suited. The office is covered in white and chrome with no wall décor. There are no sharp edges to anything in sight as every angle has a curve to it, even Nelson's desk. Angelique has brought various notes and figures, which are out on his desk to display; of course, he doesn't care. The conversation's heated with Dr. Puck aggravated and Nelson staying calm with condescension in his tone.

"This is a medical research mission, Nelson, not a firefight," she tells him.

"It's just a legality, I assure you. Since you found and brought back alien life forms, it's now required that every mission has at least one person onboard for security purposes," Nelson says.

"I haven't had to bring security for the last few missions." She shakes her head.

"Well, things change. We need to take precaution." He nods.

"They're *microscopic*! They certainly don't need firepower to get rid of!" she points out, her aggravation evident.

He takes a breath and looks at her with a smug grin and tells her, "Hey, Miss Puck...*you signed up.*"

Angelique sighs with a frown and an eye roll tightly covered by her eyelids.

Nelson stands, buttons his jacket, and walks past Angelique, leaving the office without another word. Annoyed and agitated, Angelique gathers her notes he could care less about, angrily putting them in her briefcase.

Security Feed—Corridors:
The hallways of this building look a lot like Nelson's office with

everything white and chrome with a tunnel-like curve, and like the office, it's all illuminated with bright florescent lights. What are usually corners where the walls meet the floors and ceilings are smoothed slopes. The building seems as though it was designed while looking through a fish-eye lens. Similarly, well-suited employees pass each other without so much of a nod. Angelique Puck stomps her way down the bright hallway, ever so flustered. On the other side of the curved corridor, however, is a less flustered sight. A beautiful young woman, white with short black and red hair, thin and in a suit dress. The two come across the curve, in their own worlds and not paying attention, and CLASH into each other, knocking their things out of their hands.

"I'm sorry," Angelique tells her, shaking her head.

"No, it was me. I don't know where my head is at today," the girl says with a cute laugh.

The other various people continue walking by without paying the two women any attention. The two help each other gather their spilled items, smiling throughout. They stand, looking like they want to say more, but in their busyness, part ways after another shared smile. Angelique carries on in her determination but now with her frustration deflated. The young beautiful woman whom she clashed with moves on through the bright, curved corridor with her eyes out for the destination she seeks.

Security Feed 1—Loading Bay:
The loading bay is large with random workers passing each other from all directions, all dressed for safety in padded one-piece coveralls. Some of them are moving crates: large, white, Polyvinyl Chloride (PVC). Some of them are steering lifts: a machine not really driven and hovers only a foot above the floor by air suspension. Workers pinch a button on their collars, turn their heads, and talk into it to confirm orders. It's busy but with its space not too congested.

Security Feed 2—Loading Bay:
Another section of the loading bay houses the *Capacitance*, which is being loaded and given routine maintenance checks. In a testament to the loading bay's size, the large spacecraft sits with plenty of room

around it. Various people are coming in and out of the vessel, checking things off clipboards. Amidst the crew of people working around the ship stands a couple, checking their gear. Toni, African-American, and Miguel, Hispanic, both in casual clothes. They go through their things and share a look many share while waiting. Angelique enters the loading bay; she waves. They notice her.

"Hey, guys," she greets the two.

"Hey, girl," Toni replies with a wave while her husband, Miguel, looks up.

"Ay, Angelique, finally decide to join us? You slacker!"

The three share a hearty laugh. Angelique moves on while the two continue. Angelique walks up the ramp to the ship to find Captain Harper looking over his spacecraft with his checklist on a clipboard.

"Good morning..." she greets the man, shaking his hand.

"You must be Dr. Puck," Harper says, shaking her hand. "Nice to meet you."

"How's everything looking, Captain?" she asks, eyes peering around.

"Good. Everything's looking good. We should be ready shortly."

"Great." Something catches her eye up in the ship.

Cargo Bay-Cam:
Right inside the cargo bay of the *Capacitance*, a man, Saxon, is checking over assorted weaponry. He's white and gruff with a crew cut while in all black: boots, pants, t-shirt. His dog tag is the only thing breaking the dark image of his attire. Angelique enters and approaches him.

"So you'll be looking out for us when things go awry," she says.

He looks back at her as if irritated. "Yeah, that's me. I guess they figured they needed a man on this job..." He rolls his eyes and continues his arsenal check.

"Oh, really? Then I must be here to clean up after *you*." Angelique and Saxon both turn to see who the smart mouth belonged to, and it's a homely-looking white woman a little older than Angelique with straight brown hair and big glasses.

"You must be the pharmaceutical researcher." Angelique shakes her hand not fully knowing but assuming who she is.

Whilst still shaking her hand, the woman says, "Hardly. I'm Lou Ann. I've been sent along on this little...mission by Mr. Nelson."

Angelique nods hesitantly. "Oh...*more* people? How many more from corporate are there?"

"Just me and the muscle. They wanted to add some brains and brawn to your *little medicine crew*." Lou Ann appears as condescending as Saxon. Angelique nods to herself. Another joins the cluster of crew members, a familiar young woman.

"Hi, sorry I'm late. I've been having the hardest time trying to figure out where to go. I'm Chloe."

Angelique turns around, and the two recognize one another, having bumped into each other in the corridor.

"Oh... You."

"Hi. Angelique Puck." She shakes Chloe's soft hand. Nelson's two leave, uninterested.

"I had no idea. I'm so sorry about earlier." Chloe smiles.

"Hey, don't worry about it. I wasn't thinking straight." Angelique brushes it off.

"Ladies, if we could have everyone out in the loading bay..." Harper calls, interrupting their actual moment of meeting.

Security Feed 2—Loading Bay:
The crew gathers out by the ramp to the *Capacitance* with most of

the gear already onboard. Everybody stands in their small respective cliques. Random workers continue to carry on about their day around them throughout the loading bay. Harper stands before everyone, strong and receiving the attention demanded. Stanton sits nonchalantly to the side of the captain, as chill as ever.

"All right, as you already know, I am Captain Harper and this is our pilot, Stanton."

"Yo." Stanton takes off his hat and holds it up before putting it back on.

Harper continues, "I understand this is a routine medical mission, but just in case anything was to go wrong, we've been given a couple of people from Corporate to make sure everything runs smooth." He motions to Saxon and Lou Ann briefly before pointing back to the large ship behind him. "This vessel is the *Capacitance*. We will all have more than enough resources to last us the trip and then some." Harper paces slightly, still commandeering their attention. "I do have a rule about being on my starship and no, it's not common courtesy and mutual respect. I trust you all have *some* sense of decorum. While all that goes without saying, I don't really care what you do to each *other*, but do not mess with *my ship*. Are we all clear?"

"Yes, sir," they all agree.

Security Feed—Living Quarters, Assorted:
With Stanton and Harper on the bridge, the crew boards and moves into their respective quarters, looking like children heading to class. Their rooms are nice and quaint yet blank for the most part, not that they'll see them much with the amount of work needed to be done. They'll have time to adjust their quarters to their liking later. They weren't to bring luggage full of personal clothes as they've all been given suits. The suits are full body coveralls they'll alternate wearing daily: white and silver; and black and silver.

Chloe's Room-Cam:
Chloe sets her things down and looks around. She inhales big and exhales excitedly with a large smile.

"Oh my God, I can't believe it's finally happening," she says, slightly hugging herself.

Lou Ann's Room-Cam:
Lou Ann enters and immediately sets up her work station at the desk, laying out her notes. She plugs in her tablet to charge before investigating her new living quarters.

Toni & Miguel's Room-Cam:
The couple enter and look around the room, nodding.

"Hey," Miguel says to his wife, getting her attention. Toni looks over at him, and he rubs and pats the bed while fluttering his eyebrows. She snickers.

Saxon's Room-Cam:
The former soldier enters, looking around, before laying his bags down on his bed.

"Well, it's better than the barracks..." He shrugs.

Saxon opens his luggage, revealing quite the arsenal for one man, but pulls out a black nylon square. He takes it to the center hook on the ceiling and hooks it through a loop on the corner of the square before pressing the center of it. In less than a minute, the small, black, nylon square inflates into a full punching bag. He gives it a few punches. It's weighty with solid girth. Satisfied, he nods.

Angelique's Room-Cam:
Angelique lays her parents' photo on the end table next to her bed and her tablet with thousands of books on it in case she gets time to read them. The only physical copy of any book she's brought along is a poetry book her mother had published when Angelique was a baby. After getting set up, she shuts her door and sits down to pray for a safe trip. Since they had passed, she always holds the photo of her parents while praying as it is the closest they can get to holding hands.

"Take off in five minutes," Captain Harper's voice comes over the intercom. A lot of things have changed since the days of 'fasten yourself in' galactic travel. Angelique gets changed into her uniform while keeping an eye on her watch as she doesn't want to miss the breaking through the atmosphere.

Bridge-Cam:
Harper and Stanton man the controls while the crew enter the bridge. The bridge is large enough for everyone to be there without crowding or cramping. Everyone enters, wearing their new standard issue one-piece uniforms, of course, still getting used to them with tugs and stretches.

"Ten... Nine..."

The Captain counts down as the rest of the team approach the bridge. They're all there, eight of them, holding on tight out of habit regardless of the smooth ride it is supposed to be. Everyone greets one another with smiles and nods and looks forward as the large doors open as they see the blue sky soon to be a distant memory.

"Three... Two... One..."

The jets fire up, and the engine kicks in blast off mode, and faster than a stock-car race, they're in the sky. The *Capacitance* doesn't buck or gyrate, and they all watch from the window as they pass the white fluffy clouds and pass the clear blue beyond them through a forceful fiery wall and into the black unknown. Despite the many trips astronauts have made over the centuries, it would always be unknown to them.

Resistance against the ship is felt reaching the atmosphere, and soon their orbit is a thing of the past and hopefully future. The fiery pressure doesn't look like the average flames as they appear almost like solar liquid rushing against and over the ship. Their pilot steers the ship, pushing all thrusters, and then all the struggle stops. They've arrived.

Control Panel-Cam:
Everyone stands together, individually reacting to leaving the planet, some for the very first time. It will take them a minute for it to set in and for them to realize how far away their families, friends, and the lives they know are.

"Ah, there it is... the great black yonder." the term slips from Captain Harper's lips, one he has been using for years to describe the grand universe. Harper still marvels in its awesomeness regardless of how many tours he's made and, despite him playing it down, it shows.

"Yep... It's *space*." Being a pilot on his umpteenth mission, Stanton's long lost his feeling of awe of the galaxy up close. He never blows off the notion of being up here in a sour manner; he's simply a laid back guy. To Stanton, it's another day on the job.

"Wow..." Toni says through a dropped jaw.

Miguel, beside her, pulls his wife in close.

"Beautiful... We need to conceive up here." Miguel says to Toni; not the first time suggesting it, and not the last.

Chloe steps forward. "Oh my God..." She's lit up like a child on Christmas.

"Heh, sure beats bein' in the desert." Saxon's attitude never seems to change, not even in the face of such a massive and wonderful creation as the universe.

"Oh my... I can't even think..." Even Lou Ann's coldness warms up at the sight of leaving the orbit and seeing the stark naked galaxy for the first time.

Angelique enjoys the others' reactions as she, herself, remains glued to the vision as well.

Ship Journal Continued:

I was speechless, as I was the times before. It's one thing to see pictures and to watch videos or even through a telescope at night, but *this*... this was the raw exposed universe. No picture or video could do it justice. Imagine seeing pictures of a volcano and then actually being there to discover you're the size of an ant in comparison; now magnify that times at least a trillion. We are to this open space as those atoms we were in search of are to us:

microscopic. I never thought about it until now, but I wonder if *we're* under anyone or anything's glass, under their microscope. Perhaps we're all just mites under the lens. We can't be the only ones in search for answers out here.

//

Just Another Day in the Great Black Yonder

Stem-Cam:
Asteroids of brown and gray float by the *Capacitance* in a stream-like fashion. Some hit each other, interrupting their flow along with breaking; one cracks while another crumbles into a near shatter in weightless slow motion. The bits drift out into the black in separate directions. The stars still visible in the distance shine as if attempting to get the ship's attention, perhaps intergalactic Sirens luring starships to their doom.

Top-Cam:
The wild and untamed, unclaimed, and unchartered universe seems to move about and around the *Capacitance* as it rests in the black, seemingly going unnoticed by the void.

Stern-Cam:
Through the frost, stars pulse, however tiny, while assorted rocks pass by. The *Capacitance* remains broken down on this highway of sorts with no lines, no rules, and no use for hazard lights.

DocLab 7-Cam:
The lab is currently vacant, though Angelique always keeps the light on.

Cargo Bay-Cam:
Seven full black company standard body bags lie on the floor side by side. The cargo bay's dimly lit by the glow of switches and the red overhead light which stays on when the lights are out.

Bridge-Cam:
Angelique enters, heading right for the pilot's chair. She's tired, worn out, and stressed. It may be the amount of work she's taken on by her lonesome and it may be survivor's remorse. Whatever it

is, Dr. Puck is beginning to show some wear.

Control Panel-Cam:
She looks out of the window, exhausted, and sighs, her face void of wonderment for what's beyond this ship. Angelique taps her fingers on the control panel while staring out, thinking to herself silently before reaching for the communicator controls.

"*Capacitance* to base, come in... This is the *Capacitance* sending out a distress call. SOS. Come in. This is Dr. Angelique Puck of the *Capacitance*. Is anyone out there?" With her message over, she releases the button.

//

Ship Journal
Dr. Angelique Puck: Login: 7575
Subject: **Distress**

I send out another call and wait. Here shortly, I'll have to make another walk outside to see what else I can find. There's no reason to wait around for a rescue ship or to stand outside with my thumb out; I might as well continue to see what I can get done. Though I am an accomplished doctor, it's going to be tough to continue alone as anyone in my field will tell you, a good team makes all the difference. No woman is an island, but I have to try my best under these circumstances.

I'm itching. Either before or after my spacewalk, I'm going to need another shower. I keep feeling creepy crawlies on me. Walking through the ship, I keep my eyes peeled in case it's not all in my head. I'm thankful the ship's water system is still functional. So much of the *Capacitance* is damaged. I still have plenty of power and resources to live; however, it's in no condition to travel and the communicators still appear to be wrecked. I can't call out and apparently can't receive messages either. I check the gauges again in case anything's changed since I've been on my own, and they're the same. I'm not going to lie to you and say I know exactly what all these meters do, but I figured I'd keep an eye on any changes that may come about. As I said before, I'm not a mechanic.

As beautiful and picturesque as it can be outside, it can also be just as frightening. No matter how far I get in my work up here or how mesmerized by the universe I can get, nothing can clear my mind of what I've seen and been through while up here. Looking out of the bridge's window, the asteroids are a bit too close for comfort. If I didn't know better, I would say they were trying to sideswipe the ship. Actually, the stars, themselves, are looking to be getting closer as well and not in a pleasant way. I squint, and the points of their twinkling bodies alternate between curling and extending as they walk along the black of open space. I'm seeing things. It's all in my head. I *hope* it's all in my head.

I send out another distress call, this time with only the siren beacon and wait. Not too sure a compass would help if I had one as I'm not sure if the laws of North, South, East, and West apply in space, not THIS deep in space anyway. As seasoned as I am in these trips, I've never had to be on one completely alone. At least if I were stranded on a desert island there would be things to build as a shelter or vegetation to live off of. But I suppose I have shelter and food and all, so I shouldn't be complaining too much. I'm still *alive*.

I wonder if anybody misses me; then again, I've lost track of how long I've been gone. It's something that's been discussed among crews, and they always have the same shrug followed by, "Eh, the people back home understand."

...

I checked the rooms again; though, honestly, I can't bring myself to check the cargo bay nearly as often. It's sad seeing everyone's quarters so vacant yet still have their things, almost like reopening a wound, but I feel it's for the best to do routine checks all over the ship. Frost has formed on some of the windows. I'm surprised it's taken *this* long. I keep up my routine with walking the *Capacitance*, not sure if it's to keep my head straight or to stay busy and distract my mind from the loneliness. It's a wonder I've gotten used to the magnetic strips on my boots. It's always a weird feeling to get used to. Actually...it gives me *an idea*, I have to go.

//

Possibilities

Angelique's Room-Cam:

Angelique sits in her bed while her girlfriend is on the screen extended from the wall. Serena is beautiful with light skin and short dark hair gelled back on the sides and spiked up top, her usual look. She has pouty lips and knows how to use them against Angelique along with perfect almond-shaped eyes.

"I miss you too, baby," Serena tells her, using said lips and fluttering eyes.

"I won't be up here long, besides it's for a good cause. You know that," Angelique replies.

"I know, but why did *you* have to go? Why couldn't you just tell people what to look for and what to do and send *them*?" She's frustrated, so-so understandably.

"Serena, you know how important this is to me." Angelique sighs, slumping her shoulders.

"What about me?" She pouts. "Aren't *I* important?"

"Of course you're important to me. This could be great for *us*." She tries to explain the mission's importance, but it doesn't seem to be getting through to Serena who crosses her arms in annoyance.

"Angelique to break room... Angelique to break room..." Miguel calls on the intercom.

"Look, Serena, I gotta go. I love you." Angelique kisses her hand and presses it to the screen.

"I love you too. Be safe." Disappointment is still evident in her tone.

Angelique turns off the screen as it cuts to black and smoothly returns back into the wall when the panel slides over it, encasing the screen, no longer visible.

Break Room-Cam:

The table in the center of the dining area, or the break room area as they usually refer to it, is surrounded by the crew, kicking back and relaxing. Some are eating while others only have a drink.

"Hey gang..." Angelique arrives and grabs a drink before pulling up a seat. There's little to no conversation among them.

"All right, so what exactly are we looking for up here?" Lou Ann asks with her stylus and tablet poised for note taking. She doesn't care about space or the mission's directive; this is a *job* to her.

Angelique speaks up, "We're looking for organisms similar to what was found before."

"So how do we find them?" Lou Ann continues. The others look at each other, not really expecting this downtime to be a question and answer session.

"We just gotta look. It's an *exploration*," Miguel states, taking a drink.

"It's like fishing," Toni adds right after her husband.

"So we don't know what we're going to find. What if there's nothing out here?" Lou Ann doesn't comprehend and eagerly awaits an answer to write.

"Then my job's easier." Saxon laughs. He laughs alone briefly as none of the others pay much attention. He doesn't care.

"We've found plenty up here," Angelique says. "It's all part of search and research, exploration and expedition. There's plenty of space to search, more up here than on Earth. I'm certain we'll find what we're looking for."

"So if you don't find anything, Nelson and the rest of the company is out of quite the large sum of money for this pharmaceutical trip?" Lou Ann's relentless in her job as Nelson's hound; a job she's doing quite well it would seem. Harper and Stanton share a look before going back to listening to the team, their boarders, if you will.

Unexpectedly, Chloe speaks up before the others can give a rebuttal. "It wouldn't be much more than what's being spent on RNS research on Earth. Millions upon millions of dollars are spent trying to find a cure and equal amounts are spent on treatments which have been going nowhere." Chloe isn't vicious with her speaking but isn't afraid to point out the truth of the money issues with the epidemic at hand. Lou Ann nods and makes note of Chloe's statement.

A slight pause hits the group. Harper and Stanton share a smirk and a stifled chuckle as old friends. Miguel whispers in Toni's ear as she giggles and elbows him. Angelique and Chloe smile at one another before returning to their drinks. Lou Ann continues to work, writing in her tablet. Then there's Saxon, who's thinking whilst knocking on the table with no set rhythm.

"I say why can't we just kill every RNS victim there is?" Saxon's thought comes out seemingly abrupt and eyebrows are raised around the table. He continues, "Get them all registered and put in the same place and kill them all, killing the *virus* off at the *same* time." Saxon's soldier method of a gun solving everything doesn't normally go over well in a room full of people who are trying to bring peace and not break millions of hearts.

"That's genocide." Toni's disgusted, her husband sharing her facial expression.

"It's inhumane," Miguel adds.

"What you're talking about is a *holocaust*," Angelique explains, equally as disgusted as her teammates. She puts her drink down.

"Hey, call it what you will but it would solve the problem. Shoot 'em all and burn all the bodies and their possessions so it can't get out," Saxon continues his plan.

"They're not monsters, Saxon. These are sick people who need help," Stanton speaks up, no longer wanting to sit back and listen.

"They're barely human. These people are frozen without a mind of their own, and when someone comes within a whisper's distance, they're bitten and become just like them. You don't think that sounds monstrous?" Saxon makes a valid point, revealing more brain than they give him credit for.

"What you're *proposing* is monstrous. This illness is a tragedy that we're trying to put an end to." Chloe jumps in as it seems as though it's the *Capacitance* verses Saxon while Lou Ann notates everything said.

"And my suggestion puts an end to it and any further infections of this bullshit disease. '*Rabid Neural Stasis.*' Who the hell names these things anyway?" Saxon stands by his proposal and turns his lip up at such "random" naming while they bypass his question and stay on topic.

"There are babies born RNS Positive. Do you expect to kill *them* as well?" Miguel asks.

"It's to save the rest of us, why not?" Saxon believes one hundred percent what he's saying. "Look, I've been briefed on all of this. I've heard the cases about the unresponsive babies who bite their mother's breast when their teeth come in, infecting them. And when it's time for a checkup, more are bitten. One family's infection spreads out. I'm not ignorant to the situation. I just don't see why so much work and money is put into trying to find a cure for something when it can all be taken care of so swiftly and effectively."

Like Stanton, Captain Harper has enough of being on the sidelines in this conversation and decides to jump in. "So instead of finding a cure or an efficient treatment, you'd rather just kill them all? What about everything else? What about the common cold? If someone sneezes will you blow their head off?"

Everyone laughs.

Saxon stands by his statements and shakes his head, chuckling to himself.

"Look, we'll hold a national memorial for all those lost. Better?" Saxon says with a smug smile and his hands out.

"That's supposed to make up for killing so many innocent people?" Toni asks.

"It's better than most soldiers get for fighting for their country and putting their lives on the line daily," Saxon points out.

"And what if that doesn't do it?" Angelique asks. "What if it comes from another source and the slaying of so many was for nothing?"

"Well, we'll never know, and in time while you all wanna hold hands and sing songs, those *things* will keep chomping away and the sickness will keep spreading out just like now." Saxon's blunt. "You all want to keep putting them in kennels. I'm sorry, 'care centers' just to prolong their discomfort. Now who's inhumane?"

"It's the human race we're talking about, not dogs, Saxon," Harper states.

Stanton shakes his head. "That's why these people are here, to fix the problems so we don't get to a state of medical marshal law where we shoot the sick to put them out of their misery," he says, motioning to the medical scientists around the table.

Saxon shrugs and leans forward. "You all watch, this thing's gonna get too far and soon every damn person in America and then the *world* will be infected, chair-bound zombies who starve to death because there will be nobody left to care for them. And when that happens and there still isn't a cure, you'll be thinking '*Ol' Saxon was right. We should've killed them all when we had the chance*'."

"I doubt it," Chloe mutters.

"What if you stop the disease from furthering but there's no change for any of those already infected?" a question from Lou Ann.

Saxon blurts out before anyone else can answer, "I'll tell you what's gonna happen. It's going to be an endless cycle. People get bitten and take their medicine, over and over. The price of treatments go up and not everyone can afford it; just more diversity for such *United* States. The money going to keeping braindead people alive will continue to go up leading to more poverty."

Stanton and Harper share a look before the pilot rolls his eyes and takes a drink.
"That is with the exception of those who will make money off fights they'll organize in a back alley somewhere with RNS+ victims in human cockfights. Years after it's all over, those so *fortunate* enough to survive RNS will be freaks at the circus." Saxon pulls something out of his pocket and slaps it down on the table. Moving his hand reveals a bullet. "You all think I'm some dumb soldier, but I know something you don't and that's the positive effect of a bullet. Kill them now and save yourselves the trouble and the money. You all can go back to making your trips to curing *indigestion*." His monologue's finished with the others staring at him blankly while perturbed.

"So instead of curing *PTSD*, should we kill all the soldiers who come back messed up in the head?" Angelique says, clearly digging at him. He doesn't appreciate it as his face shows. "They choose what they see and experience about as much as an RNS+ victim gets to choose their contracting it and what they experience because of it."

Before he can reply, Chloe verbally steps up. "And what about erectile dysfunction? If a guy can't get it up should we take him out back and shoot him instead of finding a cure?" The others laugh while Chloe's smug look stays strong.

"Well, I ain't gotta worry about that department, baby," he says with a sickening grin while putting his hand on hers. The others watch, rolling their eyes.

Chloe retracts giving a disgusted smirk. "I'll never know."

"We'll see... We'll see..." Saxon gets up and leaves the table and the room.

Everybody let's out a sigh and shakes their heads, except for Lou Ann, of course.

"All right, it's time we got away from childish '*nuke 'em all*' conversations and got serious," Angelique says, taking a drink.

"Okay, so what do you propose, 'Lique? Are we looking to replace the immune system completely or make an anti-virus?" Miguel asks, leaning forward, elbows on the table.

"I'm not for certain. I'm not too sure we can replace the immune system without the new synthetic system becoming infected as well," she replies.

Toni leans forward as well and suggests, "Have we tried giving a patient both the Nu-Myelin Cell and The Bouncer? Do you think both of those together might counteract the RNS virus?"

"I think it'd just be too many various organisms for one body's system to maintain," Angelique says in a shrug. "However, we could always request a test subject, but I'm leery about signing off on that."

They agree.

Lou Ann continues to take notes.

"The big problem with this virus is, while it *is* an infection and does start to show in cold and flu-like symptoms first, it *is* neurological, so I'm on the fence if the gunning for the immune system would actually be beneficial," Angelique explains as the room takes it in.

Lou Ann looks up upon hearing it before writing with a fury.

"I had a nephew who contracted RNS through a simple blood transfusion. Apparently their blood was taken early on. My nephew didn't last long with it," the Captain says to the group. "He just kept getting sicker. They tried to help, but before anything could be done, he choked to death on his foam during a fit, and he was gone."

"That's why we're here," Angelique tells him with a reassuring smile, patting his arm.

"You know..." Stanton enters the fray, "Saxon's crazy, but he does have a point with something. Is there any way to ship all of them to one location? I'm not saying kill them, but to have all of them together?"

Toni and Miguel shake their heads.

"It's inhumane, like Miguel said earlier," Angelique says.

"What do they do with other infectious diseases? They quarantine them, don't they?" Stanton asks. He knows he's out of his element, but he's still trying to help regardless if his sole job is to fly the ship.

"I don't feel like they should all be quarantined or imprisoned because they're *sick*. And that's all quarantine is, is a prison for the ill," Chloe adds. "Rabid Neural Stasis isn't airborne, so there's no need to really quarantine them anyway."

Stanton turns to Harper. "Don't they have ways of checking the blood now before transfusions?"

"If you can afford the scanning process. Most people can't and have to settle for the emergency blood and that DNA is rarely scanned," Harper says very matter-of-fact.

"That's a bunch of hogwash. I hope you all find the cure while we're up here." Aggravated, Stanton stands and returns to the bridge with his food.

"I wish there was a way to make a new immune system, but I think it might be too intensive to work. But then we need to look at the nervous system altogether. So it's all a gamble," Angelique expresses.

Miguel suggests, "What if we rewire the brain? Like if we take out someone's immune system, freeze the body and *then* replace it? Almost like we trick the brain..."

"The virus is in the blood stream though. Even though it affects the nervous system and all, it's proven to start in the blood. You'd almost have to drain someone completely and then refill them. Even if the patient *would* survive the process, which is HIGHLY unlikely in itself, there might still be remnants of the disease inside them and all it would need is a tiny bit for the new blood to become infected. We can't exactly flush them out and clean them," Toni adds.

"Yeah, it's just too dangerous." Angelique turns to Lou Ann. "And if you think *this* trip is costing money, imagine how much it would cost to surgically replace every RNS patient with a synthetic immune system."

Lou Ann thinks it over, nods, and continues making notes.

Chloe states, "So while we're up here, *are* we looking for ways to replace it or ways to cleanse the blood?"

"We're going to have to try different things. We brought along bags of RNS+ blood for that reason." Angelique continues with everyone's attention, "We've found atoms and molecules that graft to one another as well as cells that would become a powerful new white cell anti-virus. I'm hoping that we can find something up *this* alley. I say before jumping into rewiring the brain or trying for a synthetic immune system, we should focus on trying to cure the initial ailment. From there, we'll have to see how it progresses before jumping into neurosurgery."

There's a moment's pause with everyone thinking.

"You said 'cleanse the blood'. If all blood pumps through the heart eventually, is there any way to put a filter in the heart that *would* actually cleanse the blood in its passing?" their Captain asks unexpectedly as they all look at him thinking. "Sorry. I know I'm out of my element. I was just throwing something out there."

They almost forgot he's there.

"You're fine, Captain. It's not a bad idea; it's just that the moment the clean blood touches the infected blood it would go right back to that," Dr. Puck tells him.

"Ah, that makes sense." He stands up. "Well, I'm gonna get back to the front and let you all work," he says upon exiting. The team returns to work.

Bridge-Cam:
Harper enters the bridge as Stanton turns back in his seat. The beautiful Milky Way is visible outside of the window, bright with solar rays.

"Had enough science speak?" Stanton asks with a chuckle.

"That's all *way* out of my league." Harper laughs with a shake of his head and sits next to his pilot.

Break Room-Cam:
The team of experimental medical scientists, pharmaceutical researchers, and a reporter sit around the table sharing "what ifs."

"What if we put enough of the new white cells in them, a mass amount, to see if it could beat it?" Miguel asks.

"I think we'd run into the same problem as if we'd put both that and the NMC into someone—just too much of it inside. Those organisms need to be alive in order to work, and if we *did* happen to fill someone with mass amounts of them, I'm afraid it would be harmful," Dr. Puck answers. "I had an appendectomy once and what is usually an in-and-out procedure left me in the hospital for seven days. Apparently I had an infection in my stomach, and with all the medicine they were pumping in me it had caused another infection and so forth."

"Too much of a good thing..." Toni says, stating the situation correctly.

Lou Ann's having a field day with Angelique's fear of the treatment she's so proud of becoming its own parasite. She remains silent, but Dr. Puck can see it on her.

"I really don't know what happens when you end up with either an equal ratio of those cells and human cells or more of theirs than ours. I would assume that enough of them together, *too much of them*, would actually play host to a body eventually," Angelique explains.

Chloe adds, "But if they're out there in clusters already...?"

"We place them together microscopically, and after force is applied, that's when they join together," Dr. Puck tells her beautiful young teammate.

"Ahhh." Chloe nods.

"If we can't cure and fix everyone already infected, then I hope we can surely prevent future cases." Toni says.

"Well, if Saxon has his way, we won't have to worry about that," Miguel jokes as they share another laugh, albeit inappropriately.

"But that does give me an idea." Angelique holds her finger up. "Since RNS works through one's fluids, what if we could put something in one person and spread it amongst them?" she suggests her fantastical halfcocked idea.

"I suppose we could get a group together and quarantine them." Miguel looks at Chloe. "Just *briefly* and test it out that way..."

"Let's just say," Chloe adds, "that we *did* almost overload someone with those organisms and have that person spread it around the group. I wonder if the dosage or amount of those cells inside of someone wouldn't be so dangerous beyond the first person." The idea strikes the team as a good one, but they're still unsure.

"Again, we'd have legalities and other problems. We'd essentially be asking someone to be a martyr," Dr. Puck states with a wince. "Plus, at that point, we'd be banking on them biting one another to spread it, and we'd be risking the possibility of them bleeding to death."

They fall into silence.

"Everyone, we're about to pass Saturn if any of you would like to take a gander at the rings," Stanton says over the intercom.

"To be continued..." They say in unison, putting their food down to go see the dazzling spectacles that are the rings of Saturn.

Saxon's Room-Cam:

Saxon hears the pilot on the overhead and rolls his eyes. His quarters are not exactly as tidy as the others, with assorted bits of his arsenal laid out and the large punching bag in the center of the room.

He shakes his head after his eye roll. "Puh, rings of Saturn." He groans going back to punching and kicking the large bag. "I didn't even wanna come *up* here." Saxon delivers blows with a fury, frustration and anger evident in his voice. "Nelson, you better be good for the money…" He speaks to himself openly and aloud as he continues his training, keeping his physical skills up to date.

Bridge-Cam:
The crew, minus Saxon, congregate in the cockpit of the *Capacitance*. The view from the window is bright.

Control Panel-Cam:
A collective gasp. Everyone watches with mouths gaped open with the exception of the ever-laid-back pilot wearing his sunglasses. The team looks as if they were all touched by the spirit of Christmas.

Stem-Cam:
Solar rays hit the rings exactly right. The sight is bright and gorgeous. The massiveness of the planet's surrounding hoops is awe-inspiring. The stripes on the planet itself appear to merge together, overlapping one another. Upon getting closer, Saturn's exterior seems to have random creases and craters. The rings balance perfectly around the sphere. The rings themselves don't appear to have an actual color to them but are quite illuminated by the sun. It's a magnificent sight to behold.

Bridge-Cam:
Toni and Miguel snuggle up together in the light of the rings. Stanton keeps his eyes on the black "road" ahead of them as if taking tourists around sightseeing. Harper stands at the window, looking more excited than when they had seen him take the view in from the same spot previously. Lou Ann takes notes, using her tablet to take pictures. Some people would rather view life through an electronic screen than *feeling* the moment and witnessing in person. In her euphoric view, Chloe, soft and angelic, gently leans up against Angelique, however briefly. Angelique smiles at her

before returning her view to the glow and shine of just one of the non-Earth planets in the solar system.

Chloe leans in to Angelique. "I've traveled across country with my family, and I've seen beautiful plains and breathtaking mountains, and I can tell you, nothing compares to this right now." Angelique and Chloe nod, smiling with the glow of children.

Top-Cam:
The *Capacitance* is tiny compared to Saturn. Its rings are immaculate, perfect circles naturally surrounding the planet, not physically connected in any way seen. Beautiful, natural, raw universe seen in person and not from past explorations' satellite photos. Nothing man-made found in such a view, an unaltered and unfiltered galaxy. The view can be as frightening as it can be gorgeous when one considers such a size comparison.

Bridge-Cam:
The ship is passing the momentous view. Everyone smiles, happy with it. Angelique isn't done. She moves to the Stargazer, climbing up.

Top-Cam:
Angelique's smile lights up as her hands press against the glass dome, taking in the view while speaking to herself. "I need to send the recording of the footage to Serena. She's gotta see this. Maybe she'll understand then..."

//

Ship Journal
Dr. Angelique Puck: Login: 7575
Subject: **Serena**

I had returned from my last space mission not too long before when my colleagues had dragged me out after work one night. After hitting a local bar for some embarrassing karaoke, we went to a club to dance, and that's where I met *her*. Serena was dancing with friends. She struck me instantly; she's so hot. She had MOVES, and she obviously knew how to sway her hips as my eyes wouldn't leave them, gliding back and forth. When she sat down at a spot tables away from us, we saw each other and locked eyes briefly. She's black, and her skin is light with flawless complexion.

"Ask her to dance," my friends said.

I tried to play it off. "Psh, who?" I scoffed.

"Who? How about the woman you've been gazing at?"

I laughed and refused. I wanted to but really didn't have it in me. Dealing with things involved with my work such as deadly diseases were one thing, but I wasn't the most confident in my personal life. As we carried on with our drinks and conversation, a familiar pair of tight jeans stopped at our table. We looked up, and indeed, it was the woman I'd been gazing at.

"Hi. I'm Serena," she said.

"I'm Angelique," I replied, shaking her hand.

"Um, well, I was wondering if you'd like to dance." She bit her bottom lip softly.

"Yes, she would," my friends spoke up, laughing.

I happily gave up. "I would love to."

She led me out to the dance floor, and we danced the rest of the night. After that night, we began seeing more and more of each other and kind of fell into dating. It was wonderful. Serena and I laughed together, cried together, and loved together; we were inseparable. We came from different worlds but understood each other. I worked my way through college while she never went beyond high school. I wanted to cure diseases and go to space while she wanted to be a professional dancer and artist. The stage was to her what the stars were to me. She spent her time going to various auditions and performing while I spent mine researching.

I had been to several of her dances and recitals, but she wasn't ever too keen on visiting the labs. I offered to get her a pass for lab entrance, but being around sick people wasn't really her *thing*. I understood and didn't press the issue. We still spent all of our available time together, as said. Over time I got to the point where I mainly stayed at her apartment, though I kept my family's house. My friends and her friends get along fine which helps.

The sex with her had taken me to a new level of intimacy. I wasn't a virgin by any means, but the sex I was used to was a bit different, more conservative if you will. With Serena, we incorporated handcuffs, various gels, and a strap-on among various other things. Sex with Serena was amazing. We did it as often as we could, and as previously stated, we were inseparable.

The time was drawing near. I could tell she wasn't liking the idea of me going away for an undetermined amount of time. She would become distant whenever I would bring it up. This definitely became apparent when I got the word the mission was a go.

"Baby, we got approved! The RNS mission I've been telling you about! I'm going to space!" I told her at lunch outside a local café.

She didn't seem as thrilled as me. "Oh...that's great, babe."

"Well, aren't you excited?" I was hoping.

"Yeah, of course I am," Serena said coldly.

"*But...?*" She was too hesitant for there *not* to be something wrong.

"It's nothing. It's great. It is! Let's celebrate!" She blew it off and put on a happy supportive face, and we had lunch, but I knew.

The morning of the launch, I woke up in a panic, covered in cold sweats.

"You okay, 'Lique?" she asked in her groggy tone. Serena was always a heavy sleeper, and it often took her a long time to wake up.

Ever since I was little, I was prone to strange, erratic, and detailed dreams. This one was jarring. The right to gay marriage was banned nationwide, and all homosexuals had become enemies of the state. Gay clubs were shut down and locked up. Businesses who allowed gay people in their establishments were "cleansed" of their employ, and they were replaced. "No Gays" signs were put up next to the "No Pets" signs. Publishers of Gay Lit were shut down and their books were burned along with books featuring gay characters in a positive light. Production on any homosexual-based films was halted and the footage was destroyed.

I'm sure if they could've physically banned rainbows from occurring after the rain, they would've done so. It had become *illegal* and labeled a national threat to be what God had made us to be. Any touching of the same sex the government had deemed inappropriate had led to the people being red-flagged. Tolerance was no longer tolerable. Hate crimes geared toward homosexuals weren't looked at as such but as necessary police actions whether acted out by deputized lawmen or not.

Soon we were all marked, dressed in the same attire, black trash bags with holes cut out for our arms and heads, and imprisoned. Trials were held in court, but the lawyers representing the gay masses were imprisoned as well. Anyone who was openly okay with the state titled "Villainy" was arrested and held in the same prisons as the ones they supported.

Of course, Serena and I were in the dream and separated, kept in different camps. *Any* couples were separated, dragged apart, and not allowed to see one another again. All of this was to aid yet another campaign promising to "Make America Great Again." I began to hear rapid fire gunshots and screams, and they were getting closer. More panic ensued. I woke up before they got to me and the others around me. As a free gay woman in today's world to find herself in a homosexual holocaust, it was as horrifying as you'd think.

"Yeah, I'm fine," I told her. "Just nerves..." I wasn't about to start her day with such an oddball nightmare like that one.

"You'll do fine, babe. You always do." Even half asleep she was sweet and adorable.

We made love that morning after showers and coffee. She still didn't want me to go. Serena lay on the bed, and I was standing in only a t-shirt about to finish getting dressed.

"C'mon, just a little longer..." Serena pleaded with me as she crawled over, lifted the front of my nightshirt and began kissing my vulva.

It felt good, but I knew I had to get going. "Baby, I gotta go." I chuckled playfully.

I started walking away, and she grunted and sighed, falling back to the bed. I looked back at her and winked as I raised the back of my nightshirt, flashing my ass—a feature of mine she had claimed was atop of her list of favorites. I finished getting dressed and left on my journey to help better the world.

"I love you. I'll be back." Those were the last words I said to her in person.

//

"Actually...it gives me an idea...I have to go."

Propulsion Test

Top-Cam:
The polar opposite of their view of Saturn in the Milky Way galaxy: dark, desolate, cold. Angelique is suited up and on the exterior of the *Capacitance*. She's lit by the ship's lights while backed by a wall of black. There's some kind of mechanism in her hand and a satchel hooked to her belt floating up beside her. She looks around and moves toward the stern of the ship.

Angelique-Cam:
The view of her helmet camera stays mostly on the ship while occasionally looking up to the black richness of space.

"I'm outside on a walk again. After my shower, I spent the last two hours stripping the magnetic plates from the boots of everyone's suits and any extras onboard, attempting to build an apparatus of sorts. I was lucky enough to find more in the storage units. I brought excess strips in this pouch." She approaches the rockets at the rear end of the spacecraft, and they're caked with frost. She looks around, alert, so she won't get torn apart by random space debris. She's clear so she proceeds. "This test may be ridiculous. I'll find out."

"I'm hoping these are the industrial grade magnets I believe them to be. *They would have to be, wouldn't they?*" She uses her gloved hands, sweeping the surface of the rockets, brushing off any excess frost. Some won't come off with a normal wipe, so she knocks some of its coating off first. Angelique doesn't hit it too hard, enough to break it up to pull and sweep the rest of it off. The icy pieces drift up, and she pushes them away from her as they float away soon to be seen no more. The space is clear now.

"Okay, here we go. I'm going to start by setting up my magnetic strips."

The magnets are rectangular and metallic in color. It takes some force and twisting to separate them. She places the magnetic plates on, lining them up one by one beside one another. They clasp easily. She checks them; they're attached firmly.

"First part done. Thank God."

Angelique takes a breath before continuing. She shows the camera her creation. It's a white bracing with a flat end; one could say it looks like a tall, thin, table.

"While inside, what I had spent most of my time constructing. I had taken the fiberglass legs from the table of the break room and built a brace with the magnets at the end. The poles of this large apparatus should be short enough to do what I want it to do."

With her apparatus buckled to her belt, she reaches back in to the pouch. "One of the things we always keep on hand is a certain kind of putty for quick fastening. I don't know who makes it, but it's definitely strong. I'm *hoping* that it holds up the way I hypothesized."

The best she can, she glops the putty down beside the magnets on the rockets' base which was previously frosted over. Her fingers knead the putty to make sure it's sticking in place and won't float away. It's secure.

Angelique reaches for her mechanism, unhooks it from her belt, while still keeping a good hold on it and flips it around. The ends of the legs are placed firmly in the little blobs of putty. She checks its durability; it holds. Another sigh of relief.

"If it works the way the magnets are positioned, they should push against each other. I've gathered *every* magnetic strip onboard, to which there were more than I expected." Both the rockets' and the device's magnetic boards are large and look like small solar panels. It's placed firmly, and she waits *not so* patiently.

"Damn, another failure..." Angelique stays knelt down watching...nothing...but then. "WAIT!" Movement... The magnetic force is present, however slight, and movement is clearly felt regardless of its lack of speed.

Top-Cam:
Angelique raises her arms in her small victory of woman verses universe. Her white suit a stark contrast to her dark surroundings.

"It's not a full take off, but I am now MOVING FORWARD!" She declares.

Stern-Cam:
Frost chips release from the vessel as it moves. With their drifting and the ever so slight movement of the *Capacitance*, the icy bits become smaller and soon gone.

Stem-Cam:
The stars in the distance, no matter how faint, will soon seem closer as the ship is now pushing forward. She has no idea what direction she's really moving in or whether or not she's moving closer to or further away from home, but pushing forward, no matter how slowly, is better than floating and drifting aimlessly.

"I'd rather try to drive to a destination on bum wheels than stay stranded on the side of the road forever. This road, however, is made of stars. Stanton and the Captain would've been proud of me. *I'm* proud of me."

Top-Cam:
She walks across the top of the *Capacitance* toward the front of the slow drifting, albeit no longer stationary starship.

"I'm hoping I can drift to a point where contact can be made." She heads back in via the Stargazer, opening the dome and stepping down. "It's time to get a bite to eat."

//

NEWS REPORT - THE END
Streaming from the logs of the *Capacitance*.

The screen continues with cataloged news feed. The bottom of the screen scrolls with assorted news, mostly pertaining to the RNS epidemic. On the news, an older gentleman sits in an old wooden rocking chair outside of his country home wiping tears from his eyes and face. His shotgun leans up against the house beside him on the porch. His lip quivers as he tries to speak.

"I–I had to do it. Doctors said they can't do nothin' for her. I didn't want to put my wife in one of those care centers. They don't know how to take care of her." He shakes his head and talks in between sniffles and stifled whimpering cries. "I couldn't bear to see her like that. She wouldn't want to live like that, and she wouldn't want the kids seein' her in such a state. She...she just wasn't her anymore. She became somethin' else entirely. So I did it; I had to put her out of her misery. I did what I would've wanted her to do if it happened to me..." With his thumb he motions behind him, tears still streaming. "I shot her and burned her out back."

He continues to let it out when the cameraman hands him a tissue and asks him, "How long were you two married?"

The man looks up with wet eyes. "Thirty-one years." He breaks down more. "She...she doesn't have to be sick anymore."

Screen cuts to black.

//

Ship Journal
Dr. Angelique Puck: Login: 7575
Subject: **Captain Harper**

Harper, the Captain of the *Capacitance*, was older than most of us and looked to be about the same age as our pilot. He was a little shorter than me and taller than the rest of the crew, as I was the tallest on the ship. Harper was white with gray hair once a crew cut but had grown out a bit. He was stocky and despite having the compassion of a father and a husband, he was a no-nonsense kind of guy.

I suppose Captain Harper would be considered the rugged handsome type. He had the same attitude about Saxon's demeanor as the rest of us, of course with less disdain. As someone who'd been through the corporate wringer a time or two, he had little respect for people like Nelson and his cronies but still understood such necessary evils. He didn't like anyone but *him* dictating his ship but understood that without the money these missions would become more and more limited.

Security Feed—Nelson's Office:
Nelson and Harper are in the middle of a rather uncomfortable conversation as the Captain sits where Angelique has been more times than she would like with Nelson across from him.

"I...*trust* we have an understanding, Mr. Harper." Nelson says in his usual condescending tone.

"This is still *my* ship, Nelson," Harper reminds him.

"Yes, and you signed the contract for this mission so, while the vessel is indeed yours, the resources onboard belong to me." Nelson smirks.

Harper sits back and shakes his head. "See, that's the problem with you pencil pushers, you make decisions for situations you know nothing about and you throw money at people and you think you've bought them." Harper doesn't hide his dislike and lack of trust in the suits who fund such missions he leads.

"Oh, I don't think I've bought you at all, Mr. Harper." His tone is snide at best.

"That's good because I'm not for sale," Harper is adamant.

"I'm just...*renting* you is all." Nelson grins, feeling he has the Captain where he wants him. Almost a solid sixty seconds run by with the two men looking at one another.

"I think we're done here. I need to get to work." Harper groans. He stands to leave.

Nelson calls to him, "Mr. Harper, *do* take care of my property..."

Harper stops, looking back over his shoulder slightly. "Yeah, wouldn't want to lose my deposit..."

Break Room-Cam:
The crew enjoys a brief time off for a card game around the table.

"I'm out," Toni says, putting her cards down.

"Me too. I got nothin'," Miguel adds. They look at each other, giving a playfully seductive gaze before exiting the room.

"I'm still in," Angelique says.

"Me, too," Harper adds. "Stanton?"

"Yo." His usual response when most would say 'Yes'. The game continues.

"So what about you, Harper? You seem like a military man. You ever see combat?" Saxon asks the captain.

"Yeah, I've been to war a time or two." Harper nods.

"Doesn't sound like it suited your fancy...?" Saxon says taking a drink.

Harper shrugs. "I always came back in one piece, and the money was good so it was always in my mind to reenlist."

"I'll drink to that," Saxon says with pride.

"Yeah, well..." Harper says as they continue playing, "in what would've been called World War III, had it been official, my team and I had ransacked a village in search for nukes. We saw a suspicious looking man run into a small hut, and we pursued him. Upon kicking in the door, all we found was a family in panic. Whoever had run in had already left through the back. The mother of the family stood up screaming. Some of my men ran out the back after the suspicious character. I tried to talk to her, but neither of us could understand each other. While children ran around the hut crying, she had a newborn on her breast. The situation was getting more heated. She was becoming more irate when the soldier to my right stepped up and put a bullet through the baby's head and therefore through the woman's heart, killing them both. We moved on to the rest of the warzone. But no matter what happened or what was seen, the image never left my mind." Harper shakes his head, blinking hard. The others watch the conversation.

"Bravo. That's what I say. Kill them young before they can grow up to become terrorists," Saxon says.

Harper ignores Saxon and continues, "After that incident I decided not to reenlist. I opted to get in the space biz, captaining missions up here, a lot less unnecessary deaths."

"Well, I'm glad you're here to captain our mission," Angelique tells him. "However, I am *out*." She lays her cards down, defeated.

"Me, too," Stanton says. He gets up, finishes his coffee, and goes back to the bridge.

Angelique leaves the awkward room and returns to her quarters.

Lou Ann stays and continues to document everything.

Harper's Room-Cam:
Harper sits in his chair in his quarters while speaking to his wife on the video screen extended from the wall. He's relaxed and in good

spirits. His wife is around his age and pretty with red hair.

"Hi, honey, how are things at home?" Captain Harper asks.

"Oh same ol' same ol'. We on Earth have to deal with the perils of gravity." She laughs.

"Well, you wear it well." He chuckles with her.

"How are things up there in our big universe? You surrounded by hot ladies dancing everywhere and bringing you cocktails?" Her playful sarcasm comes across fully.

Harper laughs. "Of course, honey. Don't you know I run the hottest brothel in space?" The two laugh.

Bridge-Cam:
Harper joins Stanton, Lou Ann, and Angelique on the bridge. Stanton is in his seat as always, playing solitaire on a handheld device. An old world game for an old world man. The others are resting after getting back from a walk, searching for anything they can find to help them on their research. Lou Ann has her tablet in hand as always for her reports to Nelson. She questions Captain Harper while Angelique sits among the group.

"So, Captain Harper, how long have you been captaining ships like this?" Lou Ann asks.

"I've been doing this for around twenty years. Space travel was becoming more prominent, and it seemed a lot safer than what I was used to. After getting out of the military, I acquired this ship. It was a little rough, but we got 'er fixed up. I've worked with a lot of different pilots, been on more than several flights with Stanton." He pats Stanton's shoulder.

"Yo." The pilot chimes in, holding his finger up but not taking his eyes off of his game.

"Since I had flight experience, it helped me get the first job and then so forth. I've been to the stars plenty, and it never ceases to amaze me," he says, looking out of the window.

Lou Ann continues, "Have you ever had anything go wrong?"

He shakes his head. "No, thank God. I can honestly say I've been blessed. Of course, most, if not all, of the missions I've been a part of have been routine, much like this one, which is why we're all finding it a bit odd to have security onboard." Stanton and Dr. Puck visibly agree.

"It's routine for legalities and all. Just something Nelson wanted to make sure everything went safe and smooth," Lou Ann says with a plastic smile as if rehearsed.

"Dr. Puck, if I'm not mistaken this is primarily for pharmaceutical and...*surgical* purposes, yes?" Captain Harper asks, trying to find the right terminology.

She replies, "Absolutely. It's the same type of mission I've helped put together for five trips now. We've never had a use for a machine gun up here while trying to find cures."

"Oh, so this is *your* mission?" Lou Ann seems surprised.

Angelique is stunned while Stanton and Harper laugh heartily.

"For someone who seems to want to know an awful lot, you don't really seem to do your research." Captain Harper chuckles.

Lou Ann appears embarrassed. "Yes, well, I think I've got all I need for now. Thank you, Captain." She leaves the bridge, and they all continue to chuckle and shake their heads in amusement.

"Nelson sure knows how to pick 'em." Harper laughs.

Angelique smiles; it makes her day.

//

Meditation

Top-Cam:

Angelique is heading into the *Capacitance* by way of the Stargazer. She stops before completely submerging into the ship and looks out into the darkness and nods.

"After my magnetic propulsion proved successful, about as successful as can be moving this thing without rocket power, I was going to go eat. However, I *just* realized it was good time for some meditation."

She climbs out and checks her safety cord; it's tethered securely. Angelique walks across to the side of the ship on the edge and turns around. Dr. Puck reaches down, pressing the switch at her ankles, releasing the magnetic hold of her boots and pushing herself back out into the black nothing of space and just...*drifts*. The oscillating camera atop the ship sees plenty off to the sides, including Angelique floating about by her lonesome, another white speck in this otherwise stark black terrain.

"I feel weightless with nothing holding me back." She floats without purpose or a need to be *doing* something, she just *is*. "Back when everybody was still alive and our crew was at full capacity, we hit the same stressful times we always hit seeking knowledge."

Break Room-Cam:
Toni explains to everyone at the table, talking with her hands. She's got everyone's attention, except for Saxon, of course, who couldn't care less.

"Toni was big into yoga, transcendental meditation, and various other things and suggested we do meditation but with a catch."

Top-Cam:
The crew stands on the exterior of the *Capacitance* suited up as Toni is the first one to release herself from the ship, floating outward while still tethered.

Toni-Cam:
From her helmet, Toni's with the crew on the spacecraft one moment and drifting out into space the next. She breathes and pulls herself back in, showing the crew.

"*One by one we would all float and drift into the open galaxy by our lonesome eventually turning our radios off, just time to ourselves. We tried it, and it worked,*" Angelique explains.

Lou Ann-Cam:
Lou Ann's shaky in her first attempt at this but the others are supportive.

"Wait, uh, I don't know..." Lou Ann nervously says.

"You're okay. Don't worry," Miguel reassures her.

"We're gonna be right here," Angelique tells her.

They release the gravity grip and push her out while she lets out stilted breaths. Less than relaxed, her vision slings around, looking all around her with her breathing still erratic.

"*Lou Ann, as someone who was neither an astronaut nor a scientist, had a lot of troubles with it at first. She felt it was too scary being out in the unknown,*" Angelique continues while, herself, floating about, reminiscing.

Stanton-Cam:
Stanton stands before the others as they try to prep him the same way they had with Lou Ann. Unlike the reporter, he's relaxed and very nonchalant about his attempt.

"Don't worry, man. I got this." He pushes himself out. "This feels weird when you're used to *flying* a ship." Stanton relaxes in his view, and he takes a deep breath. "Oh, man, this is nice actually. I think I might just close my eyes for a minute."

"*Stanton enjoyed it a little too much as he fell asleep, snoring amongst the stars.*"

Angelique-Cam:
They're pulling Captain Harper back in from his walk. He seems relaxed and loose.

"You okay?" Dr. Puck asks him.

He smiles and gives a thumb up. "I'm good. I liked that."

"Captain Harper found it helped his peace level."

Top-Cam:
Toni and Miguel go out together, holding hands in their drifting meditation. They look like they're relaxing out in the ocean, on a vacation far, *far* from home.

"Miguel and Toni were used things like this so it was second nature to them and always helpful in keeping their peaceful mentalities."

Angelique-Cam:
Chloe's laugh is infectious as Angelique and the others laugh along while watching her out in open space doing twists and flips.

"I think Chloe was having more fun than deep thought as she was doing somersaults and cartwheels. I'm sure she just enjoyed the odd sense of freedom you'd feel when out here."

Break Room-Cam:
Around the table as Toni's explaining how to go about this, everyone's involved but Saxon, who's shaking his head 'No' before crossing his arms.

"Saxon refused to do it as it was against his security protocol, but perhaps he was too scared, we'll never know."

Angelique-Cam:
With the memories back to being exactly that, Angelique continues her solo meditation. The view of her helmet camera is simple, saying so little but so much at the same time: black, deep, deep space. The view is plain yet encompassing, unforgiving, and solid as a thick wall, which keeps one wondering what is beyond it.

"I always thought it felt lovely, like being covered in black velvet or being in a deep sleep with your eyes open. I probably should be thinking about all the sick people on Earth we had helped and the ones we were continuing to help, but more often than not, I end up thinking about Mom and Dad and Serena, among others.

Regardless of what we all thought about or experienced while out here drifting in this black sea, we all came back refreshed for the most part."

Top-Cam:
Dr. Puck floats still, being held up by the universe as if resting in the palm of God. She doesn't flail, doesn't do flips, doesn't sleep, but rests, drifting.

"This time is different for me. I find myself asking more questions than thinking of peaceful things or people. Why did this happen? Five missions and four of them benign, so why was this one so hazardous, so malignant? Where did we go wrong? I would think that maybe we really shouldn't be up here looking for answers, but we've helped so many people. Perhaps I should've listened to Serena and stayed with her, but then again, I would've gone through life not knowing. I can't think of much I dislike more than *not knowing*. I think that's one of the main reasons I went into the field I did. I hated hearing, when asked about the cures or proper treatments to various diseases, '*We don't know*.'"

She backstrokes, trying to get deeper into the void. "We always see space as white over black; bright stars over a thick dark open...but what if it's the opposite? What if the universe is really the florescent brightness and the darkness is covering most of it? When people die, they say they see a bright light; I wonder if they're seeing through the dark to the real universe, the blindingly bright open covered to most of us. Will we ever find out? I'm certain *that's* a mission which would never be funded."

Angelique-Cam:
She looks around viewing space and more space, occasionally seeing the *Capacitance* along with speckled dots of stars.

"I know he's busy, but surely God sees me out here. I'm the only one, to my knowledge, floating about the universe lost and alone. I could really use a hand right now. Even if I don't make it, I hope to at least find the answers I seek. I know I sound like a martyr right now, but I'd sacrifice myself to save millions, easily. It makes me wonder who else is up here at this moment having the same thoughts about the world. Maybe they're on the other side of the galaxy, deep in thought, pondering the secrets of the great black yonder."

She moves, looking back at the ship before looking at her hands, one at a time. She reaches them out, feeling the open space around her. "I feel like I'm being carried but the hands are so soft they aren't felt. On occasion I can feel the current, or at least, I *think* I do."

Her view looks out in the distance with her fingers almost appearing to pinch at distant stars and random asteroid pieces. "The planets used to be in the distance, looking as small as the moon does from Earth, but now they're nowhere in sight unless those are the specks I'm seeing far off." Angelique swims in place placidly.

"A million and one thoughts run through my head sporadically like stars across the Milky Way. Everything surrounds the sun in our galaxy; it makes me wonder if God resides in it. It's the largest thing in our known galaxy. Statistically, realistically, and scientifically speaking since our sun is a medium star, when it becomes a red giant and incinerates everything, I wonder if that's God taking everything back, for our galaxy anyway, as there are over a hundred billion out here. I know it's not very Christian like to think, but maybe there are several Gods in suns across this vast universe, watching over their various galaxies."

She reaches for more stars, lining up her gloved hands to where it looks as though she's holding them. "I wonder if I can actually still see the sun, as if it's just distant, like a star looks like from my bedroom window at home. Just once, I'd like to see one up close, but my luck would have it burn me alive. Still, it'd be a hell of a way to go, huh?"

Her hand taps the front of her helmet. "If it wasn't for the glass on my helmet, I wouldn't know the difference between opening my eyes and closing them. I understand it would be scary for some, like suddenly becoming blind, but for me it feels cozy like nuzzling up in a silent pitch black room."

Angelique's vision is more levels of darkness as she turns and leans in to the space around her. Soon, she turns and looks at the floating spacecraft. The ship doesn't appear nearly as damaged as it is, and looking at it, one would never assume such horrors took place aboard such a vessel. "The only light around comes from the *Capacitance* behind me. While our troubles had damaged a good deal of the ship, we managed to keep our lights, so it's a nice break from the darkness. Everything in moderation I suppose."

Top-Cam:
Angelique does backstrokes in the thick void.

"I feel free. I should do like Chloe and start doing flips, but I'm about done with my time out here. I wonder...if we do happen to cure RNS, or at least find a treatment, what happens next? There will always be diseases." She stops swimming and floats still, thinking.

"I hope someone will continue my research when I'm gone. But where do these illnesses *come from* if they haven't been around long in the timeline of it all? What if they've always been here but needed a trigger? Of course, if that's the case, what are the triggers? It's been suggested that a lot of heavy diseases have come about through medical testing for prior ailments. If this is true, have I been creating a new evil in my attempts? It's a scary thought and a double-edged sword in trying to help. Perhaps it's in human arrogance that we try to save the world. But maybe, if we were the creators of such monsters as Cancer, Multiple Sclerosis, and RNS, shouldn't it be our duty to take care of the mistakes and clean up after ourselves?"

Angelique moves around as if she's hiking. "With these thoughts within deep meditation, still I press forward on my mission. If I unleash something in my attempts, I only hope someone will come behind me to find a cure for it. Medical science is a vicious circle. We've mastered interstellar travel, but it'd be nice when they day comes we at least manage *inter-dimensional* travel. Perhaps our same doctors and researchers on another plane have already found the answers. I hope the other *us* in other dimensions are healthy and safe. Maybe there are so many different dimensions with so many variants of us that we, technically, live forever; variations of the same us stretched throughout time. Maybe there's even less war. Who knows?"

Angelique-Cam:
She looks over to the *Capacitance* and slowly pulls herself back in by the cord.

"That does bring me to another thought in this stream of conscious rambling: the universe is known as all space and matter as a whole, are we perhaps a little too 'the earth is flat' with such a human-penned definition?" The ship becomes larger as she gets closer. "Suppose maybe there are indeed more universes than this one, only we don't know where one ends and one begins. I suppose it's much like state lines, without signs you could drive or walk across various state lines and not really tell where you are. If only there were a map of the universe(s), then we'd know."

Top-Cam:
Angelique stands firmly on the ship with her boots locked on. She looks around at the surrounding universe before turning back to open the glass dome of the Stargazer.

"I'm heading back in now. I need some sleep. A good rest will surely help." Inside, she closes the dome. The *Capacitance* floats as if having its own meditation time.

//

Ship Journal
Dr. Angelique Puck: Login: 7575
Subject: **Rude Awakening**

I just woke up from a dream, a nightmare I've had on occasion. I'm piloting a solo pod: sleek, red, and aerodynamic. I stray too far from the base. Out of nowhere my instruments go haywire. I'm losing power, and I know I can't get back to base in time. For some reason, I can't reach them to send someone out to pull me back in, either. I need to bring her down.

Luckily, next to me is a small planet, about the size of the Earth's moon. Anything to land on, any port in a storm. I break through its atmosphere with violent vibrations and the inevitable flames. The pod holds together well, and I'm coming in for a hopefully safe landing. Below me, through troubled sight, almost looks to be a tropical resort of sorts. This planet doesn't appear harsh.

Resistance is met, and thankfully I land atop a body of water where my pod skis across to the nearest land, coming to a crashing halt on a beach shore. There doesn't seem to be civilization around as I've crash-landed on a desert island. I get out and check my vessel, and I'm utterly lost at what went wrong. Everything abruptly stopped in mid-flight.

I hear something, *people*, in the distance. I look around for locals when I see something. A group of women come over and down the hill, and once they hit the level ground, they rush over to aid me. There's not a man among them. The women are all drop-dead gorgeous and seem very intelligent. They approach me, and I take my helmet off. They react strangely to me at first but soon agree to help. They take me back to their city and tell me they'll send a mechanic out to fix my pod up. Their society is one of the most peaceful and advanced I've ever been to. Poverty and pollution seems to be at a low as well as violence. Not a man in sight: I'm quickly realizing this is a planet of *only* women, beautifully perfect women of different sizes and colors.

Seeing this wonderful civilization, you'd think I'd be in heaven, but I'm not feeling anything for what my eyes are taking in. Heart, mind, and body, none of which are basking in such a wonder. I find a washroom to clean up when I see myself in the mirror, and I'm a man. Having never seen this man before, despite being myself, I'm attracted to him. I'm a man but more specifically, I'm a *gay* man. I knew it was too good to be true. I crash land on a world of nothing but women in their varied beauty and intelligence, and here I stand in a washroom, a homosexual male. Once this is realized I woke up.

//

Back to Work

Control Panel-Cam:
Angelique sips her coffee in the pilot's chair while talking to the camera. She tends to use the control panel camera as her

confessional a good deal of the time. Despite being on camera all across the ship and voice recording her journal, this feels more direct and personal for her.

"Despite having such a dream, I feel rested, and it's time to get back to work. I checked for any messages, and of course, there's *nothing*." She shrugs. "Before I head to the lab, I'm going to check in on the other rooms."

Toni & Miguel's Room-Cam:
Angelique enters the couple's room, giving a look around before backing out.

"The doors thankfully still open with ease. The last thing I'd need at this point is for the doors to go too," Angelique says, glancing at the door closing on her way out.

Chloe's Room-Cam:
Angelique does the same, stepping in and peeking around before exiting.

Stanton's Room-Cam:
The pilot's room is untouched as well.

Harper's Room-Cam:
Angelique checks in at the Captain's quarters. It's like the rest of them. Before she exits, she looks down at his bedside table to see a photo of Harper and his wife. Angelique sighs, a reminder of the widow he left behind. She leaves.

Lou Ann's Room-Cam:
Her room appears more like a reporter's office than it does a bedroom. Papers and notes are scattered all over the desk and table. Angelique nods and exits.

Saxon's Room-Cam:
Angelique chuckles and shakes her head like she does every time she sees his room. Much like Lou Ann's was littered with notes, his is littered with various weaponry, though certainly not as messy.

Cargo Bay-Cam:

She opens the door and peeks in with trepidation. Angelique trembles slightly while looking in, counting silently to herself: one, two, three, four, five, six, seven bags, all still. The room is calm despite her unease. She doesn't walk in any farther and exits with a shiver. The seven bags, all full, remain still and together in their lonesome.

DocLab 7-Cam:
Angelique enters her lab with a sigh before shutting the door behind her.

"Thankfully, all the rooms look the same with no change. Eventually I'll get inquisitive enough to actually look around. For now, I just peek in and make sure nothing's changed." She walks to the large, busy table. "First, I'm going to check on the specimen I had left in here earlier, the microorganisms with the RNS+ blood in cryonics."

She does so with a droplet beneath her microscope. "It looks to be holding up okay, but we can't have everyone walking around with cryogenics in their bodies, if they'd even *survive* it. I'm going to leave it out a while and then check it again. Time to move on..."

Angelique goes to her clear casings of assorted space-mites.

"I have various samples of particles we've found up here, and as requested, I also have some from past missions." She brings samples over to her friend, the advanced *microscope*, and looks deep.

"Looking at them all individually under the microscope, it strikes me odd how they're all so similar. I still think they must be, collectively, a race unto themselves. There are obvious differences but not enough to easily spot unless you've spent time with either of them. The Nu-Myelin Cell mites were found on the opposite end of the galaxy; it *still* makes me wonder how far out these things go, and where they actually come from."

One by one she tests the new "cells" with the infected blood. "Considering Serena's reaction when I sent her a snippet of the live feed footage of Saturn, I highly doubt she'd be interested in seeing how alien life forms merge with infected human blood. I sent her the video and she said 'Wow, it looks just like in the movies.' She didn't fully feel the awe. I suppose something gets lost in translation when an image is sent digitally."

Angelique continues her eye-straining work with microscopic creatures and dangerously infectious blood. "Though we had collected some on this mission, tragedy had struck before we got to do a bunch of this work. Going at it alone will take time, but it appears time is something I have," she says, not looking up from her work.

Angelique is hunched over, more than likely feeling like a giant in these experiments. "Each of these organisms reacts to the blood in a different way, but nothing seems to affect the disease as a whole. I'm trying different combinations in hopes that all these external cells are compatible with one another because, if they're not, there's no reason to try to mix them in someone's bloodstream. I start with the Nu-Myelin Cell and The Bouncer as per Miguel's suggestion."

She retrieves the cells from two specially marked casings and returns to hunching over with her utensils. "Using my needle-like instruments, I push the little chromosomes, silver in appearance, toward one another. They're hesitant at first, but they grasp each other. ...And they appear as one cell now: stable, strong."

She sits back for a second to rest. "Looks like Miguel was right. I'll add the blood to see how it affects it. Wait a second." She sees something. "The cell is gyrating, becoming unstable. It looks to be having a seizure. The combined cells are shaking violently." Her head cocks back. The glass they're on is vibrating, tapping about. Not liking where this is going, she pulls back from the microscope.

She jumps back, shielding herself. The glass EXPLODES with a loud POP, shattering everywhere while throwing and breaking the microscope. She drops her arm, looking at the mess. "It goes without saying, but the two together proved *highly* unstable. In an instance like this, it sucks being right. Well, I'll have to clean this mess up before I get to any more testing. This is definitely where an assistant would come in handy."

Control Panel-Cam:
Angelique leans back from the control panel, exhausted at the ship's

helm.

"With the lab cleaned, I went ahead and sent out another distress call. Years ago, cell phone providers had tried to get specific satellites up, matching their towers so when the day galactic migration was made readily available to the masses there would be cell phone service up here. It never went through as it would cost too much; of course, it's been argued that if the rates went up per user it would even out in the back end. At a time like this, I would've loved it if the order would've gone through. With the ship's communicators out, a cell phone would be of great help. Being stranded out this far, it's highly unlikely I'll see a rescue vessel or even be able to get an SOS successfully released."

She stretches. "I'm gonna get a bite to eat and then get back to work."

//

NEWS REPORT - A HOLY BLESSING
Streaming from the logs of the *Capacitance*.

The screen ignites with the holy image of three nuns gathered together out in front of their convent to share a message.

"To our brothers and sisters in Christ heading up on this crucial mission, we pray you a safe trip. This disease that has taken so many of God's children from us is surely the work of the Devil. Sometimes prayer alone can't defeat him and action needs to be taken. You are instruments of God, and we know you and the Lord will make it right and bring this sickness down. Our prayers and hopes are with you. Godspeed and God bless."

The holy message fades to black.

//

Ship Journal
Dr. Angelique Puck: Login: 7575
Subject: **A Revelation**

The combination of the two cells being unstable didn't come as too much of a shock to me, no matter how helpful they were in their respective diseases, due to a find we'd made not too long before everything went south. The lack of stability wasn't a surprise, but the two similar cells coming from two different locations—that one still baffles me. Regardless, I still had to try.

Top-Cam:
The crew of Angelique, Miguel, Toni, and Chloe are out on the ship, suited up, and all with their "bags." The med team all have their industrial flashlights and pouches dangling from their belts along with the safety cable, keeping them tethered to the spacecraft in case they're knocked away or the unlikely chance of their magnetic boots were happen to lose connection. They all walk off in four different directions on the spacecraft's exterior.

"We had come to a stop and decided to go on a walk in search of the same clusters we'd found previously. It was exactly like it was put earlier, fishing. We never knew what we were going to find and where as we couldn't really find any specific place these little beings were indigenous to. My team and I would walk the length of the Capacitance's exterior in different directions. We'd had our lights and bags like children trying to catch fireflies on a summer night. We were looking out when we should've been looking down. That's just what Miguel did when he'd almost stumbled, noticing a cluster of the microorganisms right on top of the ship."

Angelique-Cam:
She looks out into the black around them in hopes to find a certain shimmer. The light catches nothing but *black*. Her light only travels so far before it's cut off by the darkness, swallowed, and digested.

"Hey, Lique'..." Miguel's voice comes through her headset.

"Yeah?" Angelique answers, still shining her light out to the darkness.

"You should see this."

Top-Cam:
Chloe, Toni, and Angelique make their way to the ship's rear where Miguel is with big, almost exaggerated steps while still shining their

lights about, looking all around them.

Chloe-Cam:
The others all walk together alongside Chloe to reach Miguel. He's crouched down. The shimmer is seen.

Toni-Cam:
Sure enough, there's quite the large amount of these tiny space dust mites. They're in a cluster, a cloud teeming with life. The mound jumps around while still stationary. While some of the nano-aliens bounce off of one another, the others seem to stay tight and close with each other. The huddle glistens beneath the four beams of light.

"Ah," Toni says. Beneath their lights they watch as the space-mites continue to move around but stick close to the outside of the vessel, still with some moving toward each other and others moving away.

Top-Cam:
They each bag up as much as they can, using their hands to scoop those evading the plastic netting. With each having bags plenty full, they head back in through one of the hatches, all of them looking around at the lack of worlds around them before submerging into the *Capacitance*.

DocLab 7-Cam:
Still suited, they enter the lab and put them in the glass cases on the counter at the back wall. Angelique takes off her helmet and gloves and sits down at the microscope to look at a select few while the mites are being emptied from bags into casings. Chloe sits down beside her to inspect some of them herself. They waste no time getting to work.

"These look like the others," Angelique says, looking up from the microscope.

"These too," Chloe adds at another microscope.

"Still look chrome?" Toni asks.

"Yeah," Angelique answers. "It's odd. All the same make at different points in the universe." She pulls back and thinks to herself.

The others wait.

"Maybe these are actually the *little green men* everyone's so interested in," Toni jokes.

"Well, maybe these are vessels and the actual lifeforms are piloting them. Can we *cut* one?" Chloe suggests.

"If we can split the atom, I'm sure we can cut into one of these." Miguel chuckles.

"Okay..." With the instruments beside her on the table, Dr. Puck attempts to make an incision on the one she has on the glass. It's tough, even for its size. Angelique's eyes readjust as she looks harder, squinting. She tries to penetrate it with a needle and then even a scalpel but it won't really go.

"Hmm..." She hums while her mouth scrunches as a child's would, curiously. She looks up to the others awaiting an answer. "I can't break through it. We'll need a laser." Angelique nods.

"I'm on it," Miguel says, leaving the lab to another to get a laser-cutter.

"These things are getting more interesting by the moment," Chloe says, crossing her arms, sitting back, and looking at Angelique.

"Yeah, I attempted to cut one before, but it wasn't happening. Everything we did was using them as a whole and using their grafting abilities to combine them." Angelique shrugs.

"I'm actually surprised that the military hasn't tried to acquire those in the NMC for armor plating. The possibilities are actually endless," Toni says, leaning up against the counter. Chloe nods before looking over to Angelique.

"Eh, not my field. I don't own these by any means." Angelique chuckles. "I don't have a patent for them or anything. They could come up here and find them if they were interested. But I'm sure it goes against protocol and regulations so…"

"We'll let Saxon have *that* mission." Chloe jokes as they all snicker.

Miguel returns with the laser-cutter-microscope combo and sets it up. Angelique hands him the glass with the same cell on it she was trying to cut. Miguel places it underneath and turns it on.

"Okay, here we go," he says as he turns on the laser.

The ladies watch with mentally crossed fingers. They see a blue light about the size of a hair and hear the hum accompanying it. He watches as it cuts, keeping the girls posted.

"It's giving a lot of resistance, this one." His face shows struggle with the cutter. The mechanism vibrates, hitting said resistance like a chainsaw hitting a knot or tough spot in a log. "Okay, it's cutting. We're through."

The others perk up as his excitement grows. He briefly rubs his eyes and returns to his view.

"Well, anything inside?" Chloe asks.

He sighs.

"Ah, *damn it*," he says looking up at them. "We lost it. It was fighting the laser, but when it went through, it seized and fell apart. Looks like a little metallic puddle now. It killed it," Miguel says, sitting back looking at the rest of his team.

"Well, that answers *that*," Angelique says.

"So it *is* the living organism and *not* a shell for one," Toni says in clarification.

Angelique answers, "That appears to be the case."

They take the information in.

"The thing's tough," Miguel says, thinking to himself. "I have a thought..."

They're all ears.

"They were huddled around the outside of the ship, they look metallic, and they seem just as strong," he says as if thinking aloud.

"Could they be magnetically driven?" Toni asks.

Angelique is glowing.

"That's actually what I'm thinking," Miguel answers, still in thought. "We all noticed how some would go together and some wouldn't." They all nod, agreeing with the excitement of a breakthrough shared. "Well, if it is magnetic, even slightly, then..."

Angelique jumps in knowing exactly where he's going. "Then some of them might be positives and some might be negatives explaining the difference in the way they cluster." The lab becomes a universal smile. Angelique couldn't be happier to have this team, *her* team. The synergism in the room is strong.

"Yes!" Toni says excitedly. "But separating these holding tanks is gonna be ridiculous." Her look is one of uncertainty.

"It'll definitely take a while," Chloe says, looking over at the clear tanks holding their little shimmering mites, bouncing around.

"Well, it might not take as long as we think," Miguel states, standing up.

"Got an idea?" Toni asks. They watch as he grabs a flashlight.

"Yeah, turn off the lights..."

Angelique moves to the lights, shutting them off and cutting the room to darkness. Miguel turns on his flashlight and points it directly into the clear case. The light glistens and sparkles as they move around chaotically. There's no color difference in the shimmers. The four lean in watching them almost dance. The team's faces are lit by the reflective light given off the mini cloud of alien life. As seen outside, only with closer inspection, some flock to each other while others bounce off one another. They watch in awe of such a thing.

"It's like we caught a bunch of stars. Makes you wonder what we're really seeing out there," Chloe says quietly to herself, watching them.

"If we kept our view like this, we should be able to retrieve and separate them," Miguel suggests. "We would have to label and assume what would be a negative and a positive but the opposites will be easier."

They all agree and get to work using small nets similar to what one would find used for a fish tank.

Security Feed—Lab Hall:
The lab's darkened but the shine of flashlights and metallic glistening are bright, escaping the glass into the hall. Lou Ann snoops around, surely wondering what they're doing in the darkened room while seeing lights flickering and shining, while some of the metallic glistening even runs across her person on occasion. Not noticing her, or simply ignoring her, they continue to work. She leaves, marking it down in her tablet.

The Captain and the pilot almost always stay on the bridge.

Saxon hardly ever comes around the lab hall; actually, they rarely see him around at all, which furthers the question, "Why is it so important for Nelson to have him here?"

DocLab 7-Cam:
It takes hours to separate the tiny beings, but Dr. Puck and her team get it done. With the lights now on, they all rub their eyes and shake their heads. A case is labeled "Positives" while another is labeled "Negatives."

"Well, gang," Angelique says, looking at the three of them. "It looks like if they *do* happen to get pierced, they die, *but*, if it gave a laser trouble in the process, I think we'll be okay. Now we're going to see what else we can find and then see what we can come up with." She smiles and claps her hands together.

"All right!" Glowing, the other three are equally as excited as Angelique.

//

Ship Journal
Dr. Angelique Puck: Login: 7575
Subject: **Stanton**

Stanton was about Harper's age and slightly shorter. He was thin and lanky with graying hair and almost *always* had a five o'clock shadow along with his baseball cap. The pilot was always a laid back guy as I've mentioned plenty. Long ago he would be referred to as an ex-hippie. He always had an easygoing attitude and didn't really take up strife with anyone no matter how annoying they were.

Stanton dealt with Lou Ann's questioning and Saxon's attitude like a champ, and even handled mine and the rest of the crew's little idiosyncrasies with charm. Actually, I would probably best describe Stanton as the polar opposite of Saxon. He's kind of the old world's working man, who had learned long ago to let things go. He was a kidder but definitely got serious and got things done when he needed to. And, most importantly, he was one hell of a pilot.

Security Feed 2—Loading Bay:
The *Capacitance* sits, docked in the loading bay. Various workers scatter about while Captain Harper stands outside of the ship, checking things off his clipboard. Pilot and friend, Stanton, approaches; his lankiness and easy going attitude is a contrast to his friend's stocky build and strong stance. Stanton looks at the Captain and the *Capacitance*, nodding.

"I see you left my ship intact," Stanton jokes.

"*Your* ship?" Harper laughs. They shake hands, *old* friends.

"I saw on the Flyers' Log that you had Taggart flyin' 'er last time." Stanton takes off his hat, rubbing his head with it before putting it back on. "Hopefully, he didn't mess with my settings." He chuckles.

"Yeah, don't worry. He didn't touch the radio," Harper quips.

"I just got done flying the Viper last week," Stanton says, nodding.

"Oh *yeah*? How'd it go?" Harper asks.

"...Smooth." He shrugs. "Kinda weird, though, everything was top secret even to me. I got my flight pattern and that was it. I think I overheard them talking about looking for alien life or something, had plenty of firepower onboard." Stanton chuckles.

"Some things *never* change," Harper says.

Angelique hears them upon walking over. "Well, I can tell you there's really nothing top secret about our mission, and the only guns onboard will be with our security," she assures him.

Stanton looks at her and then Harper.

"This is Dr. Angelique Puck," Captain Harper says, introducing them.

"How are ya? Stanton: *Pilot Extraordinaire*," he says, chuckling and shaking her hand.

Harper lets out a stifled chuckle while shaking his head at his knucklehead friend.

"Hi, nice to meet you," she says with a smile.

"Did you say *security*?" he asks. Angelique and the Captain groan simultaneously.

"I'll tell you later." Harper rolls his eyes.

"Uh...Nelson...?"

She shrugs, face slightly scrunched.

"They're *still* lettin' that guy make decisions?" Stanton shakes his head.

"I take it you know him?" She nods.

Camaraderie found through all having dealt with the corporate head who loves to flex his power, if not abuse it.

"Unfortunately..." Stanton looks at Harper and huffs. "Couldn't make it with *us*, so he's been milkin' this suit and tie thing for all it's worth."

Harper nods, agreeing.

"Ahh..." Angelique says to herself, finally getting a bit of understanding as another layer of the onion that is Nelson is peeled.

"You mind if I ask what we're going up for?" Stanton asks.

"Routine medical trip, nothing too taxing," she says with a fan of her hand.

He nods with an "okay" hand gesture and then looks at her. "Wait a second... You're the one who came up with the multiple sclerosis treatment."

"That'd be me." She nods, not sure whether it's a good thing or a bad thing to this man as she's had plenty of supporters and protesters.

He's thinking while snapping.

"The uh...that uh NMC!" He recalls, snapping his fingers. "My sister has MS and got that. It *works*. She's a lot better now." He smiles and nods. "It's an honor to fly with you."

"Well, thank you." She returns his smile and nod. The mission's already starting off well.

Security Feed—Sleep Hall:
Down the hall of doors, outside everyone's quarters, where they happen to be setting up, the pilot meets the ship's new security for

the first time. Stanton casually strolls up to Saxon. His slinky, easy-going attitude is evident in his casual movement with his hands in his pockets while speaking to the man with an obvious chip on his shoulder.

"Ah, judging by your *getup*, you must be our resident security," Stanton says. Saxon isn't catching the pilot's sarcastic wit deep within his greeting.

"Yeah, that's me." Saxon's cockiness is always in his voice, no matter what he says.

"I trust you have plenty of *firepower*," Stanton says, again, with his dry wit.

"Oh yeah." Saxon's so proud, still not catching it.

"Let me ask you something, what *exactly* do you think we're going to encounter up there?" Stanton flat out asks, with all sarcasm aside.

"Well, we might find ourselves in a hostile environment. There might be alien life...or even if the crew gets unruly, I can detain them," Saxon says very matter-of-fact.

Something in his tone says he almost hopes for one of these.

Stanton laughs. "On a vessel full of *scientists* and *doctors*, I highly doubt it. Anyway, carry on, soldier." Stanton gives a salute dripping with the same sarcastic wit he started the conversation with.

Saxon doesn't know how to reply, so he salutes, albeit confused. They part with the pilot still chuckling to himself and shaking his head.

Bridge-Cam:
With the *Capacitance* not far out of Earth's orbit, Chloe, Miguel, Toni, and Angelique are relaxing on the bridge and looking at the moon while Harper and Stanton sit, stationed in their usual seats. Stanton's playing a game in hand.

"You still gambling on those games?" Harper asks, looking over to his frequent partner in the stars. A sly grin crawls across the pilot's face.

"Nah. Got tired of losing my paychecks and, *well*, most of what I *owned*, so now I think I play out of habit." Stanton chuckles, not looking up from his game. "It's just solitaire for me these days." He turns, showing Harper.

"Of all the games that have been created and updated for a century or more and you play solitaire?" Harper asks in jest.

"Hey." He shrugs. "It keeps me out of trouble. And if I lose to myself, I can always take an IOU."

The friends laugh together.

"It's amazing to see the size of the moon this close up. It always looks so tiny from home," Chloe says, watching the gray tattered ball through the window.

"Yeah, my first time out I almost *shit* myself when I saw it. I had to check my charts again to make sure where I was," Stanton jokes.

The lively spirit of the room seems to come down as Lou Ann enters. Miguel and Toni instantly get up. They haven't had much interaction with her yet, but they're more than put off by the aura she carries.

"Well, we got work to do," Toni tells the room.

Lou Ann tries to stop them, eager like a door-to-door salesman. "Oh, I was wondering if I could ask you guys some questions."

Miguel looks at her and shrugs while shaking his head. "No Hablo Ingles."

The couple leaves while the rest of them chuckle beneath their breath. Angelique nudges Chloe, and she looks over to her, smiling.

Lou Ann walks up to Stanton.

"Hi, as our pilot, you must have an insight into where we're headed. Can I ask you a couple of questions?" she asks with her tablet poised, uncomfortably close.

"Lady, I just fly the ship. If Harper says to fly us through an asteroid field, that's where I take us," Stanton says, still not looking up.

Harper speaks up, "It was *one* time!"

Chloe and Angelique share stifled snickers.

"Uh, yes, well, can you tell me anything else about piloting in space?" she continues.

"It's no different from piloting a plane in orbit, only less rules and fewer things to look out for with the exception of nosy passengers and no flight attendants to keep them back where they belong," he says, looking over to her. Stanton's lack of patience with Nelson and his people seems about the same if not more than his fellow Captain. His laid back attitude seems to stop at corporate suits, not out of anarchistic mentality but past personal experiences.

She's struck by his attitude.

"I'm just doing my job, Mr. Stanton," she says.

"And I'm attempting to do mine," he says, with a digital solitaire game in hand. "It's hard for me to keep my eyes open for *aliens in flying saucers* and *comets* if I'm being bothered by someone with a notebook in my face all the time."

Growing frustrated, she leaves in a huff.

He looks over to the others with a sly grin, who are almost equally shocked at his change. "What? I couldn't use *Miguel's* out." Stanton shrugs.

Angelique's Room-Cam:
Angelique sits in her room talking to an older gentleman on the video screen extended from the wall. They have a good rapport; this man, gray and up in years, is her old college professor. Her respect

for him shows in her posture and tone.

"I'm so proud of you, Angelique," her old mentor says.

"Thank you. I'm *trying* to make a difference," she tells him.

"You already have, 'Lique, you already have. You're my greatest pupil," he says, smiling. The image of this proud man pixilates as the screen rattles.

A rumble. A quake. In an instant, the ship violently shakes.

Her eyes seem to grow double in size as they dart around her at her vibrating environment. It shakes harder with large jolts as if God himself is throwing punches at the *Capacitance*. Angelique is freaked out, suddenly being tossed around with the ship's turning. The man's eyes widen like hers on the screen, and he leans in closer, worried.

"Angelique, what's wrong!?" he shouts concerned.

"I gotta go. I'll talk to you later." She ends the conversation, barely able to press the screen's button as she's thrown about her room. The screen surprisingly makes it back into the wall with all the rumbling. Loud clashes are heard in the turbulence they've hit. Every clatter brings more tremors to the *Capacitance*. Angelique is shaken, wide-eyed and alert frantically thinking of what to do. This is her first actual turmoil in any mission and everything continues vibrating aggressively, turning as if the ship is on the tracks of a rollercoaster.

"Harper, I need you on deck ASAP!" Stanton calls on the intercom with obvious urgency.

Security Feed—Sleep Hall:
Though the pilot called for the Captain, almost everyone leaves their quarters and runs into one another. Frightened and confused, the crew members look at each other.

"What's going on?" a scared Chloe asks Angelique in the hallway.

"I don't know. Let's go," she tells her with the same visible shakeup. Nearing panic, they all rush to the cockpit.

Bridge-Cam:
Members of the crew arrive to the bridge not long after Harper, already standing next to the pilot, looking out. Stanton's in work mode, serious.

"What do we got? *Asteroids?*" the Captain asks Stanton.

"No. Looks like we're hitting some debris from an old satellite," Stanton answers, steering the ship. The crew watches out of the window, seeing assorted scrap metal pieces and chunks clashing into each other as Stanton maneuvers in and out of the cluster the best he can. With every turn, the ship is hit with more, bumping the crew from their stationary stances.

"Think you can get us out of it?" Harper asks.

The rest watch, clearly seeing the fragments from the window: metal pieces of machinery, old and outdated, fly past and into the ship randomly.

"Workin' on it, Captain," Stanton replies.

They're still being bombarded, shaking everything brutally while the team holds on tightly. Nobody says a word, seeing the two men are not in any mood to hear from the peanut gallery. They're barely able to stand up straight, and their hearts race. Miguel and Toni hold each other closely, frightened. Angelique and Chloe hold hands, both with terrified grips. Lou Ann has her tablet out and ready but is too shaken to write any of this down. Harper stands by, keeping an eye on meters and gauges before moving over to the viewing scope. The two men work like a well-oiled machine. The Captain pulls the scope down and looks while the rest wait on pins and needles.

"Stanton, we got an opening, but it's a tight one!" Harper yells.

Stanton grasps the handles tighter, trying his best to get out unscathed.

Top-Cam:
The *Capacitance* is in the midst of a mechanical storm. Scrap metal along with assorted smaller broken meteor pieces clash into one another as well as the spacecraft. Nothing resembles what was once hi-tech equipment, just *junk*. The ship drops down below the thickest cloud of broken satellite, albeit still surrounded.

Control Panel-Cam:
Stanton turns back to the scared crew with the controls in hand. Harper steps forward looking out.

"Everybody, hang on!" Stanton yells over his shoulder.

Top-Cam:
Stanton spins the *Capacitance* to the side in the metal cloud. More debris is abound, but there seems to be an opening, a small clearing, revealing the star-filled black beyond the whirling scrap pile.

Stern-Cam:
Stanton flips the thrusters, BLASTING forth. Beyond the blue flames, the satellite clusters get smaller in view, still colliding with other various pieces.

Stem-Cam:
The ship rockets forward, past the debris of wreckage as the mechanical bits causing such a turbulence are passed on either side while some hit the ship, reflecting off. Vacant space yet again.

Top-Cam:
They make it out of the brief albeit scary situation safely. Stanton corrects the ship upright and kills the thrusters, knocking the speed down to a snail's pace. The satellite storm is well behind them.

Control Panel-Cam:
They all catch their breath, looking at one another, still holding on tightly to the handles installed on the bridge for such a situation.

"We gotta go check and make sure nothing was damaged," Stanton says, getting up.

Bridge-Cam:

Stanton and Harper pass the still-shaken team. They open the door to exit as Saxon runs in with his flash rifle charged, looking eager and ready. His head whips back and forth with his gun poised.

Stanton, annoyed, isn't about to have any of it. "What the hell are you gonna do with *that*, son?"

They leave while Saxon stands clueless, dropping his weapon to his side. Angelique and her crew look at each other, thankful, while Lou Ann immediately writes about it in her tablet. Toni kisses Miguel while he rubs her arms, still holding her. Angelique and Chloe look at each other and hug hard, exhaling. After a moment passes, they all exit the bridge and return to their rooms.

Angelique Room-Cam:

Angelique lies in her bed holding her parents' photo with tears in her eyes and breathing deeply. She shakes her head hard at the thought of what had taken place. Still scared, terrified, she sniffles, but the lump in her throat refuses to let a cry come out.

"All right, everybody, we are officially in the clear with very minimal damage. Sorry for the inconvenience, please enjoy the rest of your flight," Stanton says over the intercom.

Angelique tries to smile and regulate her breathing.

//

NEWS REPORT - TOWN MEETING

Streaming from the logs of the *Capacitance*.

The monitor lights, revealing an angry man leading a meeting. Local News title streams "Town Meeting Discusses Medical Issues." The man is white, thin, and well-suited. He stands, speaking aggressively, while the audience and participants nod along in their seats.

"Here we sit, waiting on *them*!" He points above them all. "I tell you, we don't need *Gun* Control in this country. We need *Medical Control*! We give these doctors and '*medical scientists*' too much leeway! They do anything they want to us, to our children, and *tell us* it's for the better! We don't know what they're *doing*! How does a degree grant you *control*!? They're not trying to *fix* anything; they're trying to play *God*, changing things as they see fit! Insurance companies, experimental testing, interstellar medical expeditions—when does it stop!? How long will we let them have control over us!? They need to be reined in!"

The crowd cheers this man, who sounds like a Southern preacher running for office. He's pumped, nodding to his cheers.

Screen cuts to black.

//

On the Hunt

Top-Cam:
The crew of four searches the exterior of the ship again for more of their little friends.

"If they're attracted to metal, I wonder if they'd be around satellites," Miguel suggests.

"Could be. I don't see any around, but we'll ask Stanton when we get back in," Angelique says before stopping and looking over. "Wait! I wonder if any of them came off of the old satellite pieces we flew through earlier!"

"It's a possibility." Miguel nods.

"In one of the collisions, they very well could've jumped ship and boarded," Toni adds.

"I'm curious if there's an actual *place* they come from," Angelique ponders aloud.

"You mean like a planet or moon?" Toni asks, as she continues hunting for the little chrome-tinted molecules with her light.

Chloe chimes in, "Or even an asteroid, with as small as they are."

"Any of them would suffice. I'm wondering if they're a part of a greater whole," she ponders, looking out into the galactic open.

Toni and Miguel continue to search the ship.

Chloe-Cam:
Chloe watches as Angelique shines her light out into the open space before turning it up to its brightest setting and taking another look. Like before, the light only travels so far before it's taken by the dark.

"Angelique, what are you doing?" Chloe asks.

"Just looking," Angelique says, while peering deeply out.

Angelique-Cam:
Her light catches a shimmering flicker in the dark. It's faint, quick, but it's there: a metallic wisp in the black sky. Her light dashes back to the point; it's far, too far to reach up and grab.

"I gotta to get closer," she says.

Top-Cam:
Still tethered by her cord, Angelique kneels down and presses the little red button on her boots, disconnecting her magnetic grip from the ship. She jumps off to swim out closer.

"Angelique!" Chloe shouts.

"Are you okay!?" the others add, concerned.

"I'm fine! I'm fine!" Angelique assures them. "I need to see something!"

Toni-Cam:
Toni and the other two are still bound to the *Capacitance*, looking at each other, stuck in a mid-shrug, while their team leader has been hit with a spur of the moment recklessness.

"What in the hell is she doing?" Toni asks, as Angelique swims and pulls herself out deeper.

Angelique-Cam:
Her hands are out: one shining the light and the other reaching. She can't reach it but gets close enough to see. The little particles are surrounding a chunk of lose rock drifting about. She tries to keep her light on them while getting closer. A stray piece of meteor, perhaps broken off from a larger whole.

"What have I found?" she asks herself, baffled. She turns sharply, grabs her cord, and pulls herself back to the ship. The others wait, still curious, as she gets closer. The tiny three figurines previously seen planted on the ship's exterior grow to human size the closer she gets while reeling herself in.

Miguel-Cam:
The three of them help pull her back to the ship the rest of the way and grab her, getting her back to her feet as her boots lock on.

"What was that all about?" Chloe asks.

Angelique puts her hands out to her team, excited and takes a deep breath. They wait, curious of the answer to Chloe's query.

"Okay, this is going to sound crazy and dangerous, but I need one of you to do something with me and I need a bag." She so-so explains.

Toni steps forward as her volunteer. "I'll do it. I wanna know what you're *up* to."

Angelique detaches her safety cable, to the shock of her crew, and gives it to her. "Fasten this to your glove."

Toni sighs and does so for the safety of her friend, hooking it to the loop on her glove safely secured to her suit. Chloe looks to Miguel, who looks back; they shrug, *sometimes the only appropriate response to give.*

Top-Cam:
Angelique pushes herself from their standing point, and Toni detaches herself as well. They both drift from the ship, tethered together, as they make their way up and out. Chloe and Miguel stand, ready to pull them in at the first sight of trouble.

Toni-Cam:

Now allotted with more length, Angelique tries hard, waving her arms with large strokes, to take her out to the rock still unseen by the others. Toni looks back at Chloe and Miguel waiting on the *Capacitance* and then back up at Dr. Puck swimming out and above them while they're connected in a way surely going against safety standards and regulations.

"Angelique, this is *crazy*." Toni groans before attempting to push herself up farther as well.

Angelique-Cam:

Dr. Puck alternates between swimming and reaching. She frequently shines her light up at it to make sure it's still there as when the light moves to either side it becomes shrouded in darkness. The stone is in the distance, albeit still floating around, but she's getting closer.

"Hey, you *signed up* for crazy, lady," she replies, almost reaching her goal. "I'm almost there."

Top-Cam:

Chloe and Miguel watch, safely secured to the *Capacitance* while Toni's out as far as her cable will allow and, from her glove, Angelique's as far as *her* cable will go. Two white figures strewn across the open black.

"Now that's dedication," Chloe says, looking up at them.

"Girl, you ain't kiddin'," Miguel agrees.

Angelique-Cam:

She stretches out as wide as she can, reaching for this stone covered in microscopic alien life forms glistening beneath the light. It's within range.

"I GOT IT!" she yells, grabbing a hold of it and tucking it in her bag, trying her best not to move too swiftly and lose too many of the beings.

She looks back at the extended lines and her friend holding on to her cable between Angelique and the *Capacitance*. It's good that she catches the little meteorite when she does because she's at the end of both her line *and* Toni's.

"All right, guys, we're clear," she tells them, sighing from excitement and exhaustion.

Chloe-Cam:
Chloe pulls them both back to safety by Toni's cable as Miguel joins her while, simultaneously, Toni holds and tugs Angelique's line. The ladies get closer to the ship with every draw; a human assembly line. Space: the only place they could feel *this* strong. Contact. They're back with them as Miguel and Chloe lock Angelique's line. Both of them are fastened to the ship securely.

Angelique holds her bag out. "I think we should go have a look at this."

Security Feed—Lab Hall:
The crew's back inside. Outside the labs, Miguel and Toni help each other get their suits off while Angelique and Chloe do the same.

DocLab 7-Cam:
They rush into the lab as Angelique finds the biggest case she can before they take the meteorite out of the bag and place it inside, closing the case. They take a deep breath and catch their bearings, trading high-fives and fist bumps along with smiles. The newly acquired space rock covered in mites rests on the counter beside other clear cases of findings.

Control Panel-Cam:
Stanton sits at the helm, drinking his coffee and keeping his eyes on the darkness ahead, the galactic freeway they're driving down. The door beeps; Angelique and the others enter behind him.

"Are there any satellites coming up on our radar?" Angelique asks.

"Not this far out." He shrugs before chuckling. "After earlier, I don't wanna see another satellite for a while. You all find somethin' worthwhile out there?"

"We'll see," she tells him with a pat on his shoulder.

Security Feed—Lab Hall:
Coming back from the bridge, the four head to the lab. Lou Ann sees them from down the hall and rushes to them with her tablet out, in hopes to get a word. They stop.

"Oh, hey, do you mind if I sit in with you while you do your experiments, you know, for my report?" Lou Ann asks, with an air of desperation.

"Yes, we do." Angelique takes hold of the situation head on. "It's complicated work. We're professionals, and we'd like to be left to it." Angelique leaves it at that, and they pass her.

Aggravated, Lou Ann walks off.

DocLab 7-Cam:
The med team enters the lab where the rock was placed and go through the separation process again, turning out the lights and shining their flashlights on them. They shine as they did last time, and carefully the team watches the little space-mites before they segregate the positives from the negatives and isolate the rock using the small nets. The team's getting the hang of the process, and it's not taking as long as it once had. They turn the lights back on and examine the stone. With squints and leans, they all look over it. Angelique snaps on a pair of gloves and reaches in, picking it up. The others watch and clear a way as she passes them, placing it on the table.

"It's as cold as *ice*—as hard as ice, too. No telling how long it's been out there," she tells them. Angelique thinks hard, looking at the steam coming off it.

"But why were these things surrounding it?" Chloe asks.

Dr. Puck looks down at it shaking her head. "I have no idea."

"There's only one way to find out. I'll be right back." Miguel exits. They have multiple labs, but they usually end up working in Angelique's. For the next ten minutes, the three women examine the stone, brushing away excess frost to find a couple of slightly frozen microorganisms stuck to its outside. The door beeps; they turn.

Miguel returns with a spike and a hammer. "Gotta love how our labs are used more for storage, and we mainly work in yours." He smirks.

"I was just thinking the same thing." Angelique chuckles.

Beneath the frost, the rock is brown and gray and doesn't look too much different than the rest of the meteor fragments they've come across.

Miguel gets the spike and hammer ready. "All right, guys, watch out."

In one strong swing, he breaks the stone in half with some assorted pieces falling off. They all lean forward, looking at its inside. Beneath the brown and gray exterior shimmers with an appearance of raw iron, brass, or some other kind of metal; it's too early to tell.

"You guys see what I see?" Dr. Puck asks her crew, unable to look away.

"Is that... Is that *metal?*" Chloe asks. They all look at each other, thinking.

"That's what it looks like to me," Toni says.

Angelique immediately goes for the intercom. "Harper and Stanton, your presence is requested in DocLab 7. Captain and Pilot to DocLab 7."

Bridge-Cam:
Stanton and Harper sit at the ship's helm, hearing their beckoning. Both men have their feet kicked up on the control panel as they watch out of the window, seeing the usual. They look at each other and nod in unison before getting up.

DocLab 7-Cam:

The two men show up in no time at all. Lou Ann's behind them, trying to get a peek at what they could be called for, but of course, she's left out. She tries watching from the window but can't see through the grouping of crew members to get a glimpse of what they're doing.

Harper enters first. "What's wrong? Something happen?"

"No, no. Everything's fine," Angelique answers, her hands out.

"Man, I haven't been sent to the principal's office in a *long* time," Stanton says, coming around Harper. They all laugh before Angelique shows them what was found.

"What is *that?*" Harper asks, looking at the broken space rock sitting out on the table.

"Looks like a random meteorite." Stanton shrugs. "We see them all the time, just never really seen one inside the ship let alone cracked open like this. What's in this? Looks *metallic*," Stanton speculates, upon closer inspection.

"Exactly," Angelique says, watching both of them touch the inside of the meteorite. "Remember when I told you that we had found these microorganisms are magnetic, or at least drawn to metal in *some* ways?" Both men nod, answering her. "Okay, well, we found this floating by outside, and it was *covered* with those things. We caught it and broke it open, and, lo and behold, it looks to be metal of some kind."

"Where do we come in, Doctor?" Stanton asks, curiously motioning to the Captain and himself. The med team watches.

"Well, I need you to hear me out because it won't exactly sound...safe or procedure," Dr. Puck says slowly, almost expecting to be shot down before she can explain. With her team behind her, the Captain and the pilot give her their full attention. "Since we found these things, we've wondered if they were actually indigenous to anywhere, if they're coming from somewhere specific instead of floating aimlessly. If this piece is from something—a moon or a planet or what have you—then we may find their home. The problem is I don't know how long that piece has been out there by itself."

"Yeah, it's pretty cold. There's no telling," Captain Harper says.

"So let me just...let me see if I understand you... You want to find where this came from and, hopefully, land on it, yeah?" Stanton guesses.

"Precisely," she says, nodding.

"Have you thought about how long it would take to find it?" Harper asks, skeptically.

Angelique extends her hands in explanation. "I understand it could take a bit, *but* we're up here to find anything we can to help and up until this moment it's been random exploration. With this, we redirect our mission to solely find this, whatever *this* happens to be. I think it might actually be easier for us to find a large mass as opposed to randomly fishing the galaxy," Angelique suggests.

Stanton looks over to Harper. "What do you think?"

"Honestly, it sounds ridiculous and a bit absurd that we'll find anything remotely related to this random piece floating around out here," Harper thinks aloud.

Angelique and her team become nervous.

"With that said, I *think* it can be done. I'm assuming you'll be able to get us there. I mean, we don't exactly have a metal detector onboard and certainly not one so massive, but if what we're looking for is rather large then we'll have to look all over," Harper replies to Stanton, who's still thinking. "I know finding a large rock in the universe is like finding a needle in a haystack but what do you think?" He chuckles.

Stanton nods before looking at Angelique. "You're the boss. If it's out here, we'll find it." The team is relieved to hear it. "Well, we better get to it."

They leave, and the four scientists look at each other, thrilled, all releasing a collective sigh of relief. Excited, they hoot, holler, and high five. Angelique's euphoric. Their research has reached a new level.

//

Ship Journal
Dr. Angelique Puck: Login: 7575
Subject: **Under the Lens**

Beneath the microscope lens, the testing takes place. Even though I've worked with these microorganisms and particles like them for years, I'm still amazed watching them live and fight to survive like any other beings. They face off like chrome-plated amoebas, armored mites. With no set shape, they move about freely, wiggling and wobbling how they see fit. To be more specific, they each have a clear coating, some kind of thick lamination presumably for protection while the main "body" beneath appears polished silver with even smaller black atoms seen floating around within it, though these tiny spots in them are not always seen. There are two on the glass right now; they appear almost territorial. Cell A is on the left while Cell B is to the right. We had separated the negatives from the positives once we found out which ones clashed and labeled them to the best of our ability; both of *these* are positives.

They use their sheaths as a bumper, pushing each other away from one another. While doing so, there seems to be vibration among them as if they're agitated. I push them closer toward each other with my pin. Their shapes morph and bend into what appear to be limbs and push at each other. Cell A pushes Cell B back and vice versa. The two attack each other the closer they get. The limbs they've formed sharpen to pointy silver tentacles, and the clear cover morphs with them. While they don't pierce their exteriors, they certainly fend the other off. Cell B moves forward, knocking into Cell A sending it back though still on the glass. These microorganisms don't appear violent per se, but they do appear defensive.

Cell A progresses and pulsates as it attacks back. Cell B falls back before making its way back to center glass, slapping its opponent with the wobbly limbs this tiny metallic blob has made. They both appear an amalgamation of platinum and fiberglass melted together into living beings. With no wings or set propulsion points found on their bodies, their airborne movements must stem from the magnetic pull. The two molecules found in deep space are duking it out beneath my microscope. I know I should be making notes of this, but I can't turn away; it's actually *exciting* to watch.

If I was in the field or business to do so, I could probably make a killing off of this with microscopic cameras projecting this onto larger screens while people take bets on which cell would win. Their clear coating is never disturbed beyond a ripple and, of course, their chrome bodies, though frantically morphing and shifting, are unscathed. I haven't nudged them closer since, and they are still fighting. Microscopic punches and kicks (presumably) are thrown and taken. My eye is getting dry, but I don't want to blink and miss anything. Despite them clashing in the center of their platform, they never cross over each other in a reversal of sides.

So it's not just a matter of these things not being compatible; they are completely intolerant of each other with both species, or *classifications* of what seems to be the *same* species, fighting one another for territorial supremacy. Their pulsing before attacks reminds me of a cobra putting its hood up; they throb and pulsate and would appear to swell (if only slightly) before striking. If both of these were inside of someone at the same time, I wouldn't doubt that person would end up like the glass holding the two mites I'd tried before. The two earlier at least took to each other at first but these two are adamant about their distance. I'm going to separate these two before I have another mess to clean up.

Although, I am curious if putting them in with others in their agitated state if that aggravation would be contagious to the others. I take Cell A off the glass and carefully place it in a canister with three others of the same make and watch. The others tremble and vibrate but only for a second and then they all calm down. It would seem that being around the others took the edge off, yet, I'm sure if they were forced onto a smaller platform together, they'd end up fighting just the same. As it stands, they're peaceful with one another while keeping their distance. I'm gonna finish putting these guys away, and then I'm going to fill out my forms. I'd leave this voice recorder on, but I wouldn't want you to fall asleep at the necessary evils of paperwork. Besides, I always make copies of my files, so if and when this is all found, it'll all be here.

//

Ship Journal
Dr. Angelique Puck: Login: 7575
Subject: **Drifting**

Good morning, I guess. Ugh, even in the deepest reaches of the universe, coffee is a good friend to have on hand. I'm having the hardest time getting with it today; I'm sluggish and zombie-like. Of course, it doesn't really help that all I've been doing is working and more so than I usually would be. Then again, in my predicament, I don't have much of a choice. Since the concept of day and night is gone in this neck of the woods and with my recent sleep troubles, I feel like I'm drifting a bit from everything. Dreams that feel hyper-realistic at the time are making me question my current situation—*another* nightmare. After a cup of coffee, it'll all come back to me. For now I'm going to get up and move around. I'll do my checkups around the ship after I attempt another distress call.

Control Panel-Cam:
Angelique flips on the communicator in her tired, groggy state. Her hair's a mess, her eyelids are fighting to stay open, and her system's waiting for the magical potion of *coffee* to kick in.

"*Capacitance* to base, come in. This is the *Capacitance* sending out a distress call. SOS. Come in. This is Dr. Angelique Puck of the *Capacitance*. Is anyone out there?" She exhales, switching the communicator off. A stretch and a sip later, she gets up.

Security Feed—Lab Hall:
Angelique passes by the labs, peeking through the glass of each one. No change to the lab hall. She reaches the end and opens the door.

Security Feed—Sleep Hall:
She enters the sleep hall and proceeds with her room checks. Angelique passes her room, naturally. She heads to the next in line, which is Chloe's.

Chloe's Room-Cam:
Angelique enters the room; it's cute, tidy. A digital picture frame is on the bed where Chloe left it. Whenever she normally does her checks, she looks in and rarely actually goes in and tinkers about. Angelique picks it up, a white fiberglass frame with a black screen. Using the top button on the right side of it, she turns it on. She's still trying to wake up as she browses through these pictures. She swipes to the right, going through this gallery to find pictures of Chloe with her family, cheesy selfies, and finally, some with Angelique.

"I had actually forgotten we had taken *any* pictures together. It's nice to see, and as much as I want to take this, I'm going to leave it right here. Maybe I'll give it another look on my next check," she says to herself aloud as she exits.

Toni's & Miguel's Room-Cam:
Across the hall now, she enters Toni's and Miguel's quarters. The bed is made and everything's as tidy as Chloe's space. She looks around and nothing sticks out really besides a picture of them together on the bedside table. Everything looks normal for the room of a scientist couple. The med team all seem to like everything neat and orderly.

Lou Ann's Room-Cam:
A room over is Lou Ann's, where Angelique now enters. For a woman who appears so composed, her quarters are quite the opposite with files and paperwork laid about and random notes here and there. It's as messy as it has been upon every other check. Angelique walks to the desk and looks through some of the mess.

"She may use the electronic tablet to file and send things to Nelson, but she still *scribbles* like the rest of us on the way there. I can't make much sense of these jottings and ramblings, though. It mainly looks like chicken scratch and shorthand. Most of it looks to be thoughts of the crew: opinions, accusations, and critical reviews." Angelique looks unsure while viewing the paperwork, rolls her eyes, putting papers down before exiting.

Saxon's Room-Cam:

Across the metal walkway of a hall is Saxon's room, where he spent the majority of his time. Angelique enters. His home away from home looks unsurprisingly militarized. There are some other things, however, standing out, such as: the black punching bag hanging up, a dummy of someone's upper torso with knife wounds throughout, a plethora of weapons on a pegboard above the desk which has on it a pistol taken apart, and passing the bed, on the floor before the dresser she finds a black duffle-bag filled with hand grenades. She sniffs the air.

"Hmm... something smells like ashes, but it doesn't smell like cigarettes or cigars, or even *weed* for that matter. Ah..." In his ashtray on the dresser is a pile of ashes with what looks to be the top of a file. All that survived is the header "Mission Trajectory."

"Nelson, what were you up to...?"

Stanton's Room-Cam:
The next room over belongs to Stanton. She enters and looks around. It's pretty standard. It actually looks like quite the bachelor pad. Like some of her colleagues' rooms, nothing sticks out. The only thing catching her eye, beyond the ashtray full of cigar ends, is a calendar on the wall, featuring girls in bikinis modeling in front of various starships—hot women, hot ships. She looks at the calendar and nods, smiling, before she exits.

Harper's Room-Cam:
At the end of the hall is the Captain's quarters. The door slides into the wall, and Angelique walks in. It's nice in here, feels warm. He looks to have replaced the standard bed covers with some quilts and comforters from home. A framed photo of him and his wife on their wedding day sits on his bedside table. On his desk is an envelope, which she looks through to find old family pictures. He seemed to be quite the family man. Along the walls in digital frames are pictures of the Captain with past crews. Stanton is in quite a few of them. They look the same in the past as they did on this mission.

"With all the people in the world who hate their jobs, it's refreshing to see these pictures with those who actually enjoyed their work. It makes me question, though, with this crew gone, who will tell their families, and *how* will they tell them? I wonder who's missing *me* at this moment. Does Serena miss me at all?" She ponders aloud. "Wait a minute..."

Angelique looks closer at the pictures of past crews, and in a couple of them with Stanton standing beside Captain Harper, a younger Nelson is seen among the group of people. He doesn't look happy by any means, and his smug look is vacant, if even born yet at such time.

"Huh."

Cargo Bay-Cam:
She's walked down to the cargo bay but is skeptical about opening the doors. She doesn't know why, but she feels compelled to check it. An ominous feeling visibly swells in her being down here. She opens the door and looks at her crew, all completely still as she last saw them: all in the biohazard body bags they've been stored in, lined up beside one another. There's no movement among them, which is pleasing to Angelique; being alone on a ship full of dead bodies adrift in the middle of space can be a bit creepy, after all.

Break Room-Cam:
She's left them to rest and is now up in the break room getting cup of coffee number two, as black as the space beyond the walls of the ship. Everything looks normal; time to relax in the Captain's seat a bit.

Control Panel-Cam:
Angelique relaxes with her cup of Joe while watching out of the window, continuing her monotonous and tedious daily routine. Along with being scared and tired, she's also grown quite bored.

"I see I'm not moving much. I wonder if the magnets outside are frosted over. I may have to go out and scrape them off, if it'll do any good. I didn't think it would last forever, but any movement was better than staying still." She stops, thinking to herself. "It's coming back to me. I'm remembering my nightmare." She takes another drink of coffee.

"Toni had just come back in from meditating, and it was my turn. I was suited up and went out, pushing myself away from the spacecraft, drifting. In my deep thought, I had fallen asleep. I must've been exhausted because when I woke up seeing nothing but the surrounding black, I PANICKED. I looked around and couldn't see the ship anywhere. I screamed and shouted, flailing about, not tethered to anything. My cord was *gone*. My heart raced, and I reached for anything, but there was nothing remotely close to tangible. I was breathing harder and harder, fogging up the glass in front of my face, covering my view while trying to steady myself in this strangely stationary free-fall."

"That's when I saw it...the *Capacitance*. I had barely seen it as it appeared a large blank space in front of a wall of distant stars. It was dark with every light onboard shut off, and as I noticed something passing me in the dark, all the lights came on in an instant. It was as startling as it was blinding. I was directly in front of the ship with its bright spotlight-like lights hitting me. My heart jumped, I shielded my eyes with my hands, and through my fingers I could see the entire crew staring at me from the window. They were all pointing at me and indistinctly laughing and shouting obscenities. Chloe turned her lip up at me and shrugged before laughing along with the rest of them. I didn't understand what was going on at all, and now I was being berated, the laughing stock of my own team. Next, I heard a hiss inside my suit. I had sprung a leak from the outer layer. Panic returned while my colleagues proceeded to point and laugh, repeating in a chant-like fashion, *'Lique sprung a leak! 'Lique sprung a leak!*

"For whatever reason, I screamed, while tearing my suit off me as if it were made out of paper. The shreds of my suit drifted away like newspaper blowing down a city street. Simultaneously, the ship had blacked out and disappeared. I took off my helmet next and threw it into the darkness and watched it get smaller as it coasted away from me. Of course, being a dream, I was breathing perfectly normal among the stars without a suit or breathing apparatus. I was naked for the whole universe to see and, yet, didn't care. I floated in the middle of the black and desolate universe naked and alone for what felt like an eternity before waking up."

Finished, she looks down in thought before nodding to herself with a sigh and taking another drink.

"You know, I don't remember dreaming at all when we still slept in sleep pods. Years ago, quarters were changed to resemble more of an actual bedroom, helping create more of a home away from home feeling. I suppose some things should be left at home."

//

NEWS REPORT - THE FUTURE OF AMERICA
Streaming from the logs of the *Capacitance*.

The screen, warm from the constant stream of cataloged news footage, continues. A group of young, eager college students stand outside a community college. Young men and women of different races stand together, all in clothing containing their school's logo. The street reporter leads her camera crew, making sure the students are all gathered in frame.

The microphone is poised. "So, as the future of America, how do you all feel about the latest strides to stop the growing outbreak of Rabid Neural Stasis?"

The student up front decides to give an answer. "I think it's great, actually. They've been doing all they can and haven't really been able to come up with anything, so why not let a team go try to find something elsewhere."

The microphone stays extended.

Another student steps up. "They're trying to *help*. I don't understand the *backlash* they've been getting for wanting to go about a big problem in a different way. I mean, that's what they've always taught us—" she motions to her fellow students "—if you don't *see* an answer in front of you, *find* one."

The others seem to agree.

The reporter moves on to another student. "And do you agree?"

"I do. They're doing more about the problem than the people who are *protesting* them. I say more power to them. At least they're trying," he says casually, with the others very much agreeing.

The reporter turns to the camera.

"Well, there you have it, a word from America's Tomorrow." She turns back, smiling to the students. "Thank you guys very much for your time."

The students cheer, holding up their shirts, making sure the logos and name of their school are seen.

Cut to black.

//

Ship Journal
Dr. Angelique Puck: Login: 7575
Subject: **Toni & Miguel**

You'll see when I mention the two I usually do so with them together, Toni and Miguel. This is because they were *always* together, the inseparable couple. They loved one another deeply, respected each other, and it showed daily. They worked together, they went to sleep together, and they woke up together. They changed the world together, they lived together, and they died together. They lived for their work; one of the reasons we got along so well, as we shared the same passion and drive.

This was our second mission together. Usually we worked in the labs together on Earth, but after our last mission went so well, I knew I had to include them on this one. They were both brilliant, bringing their expertise to the table more times than I could count. I was always thankful to work with them.

Even though they were highly decorated scientists, one of the other things I'd admired about them is they had kept their sense of humor, something so many of us lose in the field, becoming a bit stiff. Both in the interracial relationship were about the same height and thin. Toni is black with short hair while Miguel is Hispanic, also with short hair.

Security Feed—Home Lab:

In the lab on Earth, Toni, Miguel, and a slew of workers are busy making examinations. The room is clean, sterile, despite the potentially dangerous things they're working with. The door's clearance tone is heard, and Angelique enters. She takes a look at the lab full of people hard at work.

"Hey, guys," she greets them, upon stepping into the lab. The couple are both hunched over, eyeing their individual samples intently.

"Angelique, what's up?" Miguel greets first.

"Hey, girl," Toni says, looking over. The two continue.

Angelique walks over to them, slightly looking over their shoulders at their work, being nosy.

"You guys got a minute?" She asks.

"Sure," they say, stopping what they're doing. They put their utensils down and follow her over to an empty table where Angelique sits down.

"How're your space legs?" she asks, giving them a sly look.

It takes them a moment.

"It got *approved?*" Toni asks, excited, subconsciously grabbing Miguel's arm.

"Yes, *finally!* After years of pleading and begging and making case after case, we FINALLY got the green light," Angelique tells them proudly. "And, *of course*, I want you two to go." Her hands are out, hoping for the answer she seeks.

"Of course!" Toni yells.

"Hell yes!" Miguel adds.

In their excitement, the three get looks from the various workers around before they turn back to the work at hand.

"Great! We leave *now*." Angelique looks at them sternly without a blink.

"Uh...What?" They're lost, looking at her and each other.

She winks at them. "Joking. We'll be starting as soon as possible, though."

They relax and laugh.

"What are you guys working on?" she asks curiously, looking around.

"Oh..." Toni says as they get up to lead her to their work station.

"We're trying to improve on The Bouncer, trying to see what else it can fight," Miguel says. The other workers continue without missing a beat.

"Yeah, we're wondering if we can alter it for the common cold. Trying to get it to where it won't be as intensive as a neurosurgery and more of an injection," Toni adds.

"Oh, cool. Getting anywhere?" Angelique asks, looking over their charts.

"Unfortunately *no*. At the moment, it's proving too strong for simple injections." Toni shrugs.

Angelique nods.

"Mind?" she asks, motioning to the microscope.

"Oh, please..." They hold their hands out.

Angelique looks through the lens and reacts; sure enough, it's quite the strong cell. "No way of diluting it, I wouldn't think, since its base is a living organism," she thinks aloud. She stops looking at the cell and redirects her attention to her friends.

"Yeah, that's where we're having trouble. Can't exactly cut it down or weaken it and have it still *operational*." Miguel scrunches his face.

"Eh, you'll get there. Maybe we'll find something on our trip to help. Who knows?" she says positively before checking her watch. "Well, I need to get going, so I'll let you guys get back to work."

"All right, we'll talk to you in a bit," Toni says.

"Later," Miguel concludes.

Angelique leaves them and lets them get back to saving the world one sickness at a time.

Security Feed 2—Loading Bay:
Outside the ship, about to board, the loving scientist couple wait while Harper continues his routine checklist. They look around and talk amongst themselves.

Angelique approaches the couple. "Guys, we couldn't get bunk beds in your room so you'll have to share a bed. *That okay?*" she asks, pointing back and forth between them.

"Aw man, I *guess*," Miguel quips, slumping his shoulders.

"You mean I gotta sleep with my *husband?* I thought this was a *girls'* getaway," Toni jokes back.

They all have a good laugh.

"If only!" Angelique replies.

"Ship looks good. So this is the *Capacitance?*" Toni asks, looking at the large ship.

"Yes, ma'am," Harper answers, walking over. "Hi. Captain Harper." He greets the two scientists, shaking their hands.

"I'm Miguel. This is Toni," he says, introducing them before putting his arm around his wife. "Anything special we should know about the ship?"

"Yep, if it gets warm, turn the air on, do NOT open the windows," Harper jokes.

They're all off to a good start. Saxon walks by with a flash rifle over his shoulder while carrying large black duffle bags. Miguel and Toni notice with raised eyebrows.

"Whoa, what's with the muscle?" Miguel asks with a chuckle.

Angelique answers, "Just one of Nelson's stipulations."

"Well, that's good. If we can't cure migraines, we can always request a bullet in the head," Miguel sarcastically says, rolling his eyes.

"Is he *aware* of what we *do?*" Toni asks her with a tone of half-jest as her finger points back and forth between them and the soldier.

"I highly doubt it." Angelique smiles.

"Well then, I guess he'll be pretty bored. Hope he brought a book." Toni laughs. They grab their stuff and move on.

Break Room-Cam:
The crew of the *Capacitance* sits around the table, minus their team leader, going through their "morning" routine. Some talk amongst themselves over their coffee and breakfast while some stay quiet, still trying to get with it. Angelique enters and heads right for the coffee; *yet another magnetic draw on this mission.*

"Good morning, everyone," she greets the crew, getting a cup.

"You just getting up, Angelique?" Chloe asks her.

"No, I got up earlier. Been in the lab." Angelique answers, pouring in her creamer.

"Do you ever take a *break*, Doctor?" Captain Harper asks.

"What do you think *this* is?" she answers, holding up her cup and smiling.

"No, it's just not a good idea, babe," Toni tells Miguel.

"What're we talking about?" Angelique asks in between sips, leaning against the counter.

"Well, I want to conceive our first child while we're up here, and she's saying it's a bad idea," Miguel answers. He looks at Angelique hoping she'll side with him.

"Ah..." She responds, eyeing the others and taking another sip. The others share the same look, unsure of how to really respond or what to add.

"I just don't think it's *safe*. Think about it, we don't know how long we're going to be up here. What if we're up here longer than expected? What if, God help us, something happens to the *Capacitance* and we get stranded out here? The kid could be born up here. What if the gravity changes messes with the birth? What about the lack of natural environments?" Toni expresses.

"She does make a pretty good argument there, Miguel," Angelique says with a sip. The others, too, take the thought in.

"If we do it on the way *back* though..." Miguel suggests. It seems while Miguel is more than eager for a child, Toni is less so.

"I don't know. Are we even *ready* yet? I mean, we work a *lot*," Toni fires back.

"Angelique, will you tell her everything will be fine?" he asks to her surprise.

She swallows her coffee hard as all eyes are on her. "Uh...This...isn't really my *field*."

Miguel looks around the table for some support but is only met with shrugs and chuckles.

"Maybe women shouldn't do these kinds of missions and stay on Earth." Saxon suggests to a table of people equally not surprised it came from him and disgusted. An awkward pause hits the table in this buzzkill moment. The silence in the room is as it is outside the ship. Eyes look around at one another while Harper's don't leave Saxon.

"Well, gang, I'm gonna go back to working with dangerous diseases...*happily*," Angelique says, breaking the silence.

"Us too. C'mon, babe," Toni says, nudging Miguel.

"I'm right behind you," Chloe says, turned off, pushing her food away from her.

Lou Ann looks around and sinks into her tablet, working. Harper and Stanton stand up.

"Yeah, I gotta make sure I'm staying in my lane," Stanton says, motioning to the front. "Don't wanna get a ticket..." He turns.

They're all about to exit when, to the surprise of everyone, Harper speaks up. "Saxon, do you have a mother?"

In reply, Saxon rolls his eyes and groans in disbelief of hearing this. The Captain turns his attention from the soldier to the scientists.

"Well, Toni, I gotta say, I think both of you would make fine parents, especially since you all are making the world a safer and a less sickness-filled world. Just think, your child may never have a cold in its life."

Toni and Miguel smile. "Thank you."

Harper's gaze stays on Saxon briefly before the crew leaves Nelson's two at the table. Lou Ann looks at Saxon over her tablet.

He looks back at her, aggravated yet oblivious. "*What?*"

She sighs and continues to work.

Top-Cam:
Four medical scientists stand on the metallic ship. Their white suits

are stark against the black background of space as they look out into the star-filled wide open. Not a planet in sight. The four seem tiny in such a vast surrounding.

"Isn't it amazing?" Miguel asks. "Long ago it was a fight to even get up here, and we've been up here *twice* now. It just strikes me sometimes." His awe continues.

"He's like a little kid sometimes." Toni chuckles, looking over to Angelique and Chloe.

"I can't say anything. I *completely* understand." Angelique nods.

"Hey, guys, is Harper out here with us?" Chloe asks, pointing over to the front of the vessel. Another spot of white out in the darkness.

"That'd be me," Captain Harper says on the headset.

Miguel-Cam:
The four walk over to find Harper outside checking something, crouched down closing an exterior panel.

"Need some help, stranger?" Miguel asks the Captain.

He looks up. "Yeah, got a jack? I think we need to put the spare on." Harper jokes.

"Oh shoot, I think we left it onboard the other ship." Toni chuckles.

"Just my luck. *Stranded in space.*" The Captain throws his hands up briefly. "Nah, just checking something. Everything's good. Heading back in now," Harper says before leaving them to look around with their bags.

"We should probably check underneath. We haven't normally." Chloe suggests.

"Yeah, she's right. I don't know why we never go under there," Toni says.

"Hell, it's probably the same as up here," Miguel adds as they start to journey in that direction.

Angelique-Cam:
Walking along the bottom of the *Capacitance*, they shine their lights, inspecting the surface. It feels strange for them walking *underneath* the ship; they know they're beneath their temporary home, but because of where they are, it feels the same as on top of it. It's not as well-lit as above as their handheld lights are *it* for beneath the ship, and there are no security cameras. Angelique's flashlight crosses paths with the others' on their search. Their beams of light cross and pass one another in the dark underbelly, literally, of the *Capacitance*.

Miguel-Cam:
His light shines against the surface of the ship. The shimmering is visible—pay dirt. The other lights join his. The four make their way to the cloud, keeping their lights on it so they don't lose site of the space-mites. Like a shattered disco ball floating in place, the microorganisms sparkle under the collective of flashlight beams. Miguel stops and looks to his teammates.

"It would cut our time down a lot if we could separate them out here." He thinks aloud.

Toni replies, "I don't know. It might take just as long, but in two different places. I don't think doing the work in there or out here would really make a difference."

"Eh..." He nods. "Yeah, you're right," Miguel replies before he holds up a finger and digs down into his pouch to reveal a small piece of metal, a shard. The others watch curiously as he sets it directly above a cluster of the microorganisms they've found. The metal shard floats in anti-gravity.

"What are you doing, Miguel? What is that?" Toni asks.

"I'm trying something," he says, watching. They hold off on bagging them, waiting to see what he has up his sleeve. The little glimmering *things* float up covering the metal piece, gleaming in their lights the whole way up.

Angelique-Cam:
Dr. Puck watches in wonder at the tiny beings magnetically drawn to the small metal piece and watches her crew, thankful to have them. If one was to see this upside down, it would look like sparks descending in slow motion.

"Oh wow," Angelique says.

Chloe agrees. "That's *genius*, Miguel." The bright mites reflect off of Chloe's helmet.

"I get it from my wife. Intelligence is an STD, don't you know," Miguel says slyly, winking to his wife before putting the now completely covered metal in his bag. "If we get a couple of these on plastic rods we might have a better chance of getting them."

"Like a magnetic metal detector," Angelique notes. Toni smiles at her man unbeknownst to him, looking as proud as she could be; it could be stars in her eyes for him or the reflection of the alien lifeforms.

Break Room-Cam:
Dinner time in the break room has the crew once again around the table. Naturally, Lou Ann is more interested in her reporting work than eating and is ready for questioning. Though they don't see eye to eye, she's as driven and adamant with her job as the med team are with theirs; of course, with conflicting personalities, interests, and goals, it's never really looked at as such. Being around the table is always a perfect opportunity for the reporter to fire questions. They're all together, not in passing, without a chance to casually brush her off and walk away. Benignly trapped, as if they're all insects in her web.

"So what's it like being married scientists?"

They're asked mid-bite and raise their eyebrows at such an odd question, one these two are not used to getting.

"Well, being *scientists* married to *each other* rather," Lou Ann clarifies, awaiting an answer while they try to eat.

They look at each other before Miguel puts his hand on Toni's and answers, "We're partners in *life*. We're married, and we work together. We both work a lot so we always see each other."

Toni nods, agreeing, before smiling at Miguel.

"Well, I mean it must get hard at times. Let's say you have a marital spat or argument, it could potentially bleed into your work, right?" Lou Ann pries. Regardless of the fact that they're all currently residing in outer space, she seems more interested in personal drama than the research of scientific wonders.

This time Toni answers, "We're very professional, and we know how to keep our personal lives separate from work, no matter *what's* going on."

"Do you ever feel in competition or leery of the other's success? For instance, let's say one of you finds something the other doesn't, does it stir up jealousy between you?" she asks. The two look at each other, scoffing with irritation. The others share a similar look, wondering why such questions are being asked. Stanton rolls his eyes.

"Like *she* said, we're very professional, and like *I* said, we're partners. Her success is my success as mine is hers. We work together *for* each other, not against, and that's a key fundamental for any good marriage, not just for *scientists*," Miguel says with clarification before taking another bite.

The others watch and eat.

"There is no jealousy between us. Now...if another *team* is jealous of us and our work, that's a *whole* other story," Toni says before she and her man fist bump. The med team, along with Harper and Stanton, laughs. The reporter's expression doesn't change.

"And when you *do* have children, will that bother you, becoming the *wife* of a scientist?" Lou Ann continues, not touching her food or drink. She's relentless. Miguel's eyes widen. Toni drops her spoon and a sternness comes over her face. A nerve is hit.

"*First* of all, I am the wife of a scientist and I *am* and will always *be* a scientist. *Second*, if and when we decide to have children, I'll still be able to work. I'm a medical researcher, not by association. I wasn't *married into science*," Toni says, even more annoyed.

Miguel and Angelique snicker.

"Okay, how does it feel getting to be in space for medical research, getting a chance to 'save the world' so to speak? I mean, this trip could make you *famous*. You could make a breakthrough in medicine." She won't stop, and it's rubbing the couple wrong. They're a bit struck and at a loss of words, however briefly.

"Do you even understand what we've *done?*" Miguel's getting heated, poking his finger down onto the table. Toni puts her hand on him. Angelique's as confused as them.

"Babe..." Toni tries to calm him. "Don't. It's not worth it."

Miguel's pissed while Toni rubs his shoulder. Lou Ann looks shocked by his mood.

"I'm sorry. I don't understand. I was just asking because you get to work with Dr. Puck, that it must be a great honor."

Angelique doesn't intervene, but watches. Stanton and Harper simultaneously scoff. Chloe eats and watches, interested in where this is going with occasionally looking at Angelique. Saxon watches them, bored, as he doesn't care about any of them or what they're doing.

"She didn't pick our names out of a hat," Toni joins Miguel. "We've known Angelique for years. We're friends, and we work together a lot. We worked with her when she brought the Nu-Myelin Cell back to the lab, and it was *our* team that helped fend off different cancers. While you're acting like this is our first rodeo, we've handled multiple diseases and have plenty of acclaim *ourselves*."

Like a tag-team match, Miguel is tagged in and enters the ring. "You don't get into this business for fame. You do it to learn and to change things. *Yes*, it's a huge opportunity to get to come back out of orbit, and we're always grateful for such chances given to us." Miguel stops and takes a breath. "You know what...instead of asking empty questions and reporting back to your *master*, why don't you try to make a difference in the world *yourself?*" Miguel puts her in her place in front of the entire crew before turning to kiss his wife. Lou Ann sits silently, dumbstruck, and puts her tablet down.

"I suggest a change of topic," Captain Harper says sternly, clearly more of an order than a suggestion.

"I hear that, brother." Stanton laughs before leaning over to Angelique quietly. "Any way you could cure 'foot-in-mouth'?" The two laugh amongst themselves while everyone attempts to enjoy their dinner.

Lou Ann pokes at her food.

//

Ship Journal
Dr. Angelique Puck: Login: 7575
Subject: **Searching**

With Harper and Stanton on board for our new mission directive, we'd changed course toward the direction I had assumed the stone had drifted from, however implausible or unrealistic it may have sounded. They'd find out eventually, but we kept it out of Lou Ann's and Saxon's ears for the time being.

Bridge-Cam:
Angelique and her team stand with the Captain and the Pilot on the bridge with the view of the great wide open beyond them.

"What do we do when we find it?" Chloe asks.

Exactly what's on everyone's mind.

"It'll depend on how big it is," Angelique responds. "If it's big enough to land on, then we'll do so, get out, and investigate. If it's too small to park the *Capacitance* on, maybe it'll be small enough to haul it," she continues as if stream-of-conscious.

"Unless it's small enough to put in the cargo bay, I think most of it would burn up in the atmosphere on the way back home, wouldn't it?" Chloe makes a good point. Everyone looks at Angelique. Angelique is struck; she hadn't thought of it.

"Oh, duh." Angelique smacks her forehead. "You're sharp, Chloe; I like that. You're *right*. Well, hopefully it'll be either really *big* or really *small*."

Angelique and Chloe chuckle.

"Well, we're a good deal away from our big nine so it should be fairly easy to spot something even if it's *close* to moon size," Stanton says from his seat.

"What's our case scenario like, Doctor?" Harper asks, standing firm with crossed arms.

"Best case scenario—we find exactly what we're looking for and save millions of lives." Angelique nods positively.

The other three on her team share the same hope.

"...And worst case?" Harper asks, leaning forward, curious.

"Heh, that's what *Saxon's* for," Stanton jokes.

"No joke. Nelson might've been on to something," Angelique says sarcastically, and they all share a laugh. "No, worst case scenario is we don't find *anything*." Her face becomes grim at the thought but doesn't want to think about worst case, only the best.

"It's bound to be out there. Where else could that rock have come from?" Chloe notes.

"Unless it's from something that dissipated long ago," Miguel answers.

"Wait a minute, guys..." Toni has a thought. "What if this is something old, like *really* old? What if this was a *previous* planet or moon, like before the Milky Way had been originally documented?"

Everyone stops to think about it. Every singular curious mind on the bridge races with what ifs and possibilities.

"It's an excellent thought," Miguel tells her.

"You think something *that* old would still be around?" Harper asks, rubbing his chin.

"Have we considered the fact that it might be a piece of one of the planets in our solar system? Of any of them, I'd guess Pluto," Stanton asks before shooting another. "If not, I think it might be from an asteroid cluster or something."

"Guys, this might be a big *if*," Chloe says, "but what if the source of that rock is not of our galaxy at all and only pieces of it made it this far?"

"Look, they're *all* good suggestions, but the truth is we haven't a *clue* of where that rock came from. All we can do is search for the source and maybe check any debris we see along the way," Angelique states.

Everyone takes it in and nods before they all turn their attention toward the window, watching the black they're moving through. Harper sits down in the Captain's seat next to his old friend while the others continue to stand, gazing. The stars in the distance look as though someone had poked holes in a thick comforter beneath a florescent light. No planets are in sight, the sun is a sight of the past, and they're keeping their eyes out for loose rock and meteorites.

Angelique turns to leave when Chloe stops her. "Where you goin'?"

"Well, *someone's* gotta go up for debris just in case," she answers.

"I'll go with you," Chloe tells her with a smile.

Angelique smiles back. "All right, let's go." She waves her on.

"I think we'll hit the lab," Toni says, motioning to her and Miguel.

"I'll keep an eye out for anything upcoming," Harper says, sitting back with his hands behind his head and kicking his feet up on the control panel.

"Good idea." Stanton chuckles, pulling out his solitaire game. "I'll fly the ship."

Top-Cam:
Suited up, Angelique and Chloe set out to collect meteorites like children hunting to add to their rock collection. Angelique emerges first with Chloe behind her. Upon reaching the top, before her boots can lock on to the surface, Chloe stumbles, as Angelique's hand *instantly* shoots out, catching her.

"You okay?" Angelique makes sure she's secure in her stance.

"Yeah, lost my balance." Chloe giggles.

Angelique helps her back up, and they're off, both with their bags. They look around their sides and behind them, shining their lights with nothing in sight. They walk to the front, looking out while the ship still pushes forward. They feel a bit odd walking on a steadily moving spacecraft but being safely fastened to its exterior by magnetic boots helps. The two sit down beside each other on the vessel, right above the front window, looking out into the star-studded sea of black.

Angelique-Cam:
Angelique looks from the stars over to her colleague, enjoying the expression she wears.

"Is this what you thought you were going to be doing when you signed up for this?" she asks Chloe, not currently interested in the stars ahead but the star *next* to her.

"Honestly, I didn't know *what* I was going to be doing exactly. I just want to make a difference," Chloe says. "I've followed your research for years, and when I saw this opportunity, I had to take it."

"Well, I'm happy you did." They smile at each other, enjoying the peaceful moment before looking out into the great black yonder.

Ship Journal Continued:

Despite the fact that we were working, it was quite relaxing for us sitting up there, if only we could have a drink while doing so. Nothing makes a discourse between two people more personal than being where there is absolutely no sound. I've always been curious as to what space feels like on my bare skin, but it's something no one will ever find out; however, if I *could*, I'd love to sit with Chloe with our bare feet hanging off the starship as if sitting on the end of a dock. We'd feel the nothingness run through our fingers and toes, watch our hair waft in anti-gravity. We'd take breaks from our research while passing the sun to lie out and sunbathe.

Control Panel-Cam:
Stanton and Harper continue to keep an eye out in their own way, relaxing on the bridge.

DocLab 6-Cam:
In the lab next to Angelique's, which had become the main lab, Miguel and Toni are catching up on paperwork. They're hard at work, individually filling out forms, catching the mission's research up to date, the not-so-fun part of their field but necessary.

Lou Ann's Room-Cam:
Nelson's reporter is at the desk in her quarters, digging through a mess of scribbled notes and typing up her report on her tablet. Lou Ann takes her job seriously as the excessive amount of notes show, whether or not this is for the mission and what it means or for Nelson's personal files.

Saxon's Room-Cam:
Nelson's hired gun, a former soldier, throws blows at the punching bag with the fury of an angry man. He's sweaty and grunts with each hit. He finishes with a jump kick before moving over to the dummy propped up on a stand, pulling the knife out of it. Holding the blade upside down, he ducks and crouches, poised to strike before lunging at the dummy, delivering stab after stab. A dozen cuts and stabs later, he plants the blade into it firmly and sits down in the chair. Saxon looks restless with his eyes darting back and forth, not

really looking at anything. His feet tap and legs jump anxiously with his hands gripped on the arms of the chair.

Top-Cam:
The *Capacitance* cruises through the universe, dark with stars. A long way from home, the sun doesn't shine on these parts of space. Two colleagues sit together at the front of the ship as if they're casually sightseeing and reminiscing.

Chloe-Cam:
An open galaxy full of stars, close to empty in its view but heavy in its silence. Chloe turns from the stars ahead to her med lead, who turns to her.

"So...do you like being up here?" she asks Angelique.

"I do." She nods, almost appearing to be thinking about it, not really having been asked prior. "It's beautiful and amazing, but at the same time, it kind of humbles me. Being up here puts me in my place in a lot of ways; it's so remarkable," Angelique says, turning to face ahead of them.

"Yeah," Chloe says, turning out to space. "I can see that. Being up here kind of forces you to stop and realize you're not as big as you make you or your problems out to be...if that makes any sense," Chloe says with a stifled snicker.

They turn back to each other.

"Oh, *totally*. That's a great way of putting it, actually."

A smile is shared.

"What about you? How're you liking it up here?" Angelique asks.

Angelique-Cam:
Chloe's eyes widen briefly. She's thinking about it. The wide open star field rests behind her, however moving, a background she never thought she would've had for casual conversation.

Chloe sighs. "*Whew*, well, it's my first time so it's a bit scary."

"Yeah. You're doing really well, though," Angelique says.

"Thanks. It means a lot." She smiles.

"So...do you have a lot of people back home missing you right now?" Angelique pries.

"My parents and some friends. I'm not good at relationships because I put so much of myself in my work that I tend to alienate that part of my life," Chloe says.

Angelique chuckles. "I know *exactly* what you mean."

They turn again, viewing the space ahead. It's open and mysterious, a long road, which doesn't end nor is there even a mirage of an end in sight. A large pitch black room with no walls, floor, or ceiling.

Chloe says, "Sometimes I wonder if I'll ever be suited for a romantic life. I get this feeling that even with all the accomplishments I achieve in my life, I'll always fail the test of love. I could end up curing diseases like you and I still wouldn't feel *good enough*. Ever feel that way?"

They completely stop looking out into the open and turn, facing each other.

"Chloe, I think anybody would be lucky to have you. You're a smart, beautiful girl with a good head on your shoulders." Angelique smiles at her, looking into her eyes through the glass of both of their helmets.

"Chloe," she says with importance.

"Yes...?"

She sees it, an asteroid in the reflection of Chloe's glass dome. The piece of rock is faintly lit by the lights of the *Capacitance*.

Chloe-Cam:
Chloe sees it in Angelique's as well; they both turn forward

simultaneously to see it, the *debris*. A few pieces about the size of the one they brought in to investigate are drifting out above and in front of them.

"Doctor, are you seeing that?" Harper asks on the headset.

"We're on it, Captain," Angelique replies.

The ladies turn to each other with a grin and nod.

Top-Cam:
They stand up, boots magnetically fastened to the ship beneath them, with their retrieval bags ready. The two look out into the great black yonder.

"Get ready!" Angelique says, full of adrenaline. The stones and the *Capacitance* are getting closer to one another, but they still seem too far away. "I'm going to have to detach myself."

Chloe looks over to her.

"Be *careful*," she says, knowing at this point there's no way to stop her.

With her cable still attached, Angelique separates her magnetic boots from the ship's surface, and Chloe helps push her upward to get closer.

Angelique-Cam:
She drifts up after a good push from Chloe. She's careful so she can get it securely and doesn't end up pushing it out farther. Dr. Puck's net of sorts bags one of the loose space stones while others float aimlessly in its vicinity.

"GOT ONE!" Angelique shouts. A net comes into view next to her, getting another. To her surprise, Chloe's joined her. She nabs one as well. They look at each other with grins and continue reaching for more as if it were a game. They have a little bit of space left in their bags to maybe get another smaller rock or so, and they get them, scooping them up with ease. Any other debris is too out of reach for them.

"All right, Chloe, let's go back in."

Chloe gives a thumbs-up.

Top-Cam:
The girls pull their way back to the ship. Hand over hand, climbing their cords to the *Capacitance*, the ladies move like seasoned astronauts along with their bags of meteorites. Midway through, they high five while still pulling themselves back.

DocLab 7-Cam:
Back onboard, Angelique and Chloe place the rocks on the table in the lab. They're as cold as the last one along with the steam and look to have the same weathered exterior.

"You guys get 'em?" Harper asks over the intercom, directly to the lab.

Angelique walks over to the small box on the wall beside the door and presses the button before responding. "Got what we could. We'll be up in a moment." She returns to her colleague and the asteroids. They look over the stones; jackpot, they have their little alien friends crawling over them. One of the smaller rocks is what it appears with no microorganisms combing its outside. They still keep it just in case, plus it'd be a nice souvenir to take home. The ladies place the asteroids in some of the bigger cases.

Bridge-Cam:
Stanton and Harper turn upon hearing the door's beeping tone. Chloe and Angelique enter.

"Okay, guys, I think we're headed in a good direction. We got a few more pieces like we found before," Angelique informs.

"Dr. Puck, in all honesty, they could be coming from anywhere. I highly doubt there's a correct direction to go out here," Captain Harper explains.

"I understand, Captain. I do, but this is our best bet. Our best chance of finding this thing is to follow the breadcrumbs the universe has left us," she says, going over to the viewing scope, pulling it down.

She can't see very far, but instead of asking how to enhance the view, she studies it briefly, finding a switch with a plus sign on it. Assuming this is it, she pushes it, and it's exactly what she was looking for. Angelique pushes it twice to go to the highest and farthest view it will give her and she seems satisfied.

"There we go..."

Viewing Scope:
Even in the deep black it's a crystal-clear view. There are more pieces in the distance among the stars. Some appear as dark spots only to be seen as they pass by in front of stars and briefly cover their twinkling lights.

Bridge-Cam:
Chloe and the men await the med lead's thoughts.

"Captain, can you take a look at this please?" Angelique asks, pulling away from the scope.

He gets up, heads over, and takes a look for himself.

While he looks, she explains to him, "As you can see, there are more coming up. I think it's safe to say we're headed in the right direction, yes?"

Chloe and Stanton wait calmly.

He takes his eyes from the apparatus. "You may be on to something, Doctor." Harper nods before looking over to Stanton, who shrugs.

Chloe grins.

DocLab 6-Cam:
Toni and Miguel continue their work at the table in their lab. Deep in thought and deep in work, they're silent. The two document and file notes compiled thus far on the mission as well as side notes, opinions, and other options. Everything the team has found and

every theory voiced since the launch is being perfectly cataloged in these forms, something these two excel at. Toni appears flustered, shaking her pen.

"Can you hand me a pen? This one's crapped out on me," she asks her husband.

"They can invent everything but the endless ink pen." He chuckles.

"I know, right?" Toni laughs.

Miguel turns and grabs one out of the cup behind him when Angelique and Chloe enter.

"Hey, watcha doin'?" Angelique asks from the doorway.

"Just getting caught up on the forms," Miguel says nonchalantly. Angelique nods.

"What's up?" Toni asks.

"Can you guys join us in the lab?" she asks, motioning out of the room with her thumb.

DocLab 7-Cam:
The team enters the lab as Toni and Miguel see the newly acquired space debris. Angelique passes flashlights around, and the four immediately get to examining them. First, the lights are turned off yet again, followed by flashlights igniting to shine on the stones, finding the same results as before. Only the one stone doesn't light and teem with life. Toni turns on the lights, and they examine closer.

"Even though they look the same and some are attracted to each other and some aren't, is there any way we can see if they're of the same species?" Chloe asks.

"I don't understand," Miguel says, with his face slightly scrunched and brow furrowed.

"I know what she's saying." Angelique points her finger out. "I haven't been able to locate an actual genetic code in them as I can't pierce a needle through them to get a sample. Not to where they'd survive anyway," she answers.

As much as she's worked with these micro beings over the years, she hasn't been able to dive any deeper into their inner workings or even their origins, which makes their new mission all the more important. Angelique found a use for these cells (or space mites) and stuck to it; though, she's tried to flex and expound on what they've been able to accomplish with them, she hasn't been able to get any further. Sometimes in science the old adage of "if it ain't broke, don't fix it" often becomes a staple with certain things, but only for so long until it's time to tinker again and this is one of those times.

"Yeah, it makes sense," Toni states. "There could be a multitude of different races among this micro species, just as we're all different 'races' but still part of the *human* race."

"That's *exactly* why I asked," Chloe says, looking over one of the rocks.

"It's an excellent point. I only wish I had an *answer* for it." Angelique shrugs, shaking her head while still gazing at the items.

Chloe opens a drawer not far from them and reveals a pair of glasses with magnified view. The others look at her and nod.

"That's a good idea," Toni says.

"Man, I keep forgetting I have those, honestly," Angelique says.

Chloe puts them on, and they open up the first case to examine when, instantly, the little guys float up in her face. The others watch them drift up in confusion. Chloe tries to pull her head away from them when Angelique realizes what's going on.

"They're going to the metal in your glasses," Angelique points out, shocked.

"Oh!" Chloe takes them off and puts them back in the drawer. The mites return to the metallic stone in the clear casing in a moseying free-fall fashion.

"Oh man..." The team chuckles.

"You guys want to separate these while I hit the bridge?" Angelique asks. They nod.

She turns and opens the door when Chloe stops her. "Angelique...?"

"Yes?" She looks back to the girl who almost had a face full of space mites.

"What would happen if someone would breathe in a cloud of these?" Chloe asks, surely hoping she didn't breathe in or ingest any before fanning them away.

Angelique thinks it over. "With the tight space they would be in within your lungs, they'd probably graft together, more than likely blocking a lot of your air ways. I certainly wouldn't recommend breathing any of them in. Good question, though." She nods to herself. "For now on we need to wear dust masks when working with them, or at least when working with a *lot* of them. I'll be back." Angelique leaves to go talk to the boys in the front.

The other three grab dust masks from the drawer before getting to work.

Angelique's Room-Cam:
Before making her way to the bridge, she goes back and makes a stop off at her room. Inside, she shuts the door behind her and sits on the bed, picking up her parents' picture. She holds it, lightly touching the faces of her mother and father. She takes a deep breath in and then out.

"I'm doing it. I'm *actually* doing it," she says aloud, with tears welling in her eyes and a lump in her throat. "If only you guys could see the things I'm seeing. I'm trying to stay strong and contain my excitement but it—it can be so overwhelming sometimes. I miss you guys, and I really wish you were here right now. I love you, Mom and Dad. Well," she says, wiping her eyes and sniffling. "I better get back to work."

She kisses the photo and puts it back on the end table before standing up. She tries to compose herself before leaving.

Security Feed—Lab Hall:
Angelique passes the labs and sees the light flashing in the dark room and continues down the corridor proudly with a confident smile.

//

Ship Journal
Dr. Angelique Puck: Login: 7575
Subject: **Chloe**

I've already described this young woman, but I'll remind you anyway, she's shorter than me, white, with short red-and-black hair. Thin but not lacking curves by any means. I could tell that, while she obviously lacked some self-confidence, there was a very strong woman within. The youngest crew member, she was a pharmaceutical researcher and tried to get on this mission to extend her knowledge and make a difference in the world. Looking over her progress in the field, I had chosen her without meeting or seeing her first. She showed a lot of promise and had the world ahead of her. Chloe was going to go places.

Security Feed—Lab Hall:
The team helps Chloe get her suit on for the first time. Chloe nervously giggles during. She's about to go for a walk and is understandably anxious. Her virginity of the stars is about to be no more. She feels the uncomfortable sensation they all get upon first being suited up.

"Does it always feel like this?" she asks Angelique.

"The first couple of times, and then you get used to it," she answers, handing Chloe the helmet before helping her put it on. "After a while, you'll be throwing it all on yourself, though it helps to have an extra set of hands."

The two of them share a smile.

"You ready?" Miguel asks Chloe.

"As ready as I'll ever be." She laughs nervously. Her heart pounds and skin jumps, knowing what she's about to do. Miguel climbs up the ladder to the hatch, then Toni. Angelique has Chloe go before her to make sure she doesn't have any trouble.

Top-Cam:
One of the many hatches on the ship opens as the crew emerges. The *Capacitance* is lit by the sun, the moon, and Earth, all glowing with radiant color. The spacecraft hovers as the monochrome spot in an otherwise vivid painting.

"It's like jumping off the high dive. You just do it," Toni adds as they climb up and out, stepping out into the galaxy—the first walk on the mission.

The team gazes at their surroundings while walking about, tiny compared to their view. It takes them all a good thirty minutes to get used to the magnetic boots, but Captain Harper explained the safety cord when he did everything else so, out of instinct, they keep a hold of them during this first walk. For a while everyone walks as though they're walking a tightrope.

"Oh, I've missed this," Miguel says, reaching his hand out for his wife.

"You've done this several times. This must be easy for you," Chloe says to Angelique, instinctively trying to keep her balance with her arms out to her sides.

"Not really. Going two to three years in between trips doesn't really help," she tells Chloe, finding her footing as well.

They're barely out of their atmosphere so the moon, the sun, and other neighboring planets are still very visible—more so than the view from home. Earth is beneath them to their left: big, bright, blue, green, gorgeous. A large, colorful marble illuminated by the golden sun while sitting on a galactic shelf in an otherwise dark room.

"Wave to everybody back at home," Angelique says to them as they all wave to their home planet. The sight of Earth from their view is breathtaking. If it weren't for being here, they would think the view is fabricated: a solid mix of models, paintings, and computer generated imagery.

Angelique-Cam:
Chloe stands with her mouth gaping open and her eyes lit up. Their planet's reflection is visible in her helmet's glass dome. They explore the outside of the *Capacitance* freely to get the feel for it. It's coming back to Angelique what it's like to do this. She frequently checks her team to see how they're doing as they're all walking about in separate directions. It's exciting, but Angelique's concerned it might be too much for Chloe, as it took *her* a while to catch on during her first trip. Chloe takes large steps and, despite being safely fastened to the ship's exterior, watches where she's going.

"You okay, Chloe?" she asks her.

Chloe turns around and gives her a thumb up. "I'm getting it."

Angelique turns.

"You guys good?"

"We're good," they answer in unison with a wave.

"It's a full moon for us tonight," Miguel says, pointing over.

Chloe turns, and then Angelique turns around, opposite of the Earth, to see the *moon*. Even the moon, with its exterior scarred from being pelted with asteroids and random space debris for God knows how long, looks gorgeous up here. Its sterile and monochrome appearance holds its own beauty. It's her fourth time seeing it.

"Of all the planets and stars in the universe, why were we in such a hurry to make it to the *moon* first? It looks really drab," Chloe says, looking at the moon, larger than she'd ever seen it before with a definition so crisp, prior footage doesn't do it justice. "Still incredible to be this close, though."

Angelique looks at her with the moon reflected in her dome.

"The moon was the closest thing. Gotta learn how to crawl before you can walk," Angelique tells her.

Chloe thinks about it, taking it in. "It just strikes me funny, like a 'grass is greener' kind of thing. We try so hard to get to *that*," she says, pointing to the desolate moon, "from *that*." She points to the lush Earth, with Angelique's view following Chloe's directed movements.

Angelique laughs. "Good observation. The unknown can be exciting and scary. I guess when you're born and bred into something beautiful like Earth, you end up taking it for granted over time. We always want to know what's out here but most of us don't even know what we have down there."

Chloe watches the Earth. "Yeah. If only everyone down there could understand what we're trying to do," she says, still looking in wonder before turning to Angelique, who nods slowly.

DocLab 7-Cam:
Toni and Miguel are working in DocLab 6, leaving Chloe and Angelique in hers. At the table, they both look through their microscopes at various particles. It's fairly quiet with the women concentrating. Chloe stops and sits up, looking up from her lens, her eyes wandering as if looking and trying to find the idea she knows is there, and then how to word it.

"I was wondering," Chloe says, "is there any way these could be capsulized for ingesting purposes?"

"I don't think it would do any good as I'm not really sure if it contains any nutrients or sickness fighting abilities in that form," Angelique answers, with an unsure shrug. "Actually, I'm not even sure if it would survive the stomach acid."

"How could we test it?" Chloe asks, looking up from her

microscope.

"Well, since the days of testing on animals are *long* over, we'd need a test subject to sign a waiver before taking it, and then we'd need to observe them. I suppose a safer route would be pumping someone's stomach and putting the mites in the bile. But, again, you'd have to find someone open to letting you pump their stomach and more than likely have to sign more papers. Since everything changed years ago, there's been more and more red tape involved with testing."

"I'll do it," Chloe says, very matter-of-fact.

Angelique's head lifts from her view. "Uh, what?" There's no sign of jest in her expression.

"We can pump my stomach and put them in the bile." Chloe shrugs. *No big deal.*

Angelique looks at her, making sure she knows what she's requesting. "You know getting your stomach pumped is no cake walk. It's not exactly the *feel good sensation* you've been seeking." She smirks, but Chloe is dead serious. Like the woman she's looked up to, and now works with, Chloe's driven.

"Yeah, but it's for the sake of *science*. This is what we do, right? Someone's gotta do it." Chloe smiles.

Of all the things Angelique had expected to do on this mission, this wasn't one of them. She can't believe what she's about to do.

"We should probably do so in a restroom," Angelique says, standing up to get the items needed, including a tube and a canister along with a mesh screen for straining. The two exit the lab to get down to it.

Bridge-Cam:
Stanton sits at the helm of the ship, alone, watching out of the window with his feet resting up on the control panel. He yawns and stretches, bored.

DocLab 7-Cam:

Chloe looks weak and exhausted, sick even. Angelique still can't believe she willingly did it. Angelique looks at her with a slight wince while holding her arm in an attempt at some kind of comfort while Chloe moves slowly.

"You really *should* go lay down for a bit," she tells Chloe.

"I told you I'll be fine. I'll lie down later. I wanna see what happens." She's determined to see the results alongside Angelique. With the canister of stomach acid on the table and any solids that came up disposed of, they're set to drop the clear-coated silver-ish space mites in. The bile is a vibrant yellow, with a tiny shade of green here and there, looking almost neon mixed along with a good amount of clear fluid.

Test number *one*: Angelique uses a dropper to get some of the bile, dripping it on the glass beneath the microscope. Chloe still holds her stomach while looking rough. Angelique walks over to the cases of microorganisms and watches carefully as she reaches in with her tweezer-like utensils to grasp one, which takes a moment to do. Chloe watches as Angelique turns, placing the micro-being in the drop of bile on the glass.

"I don't know if this will be enough to really see, but we'll give it a go," she says.

They each take turns looking through the microscope and the acid seems to eat away at the clear sheath but isn't doing much to the chrome-appearing body beneath it. The alien being shivers and vibrates, attempting to fight or evade what covers it to no avail. Still whole, and still alive, it sits, quaking.

Test number *two*: After separating some of the bile into a smaller jar, they drop in several of the living particles very similar to Angelique's NMC. The bodies are so small they don't even appear to break the surface of the bile. To the naked eye, the tiny aliens are practically invisible in the fluid but will soon be apparent. Chloe turns off the lights as Angelique turns on a flashlight before turning on another, handing it to Chloe.

Within the yellow glow, they see the shimmer of the tiny space mites, a snowy sparkle in the neon pool. With one of their glass sticks, they stir the jar's contents around. Through their lights they can still see them glimmering, floating about. There's no real change in them at this moment so they decide to let them sit in it and turn the lights back on.

Instantly, without saying a word, Chloe digs through one of the cabinets before heading to the microscope again.

"What's going on in that mind of yours?" Angelique asks.

"Just another test." Chloe winks at her before going back to work. Angelique watches her as she transfers a plethora of the living particles into an empty plastic medicine capsule.

Test number *three*: They take the pill of space mites she's made over to the other table. Angelique ladles out some of the bile from the canister without alien life into another, smaller jar. The smell of the bile is strong, near sour, but they work past it.

Chloe shakes up the pill, looking at Angelique.

"I always do this in testing because I know they're going to be shaken in transport. This way, I know the effects beforehand."

Angelique shrugs. "Makes sense."

Chloe drops the pill in and they watch it. It doesn't take long for it to dissolve, and its contents float freely like the other jar.

An idea hits Angelique. "I want to check something."

She turns off the lights and then heads back to the previous testing jar to retrieve one of the little cells. After it's collected, Chloe turns the lights back on before moving it to a glass to look at beneath the lens. She stands beside Angelique as she examines.

"If the acid corrodes their coating, I'm wondering what their lifespan is without it," she says, adjusting her lens.

"No disrespect at all, but I figured with as much as you've worked with them, you'd know them inside and out," Chloe states reluctantly.

"No disrespect taken. Truth is, I understood these were living beings and didn't want to tamper too much with their livelihood as I was able to use them without doing so. I had tried to pierce one when I had originally inspected them to no avail," she replies.

"What happens with the clear coating when they fuse together?" Chloe asks, standing over her shoulder, curious.

"The sheaths fuse as well, making one large coating over the mass," Angelique answers, still looking through the lens. On the glass, the black specks once seen floating about throughout its chrome-like body have faded as the core of this cell falls apart and *dies* on the glass beneath her eyes.

Angelique looks up at Chloe and sighs. "Well, without the coating, they die and the bile eats the casing away. It doesn't really eat into their body, but they won't live long without it."

Chloe looks at her with a frown.

"Don't be discouraged. It's all part of the job." Angelique smiles at her encouragingly. "I want to check back on the first one."

She scoots over to the first microscope. Though this one wasn't submerged like the others, the space mite doesn't last long without its shielding and its quaking comes to a stop as it melts into a little shiny puddle amidst the neon-like acid.

"Yeah, it's a no-go. So it's not the amount of acid or its being dunked in and surrounded but losing their cover altogether."

Chloe crosses her arms, thinking hard; the wheels are turning. "Well...can we see what this looks like in blood?" Chloe motions to the dead cell on the glass.

"I suppose we can try... *However*," Angelique says with an unsure expression, "I tested it when we discovered the others, mixing the live particles with blood, but there was no reaction. These aren't the same *cells*, but they're definitely of the same *species*."

Angelique retrieves a blood bag from the refrigerator before filling a vial halfway. Using a dropper, Chloe collects the liquid corpse of the microscopic alien and drips it into the blood. It stays together for a very brief moment before dissipating in the DNA, the silver glimmer no longer visible under their lights.

"Well, that does in my pharmaceutical theory." Chloe sighs.

Angelique pats her shoulder, and they get back to work.

Ship Journal Continued:

Along with times of work, I also remember sweet moments with her when she'd join me for prayer in my quarters. She said it helped calm her nerves as it was taking her a while to get acclimated to space life; though the prayer sessions continued after she got the hang of it. She always appeared so sweet and innocent to me. I don't have to explain to you the benign crush I had on this girl. She was incredible, pretty, *and* smart. I saw so much of myself in her with her willingness to explore, experiment, and advance her knowledge; we really *got* each other. Despite the workplace attraction I had felt for Chloe, I was in a committed relationship and wasn't about to do anything to ruin it. Although I was deeply devoted to Serena, it had turned out the feeling was not mutual.

Angelique's Room-Cam:

Angelique relaxes in her room, lying back in her bed, decompressing from her often tedious work. The light on the outlined panel on the wall blinks as a series of beeps emits from it, loud enough to catch but not jarring. Tired, she groans briefly upon hearing her incoming call. She presses the button below the blinking light and the panel slides over as the video screen extends from the wall. Angelique turns on the screen, revealing the sexy Serena.

Angelique's tired demeanor lights up.

"Hey, baby," Angelique greets her happily though beat from work.

"Hey, 'Lique. How's everything going up there?" Serena asks through a forced smile.

"Everything's going well." She shrugs before shaking her head with a chuckle. "Girl, I'm just *exhausted*. How're *you?*" Angelique's hoping for good news while stroking her long hair.

Serena, though as beautiful as ever, hesitates and looks almost sour. "Things are...okay. They're fine," she answers hesitantly. An air of unease is evident in the call, an emptiness in body language and tone.

Angelique stops stroking her hair, and her hands drop to her side. She asks, "What's on your mind, Serena? You sound like something's up."

Serena seems nervous and is growing flustered. "It's just..." She sighs in a defeatist tone with a long blink as her shoulders slump down. She trembles slightly before taking a deep breath and straightens up. "Angelique, we need to talk."

Any glimmer of a smile from Angelique straightens. Her expression becomes blank, but her body slumps slightly as if deflated. Like the turbulence from the satellite debris, it's another jolting surprise she wasn't prepared for on this mission.

Angelique, in one of the scariest places for humankind to be, used to dealing with the unknown and the dangers of medical experimentation and heinous diseases, is shaken from this single line. This is a kind of fear of hers which tops the risk of contracting RNS while attempting to cure it. The kind of fear she's not used to even when delving into the dangerous unknown. Her eyes water, and her hands tremble. She swallows hard and takes a deep breath as she closes her eyes tightly for a brief moment and nods before opening them, wiping away already formed tears ready to roll.

"Okay. Go ahead," Angelique tells her calmly.

There's nothing to do now for Serena but to spit it out. "Look, I'm sorry, but I...*I can't do this anymore.*"

Angelique gasps.

"The distance is just too *much*. I can't have my girlfriend more than a world away from me. I'm...I'm sorry. *It's over.*"

The words strike Angelique as if she's the punching bag hanging up in Saxon's quarters. She's frozen, bordering on the catatonic state of the Rabid Neural Stasis victims back home. Serena seems as though saying it was tiring while at the same time relieved to get it off her chest.

Angelique made it clear numerous times how important this mission is. Along with being heartbroken and struck down, she doesn't bother making a case for herself and leaves it at silence, nodding with tears. The water thickly coats over her brown eyes. She couldn't get the words out if she wanted to. Even if she would've had a comeback speech prepared for such a situation, she *still*, in *this moment*, would choose not to speak and lean on the shoulder of silence.

Serena watches coldly as Angelique falls apart in front of her from the inside out. Her breathing is stilted. Her heart jolts back and forth between skipping beats, stopping, and racing. Angelique's eyelids won't close, not even for a natural moisturizing blink, as the tears stream, glistening on her brown skin. Her body shivers however stationary. Serena's silent, awaiting an actual verbalized response.

The loss of the love Angelique feels for Serena nears the loss of her mom and dad; the taillights of her parents' tragedy are in view of her broken heart. Her mind races. Her hands grip the bed sheet beneath and to her sides.

Serena sighs and can't watch anymore. "Goodbye, Angelique," she says, hanging up. The screen goes black and descends back into the wall covered by the panel.

Angelique lets out a gasp for air like a woman who's been to the bottom of the ocean, fighting her way to the top. Her face slams down into her hands as she sobs. Her nose runs as her eyes do, and she cries. Dumped from off-planet with no possible way of going to

Serena and talking to her face to face. She holds her stomach, hurting from the sobs. Her eyes close tightly, stinging from the tears. She can't regulate her breathing, and though she tries, she can't get a coherent word out.

The lump in her throat is seemingly blocking anything from releasing from her lips. Angelique falls back onto her bed and curls up in a fetal position, stuffing her face in her pillow as she lets out a bloodcurdling, albeit muffled, scream. Angelique continues to scream and sob with the occasional slapping on her bed and pillow—heartbroken, angry, hurt, crushed, thrown away. She screams and cries until she falls asleep, passing out from exhaustion. In her sleep, her body still jumps and twitches.

Ship Journal Continued:

There was no feasible way of holding her and expressing everything I felt, how much I loved her, what Serena has meant to me over the time we've shared. Millions of light-years away in the cold, desolate universe, I had to lose someone else I've cared about and not to an illness I couldn't cure but to a need (or neediness) that I couldn't cure without having skipped the mission, putting millions of lives at risk. It hadn't crossed my mind before, but I've sacrificed my heart and the love it holds for the health of the world. I felt defeated; smart enough to find the previously unseen and help millions but not smart enough to hold down a relationship.

I don't know if she was seeing someone else while I've been up here working, but it was clear that she no longer wanted *me*. I've tried my best to get past it. I still miss her; though, I don't like to think about it. I loved her, but maybe I didn't convey it enough. Maybe *I* wasn't enough, period. I did what I had always done and dove headfirst into my work, not letting any personal woes interfere with my goal—of course, work is also a wonderful distraction and always has been for me.

I often wonder if I've been subconsciously experimenting with my heart throughout the years, exploring and looking for what ails it. I thought I'd found the cure in Serena, but I was wrong. If something would happen to remind me of Serena or the job she did on my heart, I would say I had to go check something and cry alone in my quarters. I didn't tell anyone about the breakup and kept it to myself, though I had ceased feeling bad about my little crush on Chloe.

Angelique's Room-Cam:
With another day of work completed, the team has separated, and it's time to turn in for the doctor. She lies in her bed, saying her prayers in between reading her mother's poetry book for what seems like at least the hundredth time, which is propped up on her chest. She knows it by heart but still finds comfort in *seeing* the words concocted by the woman who gave birth to her. There's a buzzing at the door. She would say "come in," however, whoever it is wouldn't hear it through the door. The electronic buzz repeats. Angelique puts her book down and moves to the door, pressing the button to the side. It beeps and the heavy door slides open effortlessly, revealing the beautiful, young Chloe standing before her looking sleek in her one-piece uniform.

"Hi. Do you have a moment?" Chloe asks Angelique in her ever so innocent tone.

"Of course, come on in." Angelique lets her in and the door closes behind her.

"I wasn't interrupting anything was I?" Chloe worries.

"Not at all. I was just reading. Have a seat," Angelique says casually, friendly.

Chloe could sit in the chair at the table or at the desk but sits on the bed. "Oh, what were you reading?"

Angelique hands the book to her as she instantly looks it over. Chloe thumbs through it with a glow, surprised, as she expected Angelique to probably be reading up on something along the lines of new methods of molecular structure or nervous system treatments.

"It's a poetry book my mother wrote when I was a baby." She sits down beside Chloe.

Chloe reads the acknowledgment *"For my Angelique"* and smiles, looking up at her.

"You can borrow it if you'd like. There's something in there for everybody," Angelique says, watching her, proud to see her mother's work extending.

"I'll definitely give it a read, thanks." She holds the book close to her and looks like she has something else on her mind. The last time Angelique had heard and seen this action, it was before getting dumped via video phone while millions and millions of miles away.

"Chloe, is everything all right?"

Chloe's hands are fidgety, and she appears nervous. Her breathing becomes brief and shallow as Angelique's brow furrows. If she's getting cold feet about the mission, it's a bit late.

"I can't keep going on without saying anything." Chloe's shaking, anxious. "I'm...I'm *deeply* attracted to you."

Chloe tries to look Angelique in the eyes but struggles. Angelique's visibly struck and caught off-guard as this beautiful younger woman expresses her fondness for her while flying through deep space.

"I mean, I–I know I shouldn't be saying anything because I know you have a girlfriend, but I just had to *get it out*." Chloe fights to keep everything from pouring out to her but can't help herself, explaining with her fidgety hands. "You're amazing and gorgeous and I just... *needed* to tell you," she finishes, prepared to be shot down. However, once the young woman states that she knows Angelique has a girlfriend, Angelique's head immediately shakes.

"No, no, that's all done with." The memory of being cut loose like a low level employee comes back to Angelique as she looks down, still shaking her head. She looks up, redirecting her attention to Chloe.

"*What?*" Chloe asks.

"Sometimes," Angelique says, "you think you've found the right person and that you both are on the same page, and it turns out that you're reading *alone*," Angelique says with a slow nod, almost as if putting those very pieces together herself for the first time.

A moment of understanding grows between them, however silent. Chloe and Angelique inch toward each other in their silence about as slow as they feel moving through the galaxy and just as smoothly. They can practically feel their auras touch when they get close enough.

Chloe's breath hits Angelique's lips as Angelique's does hers. Their eyes close in unison as both of their heads tilt slightly and go in for a breathtaking kiss. Angelique's heartbeat pounds like tribal drums, and she finds herself as shy and nervous as Chloe had appeared before her confession. For a brief moment, she feels her heart lose its sense of gravity and jump in the excitement. Chloe's kiss is strong, yet by the use of soft lips, a kiss of pent up passion.

Their lips interlock, and their tongues touch. The kiss tastes amazing to Angelique. Hot and unexpected; Angelique's never done anything like this. Without breaking their lip-lock, Chloe sets the book on the bedside table. They instantly begin unzipping each other's uniforms. Chloe kisses down Angelique's neck while unhooking her bra before revealing Angelique's breasts: chocolate brown, flawless with dark nipples hardening by the second. Chloe's hands sensually squeeze them. Her soft hands caress Angelique while rubbing her thumbs on the tips of her nipples while gazing at them.

Angelique releases a slight moan and bites her bottom lip. Seeing Chloe's eyes light up at the sight makes Angelique feel good, wanted, and attractive. Chloe moves in, and her head drops as she takes the end of one of Angelique's breasts in her mouth, collecting her nipple with her tongue and lips. Angelique's eyes shut, and her head leans back as Chloe sucks on her nipples. Angelique's hand cups the back of Chloe's head as she tastes and suckles on what look like chocolate candy drops. Her hand grips a handful of Chloe's black and red hair.

Chloe stops and stands up while Angelique wants badly to tell her not to stop. Chloe gazes at her seductively. Any sign of playfulness is gone, and the look conveys almost a stern passion. Chloe, the cute pharmaceutical researcher whom she'd met right before taking off, stands before Angelique, stripping off her silver and white uniform. The bodysuit falls to the floor, revealing her natural shape. Her bra and panties are black, a stark contrast to her porcelain skin.

Their gazes never break as Chloe removes her bra, dropping it to the floor. Her breasts are a little smaller than Angelique's but supple with erect dark-tan nipples. Chloe slides her underwear down to the floor and steps out of them as Angelique eyes her from head to toe to head again. With only the top of her uniform down, Angelique smoothly drops to her knees, kissing all over Chloe's young tender body. Chloe is shaved and very clean: a benefit to the rule of mandatory two showers daily.

Chloe trembles with every kiss. Her hands stroke Angelique's long dark hair. Angelique stands up, looking down to her, and leads Chloe to the bed, laying her down. Angelique strips the rest of her uniform down and joins her in her bed in their little galactic hotel room with her dark skin touching Chloe's white skin, soft surfaces brushing against one another. Chloe eyes Angelique's sleek, smooth body as Angelique did hers. They kiss passionately, running their hands up and down each other's bodies.

Neither of them ever thought they'd have part in an intergalactic hookup, but it feels like *more*.

Chloe bites Angelique's neck as Angelique's hand slides down her gorgeous white skin and her fingers enter. Chloe moans. Angelique's wrist gyrates, and her fingers work in a "come hither" motion while Chloe becomes louder, grasping at Angelique's body. Her fingers vacate Chloe's moistness as she kisses Chloe hard and sits up, pushing Chloe back. They share a smile. Their breathing is heavy. Their eyes glued, an unbreakable stare.

Angelique licks her lips, and Chloe nods. Angelique slides down as Chloe's legs lift and open simultaneously. Chloe grips the pillow and gasps as she feels Angelique's tongue for the first time. Angelique moves slowly with caressing licks and soft kisses. Her hands, dark against Chloe's skin, run up the side of her body to where she squeezes Chloe's breasts. Chloe's eyes roll back, her breathing escalates, heart races, fingers grip the pillow beneath her, and lets out a series of moans, whimpers, and pants.

Angelique speeds up, and Chloe's breathing matches the pace. Her hands leave the pillow and grab Angelique's hair, thrusting hard into her mouth. Ecstasy rising, Chloe trembles, before screaming out in orgasm.

Sensitive and even slightly exhausted, Chloe looks down to Angelique, who's smiling up at her. A few breaths and Chloe grabs Angelique, pulling her in for another passionate kiss on her wet lips before pushing her back. Chloe slides off the bed and stands as Angelique watches.

Chloe's hand extends, and Angelique takes it and stands. Without a word spoken, they kiss. Chloe looks up at the taller Angelique and physically, sensually, directs her to bend over on the bed. She does so, laying her arms and the side of her face down on the bed with the rest of her propped up and presented, well positioned for Chloe. Chloe's eyes widen with the sight of Angelique's backend, and her hands caress her cheeks, soft and flawless like the rest of her with, of course, the same delicious brown skin tone.

With her head rested against the sheets, Angelique smiles and bites her bottom lip, feeling Chloe's hands. The young woman's index and middle fingers together slide in and then out of her mouth before sliding them inside of her colleague. Angelique moans upon feeling her enter. Inside, Chloe starts with soft strokes to which Angelique equally responds with sounds of pleasure and gyrating her hips. She grinds back against Chloe's hand before the grinding becomes almost a bucking.

Chloe takes the hint and pounds her two fingers into Angelique. Angelique loves the pressure of the thrusts, letting out screams and cries of passion. Chloe stands, nude, working her wrist while the other hand grips the cheeks in front of her intermittently. Angelique stops pushing back and shivers hard, releasing the orgasmic scream of a wild woman. Chloe slides out, and Angelique falls over, back into the bed.

Chloe lies down, holding her from behind. Angelique pants, catching her breath while Chloe kisses the side of her head.

Angelique wraps her arm over Chloe's, holding her tightly.

Angelique looks back over her shoulder with a sly smile. "I've heard of people in the Mile High Club, but I think we topped them tonight."

Chloe shares her smile, and they laugh together before leaning in for a kiss.

Stem-Cam:
Merely coasting, the *Capacitance* moves through space. Stars watch as onlookers from a distance while the ship casually strolls through the universe. Random debris comprised of meteor fragments of various sizes are seen with some drifting and some clustered while stationary. The universe: empty yet full, weightless yet heavy, cold yet passionate, open yet seemingly closed off by the black walls encasing everything. Its contents massive yet tiny in their surroundings.

Top-Cam:
The *Capacitance* looks peaceful. With everyone onboard tucked in for the night, the exterior of the ship is clear. Despite the darkness and the cold desolation of the open universe, all appears safe. Nighttime within the deep, dark woods with the ground, trees, and anything else physical taking a sabbatical while all that's left is the starry night sky.

Angelique's Room-Cam:
Chloe and Angelique lie beneath the sheets of Angelique's bed, wrapped around one another, looking up at the ceiling, enjoying their euphoric moment.

"So, tell me, how did you become you?" Chloe asks like a child asking their favorite athlete. Beyond her *attraction* to Angelique, she looks up to her as an idol in their field.

Her face scrunches. "I've always been me." Angelique laughs.

Chloe smiles, pushing her in jest. "You know what I mean, 'Lique. What's your story? How does a little girl grow up to be Dr. Angelique Puck?"

Dr. Puck thinks for a brief moment before responding. "Well, I grew up an only child and always wanted to be a scientist. I was a happy child, always looking to the sky. My parents were good people, and I loved and admired them dearly. They always believed in my constant search for knowledge and were patient and gracious enough to put up with my constant questions, no matter how inane, which there were plenty."

The girls giggle together.

"I don't know, I—I just wanted to help people, to find the cures that seemed out of reach. I was constantly hearing about advancements in science and was so desperate to be a part of that, I had to sacrifice a lot of material and personally *physical* wants to get there."
Angelique lightly touches Chloe's hand.

Chloe watches with stars in her eyes as the object of her affection speaks.

"Whenever I'd have friends, I never really found one with those same interests, so I spent a lot of time alone, studying, growing, and learning about everything I could. I would listen to podcasts about scientific finds and studies, daydreaming about making discoveries *myself*. It seemed every year there were more advances in medicine, yet every year there were new diseases and illnesses. Even as a kid I realized they were treating problems but not really finding cures. Although, I know the money is in the treatments and not in the cures, I wanted to be one to cure and not just to assist or treat. Our space program was advancing in galactic travel, and trips out of our atmosphere were becoming regular occurrences by the time I was a teenager. I couldn't help but to think the answers that doctors were seeking weren't being found because they weren't of this world and we'd have to go out and find them." She looks back to Chloe. "And that's pretty much it."

They smile and share a brief kiss.

"And what about relationships?" Chloe asks with a smirk and wink.

Angelique smiles and nods. "Though I've been in a multitude of relationships, I've always been married to my work, which rarely gives me time for a social life."

Chloe nods. "I know *exactly* what you mean."

"So what's *your* story?" Angelique asks, gently stroking her arm.

"Strangely enough, about the same. Only child. Wonderful parents. More into learning than living, things than people. I had always dreamed of going to space, and now that I'm here, it feels *odd*. It seems like once you get what you've always wanted, it's exciting for a short time, and then once you get used to it being a part of your life, it loses its wonderment."

Chloe pauses briefly, thinking.

"Why do we do this? I've always wondered why we take everything for granted as we do. The old saying 'You don't know what you got 'til it's gone' is very true and makes a lot of sense but...wouldn't you get used to being alone eventually?" she asks aloud, in an almost stream-of-conscious thinking. She turns to face Angelique, who shares the same stars in her eyes for Chloe.

Angelique touches the young woman's face softly. A light and probably a throwaway and forgetful moment to some is heavy, so heavy the lack of gravity in the universe around them couldn't hold it up. They get it; they get each other, like two cogs fitting perfectly with every turn. Their moment is loud in its silence.

Angelique smiles at her. "Hey, let's get out of here."

Top-Cam:
The ship is peaceful, floating in the star-studded black. Beneath the dome of the Stargazer, Angelique and Chloe watch the universe, not working or researching, just *enjoying*. It's closer than any telescopic sight—a front row seat better than the large videos displayed at science centers. The researchers get to take a break from fighting the deadly illness long enough to replenish their mutual love for the stars and the unknown beyond their world.

//

Ship Journal
Dr. Angelique Puck: Login: 7575
Subject: **Stargazer**

I'm standing in the stargazer, *alone* of course, looking out into the black, and the stars in the distance winking at me while thinking of things past, present, and future. Looking out of this at the wide open universe is like being in a room with gorgeous people who don't acknowledge my existence; I'm invisible. It's so pretty and perfect, and it doesn't care. Along with no sound, space carries no emotion. It doesn't need us. It doesn't require anything from us to keep it going. It just *is*. Who would've thought something so beautiful would've brought so much pain?

Space, the black widow. What will the families of *Capacitance* crew members say when they hear the news? I try not to think of the horror we encountered and the tragedy that befell my determined crew and ultimately left me alone to fend for myself in the great unknown that is our universe, but it's hard to shake. I think about Chloe and her parents' and friends' loss: a bright young woman with the world at her fingertips taken from them after accepting the opportunity of a lifetime.

I think about the child Toni and Miguel will never have. Surely Saxon and Lou Ann had families, people who will miss them terribly upon hearing the news. Though Saxon will no longer have to deal with his anger and the demons he obviously had, and Lou Ann will never get to write her exposé on the interstellar mission—and any awards that might have come to it are no longer in the cards.

I don't know if Stanton was ever married or not, but he didn't die without a single soul on Earth thinking of him. His cool and calm, often sweet, demeanor was a stark contrast to the terror he met. Captain Harper's wife will no longer be able to trade loving and joking jabs with her husband as her laughter will soon be obsolete as soon as she finds out that the man she loves doesn't live anymore. She's a widow now because her husband went to work, putting food on their table, and making sure their bills were paid.

Harper and Saxon were both military men who had seen war and had made it out unscathed only to meet their demise on such a simple space mission where there are no terrorists with nukes and catastrophic agendas. They're dead; they're *all* dead. I can't shake the feeling that this is all my fault. Had I not pressed to go deeper into the unknown they'd all still be alive, families wouldn't be destroyed, and I wouldn't be an emotional wreck. I know it sounds like a pity party, but I'm calling the situation like I see it. I couldn't even save the *healthy* people on this ship, how am I supposed to save the millions sick on Earth?

I'm all alone. Though I'm technically unhurt, I'd argue if I'm safe or not as I am completely vulnerable in my current situation. I know now that anything can happen at any time; something usually exciting in my line of work, but not so much when it comes to my personal safety. Since I've been here, I've gained friends, only to lose them. I lost someone I loved as I was thrown away like unwanted leftovers, only to find new a new affection in a friend. Of course, she was taken away from me as well.

I was trained and equipped to do my job on this expedition, not to survive under such circumstances. Beyond the lab, I don't even know what I'm doing and not sure if I ever did. I'm trying my hardest; I *am*. I'm trying to keep it together, distracting myself with numerous tests. Part of me is starting to feel calloused, as emotionally cold as Lou Ann, while the other part of me wants to curl up in a ball and cry my eyes out, screaming for help. If I happen to run into the same monstrous trouble that had left me solitary, I don't know what I could do to really protect myself. Saxon's room is full of weaponry, but it's no match for what's out here.

Sadly, I've seen dead bodies on my exploratory medical career, but nothing matches the morose, depressing, and downright heartbreaking feeling of having to physically wrap up my freshly dead friends and colleagues, whom I watched die before my eyes, into body bags after hauling them down to the cargo bay. Sometimes I think I would've been better off joining them in death rather than being forced into survival, alone to face whatever may be out here in the black, awaiting its opportunity to strike. I'm going to keep working as there's not much else to do. If I make it through this, I know I'll never forget it: amazing scientific discoveries, a night of unbridled passion, and the pure terror that took place. Who *could* forget this trip?

I'm sure it's my last space expedition whether I make it or not. The thought makes me think of the universal timeline. I've done so much in my life, but I fear that, in the long scheme of things, it doesn't mean anything. You can do a lot in a lifetime of, say, eighty to ninety years, but honestly, what does it all mean in a span of billions of years? In all this around me it seems to be just another collective of particles and molecules; territorial, much like my test subjects, we're all fighting for our own space without realizing how small we really are.

I press my hands and face against the glass, feeling its cold flat texture on my skin. With the tears in my eyes, the light of the distant stars distort as they stretch and become neon streaks across the black skies that go from white to multicolored. I'm smiling as my surroundings' blank exterior is fluorescently pinstriped. I blink, wipe my eyes, and the beams return to their pinhole state.

It's nice when the stars don't look like crawling spiders made of light.

Something Chloe had said repeats in my mind. "If only everyone down there could understand what we're trying to do..." We tried; I'm *still* trying. My crew came up here in hopes to help the world, to cure the sick, and to prolong life in the human race. We're trying to stop an oncoming apocalypse, to secure human evolution.

Some people don't believe in evolution or growth beyond the standard. When people say they don't believe in evolution, it strikes me as kind of an ignorant notion as evolution means growth. We see it and live it every day. Explorers were constantly pushing our stagnant race to new levels. Scientists and researchers were always at work, trying to improve on our often sickly designs. Most people attribute the thought of evolution to the notion of all of us coming from apes and nobody thinks about the idea of us growing into a new and better human being.

The notion is a bit confusing as apes are still here and not becoming anything other than older apes. But where are WE headed? *That* is what we were and what I'm *still* trying to secure. I predict that someday there will be a whole different species, and they will trace their roots back to humanity as opposed to primates, a race evolved from human beings. There's no law against *making* yourself evolve. I'd always read, "If you can't find a door, *make* one" so why can't the same be said for our evolution?

Space: squid ink swirled with glitter and gravel. Black, cold, and seemingly desolate; it first appears so beautiful and breathtaking, and then it becomes something lonely. Being up here is not unlike my relationship with Serena. Though I've had my share of loss and regret, I've always had my career by my side: my work, my best friend. Science has always been the true love that never leaves and never dies. With that said, I never thought my work would ever lead me so far from home and leave me lonely, and being completely alone on a vessel in a place where there's no other human life makes me feel it all the more.

What does it all mean? What are we really? Is there a purpose to our lives in the long scheme of things? Are we just wandering around looking for questions to the answers we already hold? What have I been *doing* with my life? Instead of trying to help a sinking ship, should I have left Earth long ago and set sail only to keep going until I find land? Am I destined to wander the stars for forty years to learn? Does God seem to not be around in times of distress because he has so many other worlds and galaxies beyond the man-named Milky Way galaxy to spiritually govern?

In a world divided between the concepts of God and science, I ask "Why can't there be *both?*" And why can't they both exist without friction, with the belief of God on a spiritual plane and the belief of science on a physical plane? There's no reason they can't coexist. It's all in perception. I am a woman of science, and I am a woman of God, no matter how hard that is to fathom.

Maybe I was wrong about my thoughts of God and the universe earlier upon my lonesome meditation.

Maybe we're *inside* of him and *that's* why there's no light out here. Maybe we flow through the galaxy weightless because we're flowing through his bloodstream, which isn't wet like ours but comprised of stones and stars of various sizes. Perhaps the sun isn't a medium sized star at all, and it's actually his *heart*, radiating with heat and giving life. Perhaps it *is* all in perception, and we've decided to name and label things, but we don't understand that we're all the same—various kinds of cells within God's body. Like how we have red and white blood cells, viruses and anti-viruses, nerves and myelin, immune systems, nervous systems, etc., etc.

Of course, it's a theory that would surely cause more panic and controversy than interest and intrigue, learning we're all nothing but a living cell, a mite, part of a larger whole. If the Nu-Myelin Cell and its very similar looking brethren across the galaxy can indeed think, I wonder if it's a feeling that's hit them. I never thought about how they feel or if they can feel.

Even if such a theory would turn out to be too farfetched, we're all still microscopic in comparison to our otherworldly surroundings regardless. If we, and even the large animals on our planet, are actually the mere size of a cell then where are the larger beings? I've always believed that "There's always a bigger fish," and so I ask you, where are the bigger fish in the universe? Is the blue whale the biggest being in the known galaxy? Are the specks of dust known as human beings really the smartest amidst this vast terrain? Is our size offset by our knowledge and vice versa?

Looking beyond this glass brings up too many questions. I'm already scared enough. I have nightmares of star-shaped creatures, chrome-covered in appearance when I'm not dreaming of becoming even more lost than what I am. Who will find me? I fear by the time someone does happen to find the *Capacitance*, they will find a withered skeleton sitting at the helm of a frozen metal box that drifts no differently from the asteroids around it: a skeleton of a woman who tried, only to meet her end.

Life is indeed a circle; it starts out here, and it ends out here. How do we know we haven't been living in a black hole this whole time? Part of me finds science and what we perceive as knowledge to be a curious thing; someone long ago names something, describing its attributes, and the rest of us keep that information and take it as gospel. There are seven recorded planes of existence, but of course, these are man-made observations—there very well be more, as we're constantly finding more and more out about our universe.

How do we know they weren't wrong when they decided to put a label on things? How do we know what they had discovered or collected information on was correct or just correct to their particular perception? How do we decide what to name and how? As we don't really know anything beyond our galaxy, can we really make that call? Maybe we're all survivors and the lively unknown universe we all dream of is somewhere on the other side.

Perhaps on those worlds beyond the black, the human race ARE insects beneath the feet of their dominant beings, or we even appear the oddly shaped creatures we see in the movies and comic books. Maybe the "alien beings" first found over a century ago that caused such a stir weren't *alien* to our planet at all, but our ancestors returning, essentially *Adam and Eve* if you will, not apes or Neanderthals. Maybe all the fantastical science fiction writers are on to something, and the ones who scoff at them are just ignorant, refusing to believe a perception different from their own. Maybe they see something we don't, and as scientists, we try to make tangible sense of it all.

It all raises so many questions, the universe, questions that go against being a scientist as well as being a Christian. Who *knows* why we're here? Who knows where we're going? Why do we feel the need to control and label everything? We ask "What's out there?" when we really don't even fully know what's in the Earth. Is Rabid Neural Stasis a new beginning, taking humanity into a new predatorial and territorial stage? I fear RNS is a transitional phase and what's coming is even worse, if that's possible.

In my ranting I've fogged up the glass with my breathing and subconsciously have written "HELP ME" with my finger. If only a beautiful stranger would stop by and ask if I need a jump.

For as long as I can remember, people of Earth have tried to migrate to Mars, which is interesting to me because they could just as easily make the move for Venus, often times a closer planet. If only there were countless movies and books about Venus as there are about Mars and Martians, I suppose such a move would be talked about. Nobody desires to be in this spot right *here*; everyone wants to go to a nearby planet or beyond this point.

As it stands, I'm currently stuck in the in-between of the known galaxy and the exciting galaxies beyond. Trapped in the walls between rooms containing the knowledge sought out and the only light in such a dark place is coming from the nail holes in the walls on either side.

I am but an insect, crawling within the structure of the cosmos in attempts to bring something worthwhile back to my hill or hive.

I wonder if anything could ever disrupt the flow of our spiral galaxy, perhaps causing planets to shift around. What would happen if the planets Mercury and Pluto would change places? What if Mars was sent farther out? Would it still be as desirable? Worse yet, what would happen to us if we went closer or farther from the sun? Perhaps, as Earth, we have what we have due to our perfect location in the solar system. Would some of the other planets develop life if they were in such a location? You start to question everything when you're up here long enough.

This all feels like one of my nightmares. I hope it is. I hope I wake up soon. I don't know how much longer my psyche can take this. The horrible death of my crew, the constant questions forced upon me by my surroundings, the work needing to be done, the people of Earth counting on me, the loneliness, the heartache, along with the frequent tears and unexpected anxiety that comes with all of them are always ever-present. I'm done thinking about it all—it's too overwhelming.

Pity party over, I'm going to get back to work; there are other people who need saving besides *myself*.

//

Pressure

DocLab 7-Cam:
Angelique and her med team work. Toni and Miguel show Chloe the paperwork, running her through the forms, while Angelique sits

with a large magnifying glass extended from a mechanical arm. Angelique has one of their little mites under the viewing glass with a pair of pincers as she inspects it closely.

"Dr. Puck to the *break* room. Dr. *Puck* to the break room," Harper requests on the overhead. Her eyes look up before she places the microorganism back with its brethren.

"I'll be back," she tells the others.

Break Room-Cam:
The door beeps, and Angelique enters. Captain Harper stands while Stanton sits at the table with his coffee as they're both looking to one side of the room.

"What's going on?" she asks.

Harper points over to the mounted screen. "Thought you might wanna see this, or *should* see it."

Angelique sits across from the pilot as they watch the screen catching the middle of a newer news feed.

The image is in split-screen with an anchor on one side and the head of the Center for Disease Control on the other, their titles printed beneath them.

"Since the RNS Cure's expedition has started, the rate of new patients with Rabid Neural Stasis has doubled, and it's steadily increasing," the man from the CDC states.

"So, given that rate, what's our 'prognosis' so to speak?" the concerned anchor asks.

"I wish I could tell you, honestly. It's not looking good at the moment. Without a cure or treatment, it's not something we can keep at bay. While the *Capacitance* and its crew are searching the skies, we still have doctors on Earth looking for an answer. It's my sincere hope that between different factions working for the same goal, we can find something to help," the man says in all seriousness before adjusting his glasses.

"What can you tell the viewers out there to stay safe in this troubling time?" the anchor asks.

"Stay clear of *anyone* infected with the RNS virus. If someone close to you is infected, leave and seek out an RNS Care Center. Do NOT attempt to address the situation yourself. If you happen to get bitten yourself, get to the nearest Care Center before the change so you don't risk the chance of spreading it," the news guest tells the viewers. "As a society, we all have a responsibility."

"Well, thank you for stopping by, and please continue to keep us informed. Ladies and gentlemen, you heard him. Please keep a distance from the infected, no matter your connection, and report any cases not currently documented." The anchor closes, "And please, stay safe and goodnight."

The image of the man disappears as the screen preps the next feed.

"Huh..." Angelique thinks to herself while the guys look to her.

"No *pressure*, though." Stanton huffs to her in a stifled chuckle.

"Yeah, *no shit*." She shakes her head, still processing.

"Didn't mean to take you away from your work, but I thought it was important," Harper tells Angelique. She nods and looks back and forth between them before standing.

"Well, I guess we better get to work." She sighs. "Gentlemen," Angelique says with a nod which they return before she exits the break room.

//

A New Test

DocLab 7-Cam:
Angelique is in her lab wearing the necessary protective gear, with a table full of things needed for a new test, a new hypothesis. She looks over all of her items: a plethora of space mites and NMC-like

cells in their canisters, jars of various levels of acid she's retrieved from DocLab 6, along with her assorted utensils and her trusty microscope. Without it, Angelique would never really see these tiny beings and what they can do. She displays them for the lab's camera along with narrating her actions for her journal as it seems as though the *Capacitance* is her only colleague.

"While reminiscing about my team and the mental goods they'd brought to the mission and my life, something Chloe and I had toyed with has crept back up into my curious mind. We tested the ingestion and the compatibility of these molecules' insides with blood to no avail. While I was skeptical about pushing the limits of how many *living* beings we could safely put in the human body, I never really thought about *deceased* beings, hadn't really put thought into killing that which has helped me so. Using the single dead microorganism proved to do nothing in the blood it was added to, perhaps maybe more is more in this instance. I get the feeling there may very well be some kind of nutrients or vitamins within these little silver-tapped mites," she says with her hand on the case of microorganisms. "After all, we eat dead animals and dead plants and get at least something from each of them."

She looks over all of her items while running through ideas for different processes. "I know I can't pierce them or split them unless I want to wrangle with the laser-cutter, but if I simply add a drop of acid to eat away their protective coating, I can mix enough of them together for a sample. Of course this is all in theory." Angelique sits down at her microscope, her workhorse. "First one up."

With her pincers, she gathers a chrome mite from the casing to place it on the glass beneath her. With her dropper, she fills it with the necessary amount of acid and drops it on the specimen.

Dr. Puck examines. "In no time at all, the thick sheath melts away, leaving the chrome microorganism with black specks freely floating within it." She adjusts her view. "The black dots fade in minimal time, and its firmness falls flat into a thick metallic goo. There doesn't seem to be anything left of the acid but remnants as I used just enough to melt the protective barrier. Apparently the acid is stronger than Chloe's bile so the little *thing* died sooner. I'm going to try to pick it up."

She tries with the pincers, and despite its thickness, it's far too loose to be retrieved in such a way. "Well, that doesn't work. I'll try another way. Let that be a lesson: always have a contingency."

She puts them down and grabs the unused dropper. "I think this is what we used last time anyway, but with everything going on, I'd forgotten." Using said dropper, she manages to get all but a speck or two of its liquid corpse and empties it into her nearest beaker, looking like liquid metal with no possibility of solidifying upon cooling. "I'm going to keep doing this batch with all positives, which I'll do one at a time so I don't have to struggle with their fighting."

Testing is tedious and monotonous. She repeats this nineteen more times to make an even twenty with the same type of cell. "I'm hoping, with both of their life forces gone, they'll be able to mix without pushing each other away. However, they're not in the dropper long before I place them in the beaker."

When finished, she stretches and blinks several times, rubbing her eyes. Angelique steps over to the fridge, taking out two bags of blood, and returns to her table. "I have two bags of blood here, one of a standard untainted blood type and the other RNS+," She says, pointing to each one as she describes them. She fills two tubes with the new test fluid along with the regular blood and labels them before doing the same with the infected DNA. She puts them in their places on the rack, which holds up to fifteen vials, and lets them sit while she cleans up any of the mess in the protective sheath melting process. Disinfectant and another cleaner are sprayed before she wipes everything down. She takes a breath and moves on to the next idea.

She reaches in one case and removes one of the mites, so small the lab's camera can't see it and she looks like she's collecting nothing, and places it on the glass beneath her lens. She does this again with a separate case. "I have two separate molecules, a positive and a negative, in our magnetic terms for them, and have placed them beneath my lens. With my utensils I force them closer together, and of course, they aren't as stubborn and intolerant as their compatriots were earlier. Being opposites, they're attracted to each other. However, they still need that little *push* before they'll grasp on to fuse."

Angelique returns to her dropper for the acid and retrieves some from the canister. "The two cells are almost close enough to connect exactly like the ones we use to fight Multiple Sclerosis. They don't need to fuse at this moment as they'll be mixed together shortly. I drip the acid on the both of them and their shields melt at the same rate. I wait for their end to be official before mixing both within the same dropper."

To match her first test, she mixes one of each together nineteen more times before putting the mixes of the separate blood and liquid chrome cells into the tubes, labeling them. More stretching, blinking, and eye rubbing. "Having done the test setup with only positives and a mix of the opposites, I'm now going to do the same with the negatives. I'm sure it's not much different from whatever I've gotten from the positives, but I still want to cover all the bases." She goes through the exact same process: mite, acid, collecting with the dropper, mixing, labeling. She places them all in the rack, cleans up, and looks at it all with a sigh before putting the rack in the fridge and leaving the lab.

Security Feed—Corridor:
Angelique enters the empty corridor and heads up to the bridge for an attempt at a distress call. With a large metal strip down the middle on both the floor and the ceiling, the rest of this large tube is lined with florescent lights, and one of those lights are beginning to flicker. Angelique stops to look at it. Could simply be a light, but she doesn't need anything else going out on this ship. She taps the light and gazes around at the others in this section with a curious look about her before moving on.

Break Room-Cam:
Passing through the break room, she grabs a bottle of water from the fridge.

Bridge-Cam:
In the cockpit of her home, she tries to get another SOS out when she notices frost forming along the edges of the window. She touches the ice on the opposite side of the glass and wonders if this is what Christmas looks like in space.

Control Panel-Cam:

She sits down, leaning forward, turning on the communicator.

"*Capacitance* to base, come in. This is the *Capacitance* sending out a distress call. SOS. Come in. This is Dr. Angelique Puck of the *Capacitance*. Is anyone out there?" When her message is done and sent, she reaches for another switch, flipping it before looking into the security camera in the control panel. "I turned the heat up. I don't really need a cold while trying to find cures for illnesses."

Bridge-Cam:

The heat kicks on with an unexpected audible hum. Angelique looks back, staring at the door with piercing eyes. The visible feeling within her swells and throbs like the sound of the heat pumping through the vents.

"I have this horrible, eerie feeling the corpses of my crew will be walking through that door at any moment to hold me responsible for their untimely deaths. The door's clearance tone will beep, and the door will open. They'll come through just as they were when I had the displeasure of putting them in the body bags. They'll demand answers before throwing me out of the ship. I'm waiting."

Nothing happens.

She shakes her head. "I'm losing it. When I open the door, there will be nothing on the other side but the same vacant ship that I'd left behind coming in here." She exhales. "I need a break from thinking. I think I'm going to curl up with Chloe's pictures for a while." Angelique stands and approaches the door with trepidation before exiting.

//

NEWS REPORT - WHAT ARE WE FIGHTING FOR?
Streaming from the logs of the *Capacitance*.

News continues across the screen. A rather aggressive man stands in what seems to be down in a basement of some building, fairly dark besides the swinging shop lights briefly lighting various cleaning equipment and storage. He appears angry, constantly grabbing and straightening the camera, looking directly into it.

"You wanna see what you all are *fighting* for, huh? HUH!? I'll *show* you what you hold so damn *precious*." He turns the camera, showing a man stricken with RNS. Though he's strapped to a chair, he's foaming at the mouth and slinging his head violently, snapping his jaws. His teeth click together loudly, so hard one would imagine his teeth eventually breaking. His saliva slings around as he growls with gargles. His intensity builds as the angry man takes center frame again. "That! You see *that*! You all wanna save the world? Then help *us*, not *them*! Don't *pamper* these things. *Kill* them! This is the only way to save us all, the only real medicine."

The man steps back and pulls a revolver from the waistband of his pants. He points and fires. The rabid man is shot in the head, stopping instantly, as blood hits the wall behind him. The gunman turns to the camera angrily before reaching over and turning it off.

Blackness.

//

Ship Journal
Dr. Angelique Puck: Login: 7575
Subject: **The Dark Side of Science**

I spend my life working. I live for it; I love it. Even when I had found romantic love, I lost it due to the very same work. I search, research, explore, discover, test, and do it all over again until the required results are found. Of course, there's so much more to it once one digs down into it: a lot of lengthy red tape, paperwork, phone calls, emails, corporate suits, meetings, and plenty of patience needed. There are wonderful days in my job, my career, more so than bad days. I get to see a lot of great things and meet awesome people; then again, I also see a lot of ugly things and meet even uglier people.

There's always the dark side to science. The nasty diseases we have to handle, the sight of those infected, and the bad news that often follows, to name a few. Beyond the dangerous finds and the heartbreak they cause, that dark side usually entails the weights trying to hold us back or the leeches latching onto us during our journey. Unfortunately this world of exploratory medical science I live for is full of necessary evils.

When I had first met Nelson, I could sense something about him, something I didn't like. Tall and white with short black hair, Nelson also keeps a clean shave, so you can clearly see his devilish grin at all times. He can usually be seen wearing suits more expensive than equipment we vied for. Besides his incessant condescending tone, it felt like not only did he not belong but that he knew and didn't care.

I could tell he didn't care about science of any kind (or growing knowledge for that matter) and only wanted to control with his money while those in his position before him were all actually in the field and cared very much for what they were funding. We all questioned how he came into his position but never found out the actual origin of this financier: this producer who wanted galactic medical research, or the cures to national problems on his resume. He was open with not caring about the RNS patients as it was "Their problem," but he did like the idea of being their savior. I passed on his initial offer, in search of someone who shared the same views as me. After being turned down by countless companies for the mission with claims of it being *"Too risky"* our team came back around to him, and he loved the thought of his name being above the cure for the growing plague.

He never came down to the labs, as most of his doings were in his paperwork, such as including Saxon in the mix. Of course, most of that was signing off on things: simple signatures and not actually filling out said paperwork. Lou Ann was a surprise to us all and wasn't in the forms, a last minute addition. Neither of which had ever been to space or on a shuttle of any kind nor had they had any experience in medical science, whether it be experimental or not. Despite having my chances, with Saxon and Lou Ann both keeping in touch with him, I never spoke to Nelson during the mission, and I didn't mind one bit.

Stem-Cam:
Blazing fire. Immense pressure. Heavy vibration. Soon, space. The

flames give way to the black openness of the galaxy beyond the Earth's atmosphere. The pressure's subsided.

Control Panel-Cam:
The crew stands on the bridge, having passed through the atmosphere. Now in outer space, some of the crew is excited while Lou Ann is visibly shaken. Harper notices.

Captain Harper asks her, "You okay?"

"Yeah, I'm fine. I just have a problem with heights," Lou Ann says, trying to brush off being scared. She steps away from him with a look of unease, as if he were the help and having the gall to talk to her.

"You'll do fine. It's not something to worry about up here," Harper assures her. It doesn't take long at all for her to pull her tablet out and start taking notes to report back to base. The tablet is about notebook size, the same white as Chloe's picture frame, and Lou Ann's hand is always firmly holding her stylus. She often keeps her blinders on during her work, not paying attention to her surroundings.

"Whatcha writin' there?" Stanton asks her, noticing she's the only one taking notes. He stands casually without the wit or sarcasm he usually has on hand, being nice yet curious with the lanky rocking on his heels he often has when speaking.

She looks at him. "Just...taking notes." Lou Ann steps away from the pilot after looking him up and down as if he were a dirty grease monkey.

"Ah..." he replies before going back to work, sitting in his seat to man the controls. This is Stanton's and Harper's first actual encounter with the reporter beyond educating the crew on the ship.

"For the first part of the mission, she had the same scowl across her face and cold demeanor, turning her nose up at everyone like she was suddenly in a dirty alley with homeless people. Her attitude didn't lighten up or warm up much more throughout." Angelique remembers. *"Of course, Saxon was a real prince, too."*

Angelique's Room-Cam:
Not long into the trip, Angelique is in her quarters. Her door is open, and she's laying out the different one-piece uniforms on her bed. Angry yelling is heard beyond her room. Just out of orbit, and there's already fighting.

"What in the hell are you doing in here!?" Saxon is heard, screaming from the other room to which Angelique's head whips over upon hearing his irate shouting. She drops the suit in her hands and rushes out of her quarters to see what the screaming is all about.

Saxon's Room-Cam:
Angelique arrives through the open door of Saxon's room to find Chloe standing in the soldier's quarters with him berating her. Chloe's scared, and Saxon's heated.

"What's going on in here?" Angelique asks, concerned. Chloe appears as nervous and bothered as Saxon does angry. Angelique steps in farther.

"I...I was walking by, the door was open, and I heard something in here, like a crash or something," Chloe says, shaken. "I just wanted to see if everything was okay." She shrugs while still frightened by this man's sudden manic and hostile nature upon simply finding her here.

"You were meddlin' around, is what you were doin'!" Saxon continues to yell while aggressively pointing at her. "*All* of you stay out of here!" He motions to the crew beyond them.

"C'mon, Chloe, let's go." Angelique motions. Chloe leaves, but Angelique stays as Saxon and she eye each other. He approaches her in his bravado. She stops him. "You don't *scare* me, Saxon, so you can drop the act. Nelson might've sent you, but it's still my mission, and I won't have you terrorizing the members of my crew."

She's not backing down or giving in to his attitude which he presumably uses to get his way.

He smiles and nods. "Tell me, Doctor, with all the women on the same ship for months at a time, are you all on the same...cycle?" he asks as if he jabbed at her pretty good.

She rolls her eyes and leaves.

Break Room-Cam:
With Harper and Stanton on the bridge, the rest of the crew sit around the table like normal. They should expect it but don't when Lou Ann turns her tablet and questions Angelique.

"So, Dr. Puck, I'm curious as to why you've chosen RNS for your current mission. With the amount of heat you've caught in the past as a gay woman curing diseases, is this a way to clear the negative press and show you can fix the big problems the same as the straight doctors? Is it the homosexual connection that you feel an obligation to?" Lou Ann asks and notes, oblivious to how the words sound coming out of her mouth aloud. Angelique's caught off-guard with widened eyes, and her teammates are as stunned as she is.

"I'm sorry?" Angelique asks.

Lou Ann, still clueless, awaits answers.

"Well, I'm not a scientist for homosexual problems of the world. I'm a scientist to help world problems. I'm not doing this to be a hero among the gay community, nor am I trying to prove I can be as good as the next straight person in my field. I'm doing this because of all the unfortunate people infected with this disease daily. If you'd done your research, then you'd know that Rabid Neural Stasis is extremely deadly and is spreading at a terrifying rate. There are people out there bitten every day, and if they're not dying from the blood loss, then they're biting the next person.

"RNS doesn't care what your sexual orientation is, what color you are, what gender you are. It's just here, and it's spreading as much as it can. We're here to stop the world from becoming one big quarantine zone. There are sicknesses in the world that are killing us all, and with the advancements in medical science, it's our job to eradicate them. Average doctors can't and don't have the time to search for such cures. The military fights another country's military.

The police enforce law and order in society. Everyone plays their part in the world and this is ours. This is what *we're* here to do."

Her team agrees with her; however, they are obviously still hung up on the reporter's words.

"If it was some *gay agenda* she's after, why would she choose a worldwide problem such as Multiple Sclerosis to go after first?" Toni spoke up. "She chose a growing illness with no found origin that's affecting the world, not just a community."

Miguel adds, "I think you're trying to make something personal out of this mission. Is that your job, to spark some kind of drama? Did Nelson tell you to get under her skin and try to tear her down while she tries to do what he can't do?"

Everyone's attention is on Lou Ann, and she doesn't like it. "I'm just doing my job and asking questions. It's for my report, an exposé on medical space expeditions."

"Did your boss give you these questions to ask or are you choosing to harass people?" Chloe asks. Before the reporter can retort, she continues, "Let me ask you something, Lou Ann, is there a reason why you're doing this and not working as a tabloid reporter?"

"I'm not harassing anyone. I'm supposed to ask questions, get answers, and report back. Just like you all have a job to do up here, so do I. If you don't like it, you can answer to Nelson and get off my back," Lou Ann snaps back.

"Let's get something straight, we don't answer to Nelson," Angelique says, motioning to her and her team before pointing to Lou Ann and Saxon. "You two answer to Nelson, and if he can keep his dogs on a leash while we continue our work, it would be much appreciated."

Lou Ann looks as though Angelique had slapped her across the face while Saxon sits and snarls.

"I don't have to take this shit." Saxon stands and storms off.

It's not long before Lou Ann leaves as well. "To be continued, I guess."

The crew looks to Angelique. "You okay...?"

"I'm fine." She chuckles and shakes her head.

Angelique's Room-Cam:
Angelique sits at the table across from her bed. In deep thought, she taps her fingers, appearing to be waiting for something.

The door to her quarters buzzes and pulls her eyes to it. She gets up and moves to the door, opening it. Captain Harper instantly enters with a file in hand and shuts the door behind him. It would appear this is who she was waiting for. The two sit at the table.

"Being Captain has its advantages," Harper says, putting the file down in front of her.

"What did we find?" Angelique asks, opening the folder.

"Well, the assumptions aren't far off. She's not a tabloid reporter per se, but certainly has done her fair share of trashy paperwork. Lou Ann's a freelance reporter. She gets jobs when she can but never really got her 'big break.' Years ago, she did a piece on Nelson when he was still a navigation officer," Harper explains, as she reads through the file.

"Well, that explains *that* connection. What do we have on Saxon?" she asks, looking up.

"Nothing. I couldn't find *anything* on him. It's as if he doesn't exist," he answers.

"Makes a lot of sense. I'm sure they like to keep it that way. Good work, Captain," Angelique says before they shake hands.

"I'll go ahead and dispose of this," Harper says.

Security Feed—Nelson's Office:
The phone rings in a series of beeps. Nelson stands in his white,

sterile office, leaning against, almost sitting on his desk while he picks up the phone. Even by himself, his smug look stays plastered on his face.

"Nelson," he answers with the love of hearing his name even from his own mouth.

"Hi, it's Lou Ann. I got your message. You wanted to speak to me?" she asks.

"Yes. I believe I've got something you may be interested in," Nelson tells her.

"Got a job, do you?" Lou Ann asks, audibly perking up.

"Oh, do I. How would you like to go to space?" he asks through his arrogant grin.

"SPACE!?" She freaks out over the phone.

"Come by my office later this week, and we'll discuss the job." He looks over as Saxon, all in black of course, enters his office. "I'm going to let you go for now, I've got an appointment. I'll talk to you later." Nelson hangs the phone up and motions to the seat in front of him. "Saxon, have a seat."

The soldier sits down.

"You wanted to see me, Mr. ...?" he asks.

"Nelson, and yes, I did," Nelson answers, still leaning against his desk.

"How'd you find me?" Saxon asks, with an unpleasant look.

"I have my ways. Now, I understand you were discharged and, well, pretty well blacklisted."

Saxon's anger is evident beneath his placid exterior.

"Apparently you have a penchant for *friendly fire* and a real *nasty* streak," Nelson explains.

"I don't need this shit." Saxon shakes his head and attempts to stand.

"Hold on, now." Nelson holds his hand out to him. He doesn't know why he does, but he sits back in the chair. "I'm offering you a job and those attributes could be handy."

Saxon sighs, thinking. "I'm listening."

"You've no doubt heard about the upcoming intergalactic mission to stop the RNS crisis."

Saxon nods and shrugs.

"Right, well, I need a contingency plan, CYA and all."

"Cover Your Ass," Saxon says.

"Exactly, and that's where *you* come in." Nelson stands and walks around the seated man. "You see, this mission is very costly, and it's got the eyes of the world on all of us involved. If Dr. Puck and her little *science friends* were to go up and come back with nothing, it would be quite the blow, both financially and to my career."

"I don't get it. What am I supposed to do about it? I'm not an astronaut," Saxon says.

Nelson pats Saxon's shoulder in his rounds.

"The attributes I spoke of. That nasty streak of yours. These are talents not appreciated by your former employers." He stops in front of Saxon and kneels down, locking eyes with him. "I want you to go on the mission with them, and if they don't do what they say and don't find the cure, I need you to make sure they don't make it back alive."

They nod together.

"What exactly would you have me do?" he asks Nelson.

"An unfortunate accident would need to occur. I'm sure you could think of something. I'll be putting you onboard, listed as their security," Nelson explains.

"Sounds like I'm your security." Their eyes still locked.

"Precisely. You go on the mission, they think you're there for 'just in case' situations, and you make sure they do what they say they can do. If you were to happen to be the sole survivor of the mission, you chock it up to your military expertise." Nelson stands.

"What's in it for me?" Saxon asks.

"By taking part in such an important expedition, your blacklisting will be lifted and—"

"Money." Nelson's interrupted. "I'll do it, but I wanna get paid."

"Ah…" Nelson nods. "Did you have an amount in mind?"

"Two-point-eight million." Saxon spits it out almost before the question is finished.

"That's quite specific." Nelson's brow furrows.

"A man's got debts," Saxon says, not moving.

"You'll get your money," Nelson says, extending his hand only to lift it when Saxon reaches to shake it. "When the mission is complete."

Saxon snarls his lip.

"I'll supply you with everything you'll need."

"When do I start?" Saxon asks with a grunt.

Nelson walks over to the door, opens it and motions out. "I'll be in touch."

Security Feed—Sleep Hall:

Heading to her room, Angelique walks down the sleep hall when she finds Captain Harper standing outside his quarters, against his door. Saxon's door is open. She gets closer as Saxon's door shuts, and Harper steps away from his door, looking bothered by something.

"What's going on?" she asks.

After a couple of false starts of him trying to explain, he finally says, "Let's talk."

She leads him to her room, opening the door.

Angelique's Room-Cam:
The Captain and Angelique enter her room and sit down at the table.

"Saxon ain't *right*," Harper says with a worried look.

Angelique laughs. "Well, we know that, Captain."

He shakes his head in all seriousness.

"No, he left his door open, I guess by accident, and I had overheard him. He was like a madman; feral, going around his room screaming random stuff about 'First the discharge and now this!' While he was shouting random stuff about his brothers being killed, he was going around his room, punching everything and throwing things around. His cheese has seriously slipped off his cracker. I know it's too late to do anything about it, but we gotta keep an eye on him. Having him up here with us is dangerous."

"I agree, Captain." She nods, looking out into her room. "I'm assuming Nelson just picked the easiest pawns he had access to."

"I wouldn't be surprised if pickin's were slim for Nelson, so he threw some cash at someone recently discharged. It would make a lot of sense," he ponders.

"Or at least promised him the money," she notes. "I'm honestly curious if he did the same mental testing we did or if they bypassed it to get him onboard. I'll keep it in mind, and I'll let the rest of them know to keep their distance."

DocLab 6-Cam:
Toni and Miguel fill out forms at the table in their lab. It's quiet as both of them have their heads down in their paperwork. Pages are finished and placed on the stacks beside them, and they're onto the next sheet. Saxon walks by the window slowly, peeking in, when Toni notices him.

"Hey," she says.

Miguel looks up to her, then follows her line of vision to see the peering eyes of their security. The couple and the soldier lock eyes when Saxon snarls his lip, rolls his eyes, and moves on.

They laugh it off.

"Creepy ass dude," Miguel says, getting back to work.

"That guy is so weird," she adds.

DocLab 7-Cam:
The med team of four discusses something indistinctly while looking over their tiny friends. Lou Ann stands in the window, writing down what she sees. Chloe taps Angelique's arm when they all turn to see her. The reporter moves her head, trying to see what they're working on. With a calf raise, Lou Ann tries to get some height to get a better look. The team ignores her but moves, turning their backs, blocking even more of her view, knowing she doesn't have a clue of what they're doing.

Bridge-Cam:
The crew has reconvened on the bridge on the lookout for the home of the microorganisms.

"With everything as black as it is, and as far away from any known planet, we should be able to see anything coming up," Captain Harper informs them.

"So the lights will be able to catch it?" Miguel asks.

"Yep, and with the camera and the scope back there, we're bound to not miss it," Stanton answers, turning the lights up to their brightest. A sharp beeping emits. The team thinks it's something with the ship, looking around and to the Captain, but even Harper and Stanton look over, not knowing the sound.

Lou Ann reveals a small device she has on her. She takes it out, looking down at it, not paying the crew any attention. It continues to beep as she looks up at Saxon. "Let's go, time to report back."

She leaves, and Saxon groans before following like a puppy.

They all watch in suspicion before redirecting their attention to their conversation as they watch the deep black. Small pieces pass by them, or the *Capacitance* passes *them* rather. None of the fragments are of a nature requiring their attention; random space debris but not the debris they're *after*.

Lou Ann's Room-Cam:
With the screen extended from the wall in Lou Ann's room, Nelson checks in.

"Redirection? Hmm." His brow furrows, and he asks out in the open, "What are you up to, Dr. Puck?"

Lou Ann stands like an assistant awaiting her orders while Saxon stands cross-armed.

"Lou Ann, will you leave us alone for a minute? I need to have a word alone with Saxon."

She exits, and Saxons hands come down to his waist.

Bridge-Cam:
The crew of the *Capacitance* watches from the window as they delve deeper into the great black yonder. Stanton and Captain Harper haven't been out this far, and don't know where they're headed, but go deeper nonetheless. The two men at the ship's helm share a look before pushing forth even more as the ship picks up speed.

//

NEWS REPORT - LAUNCH
Streaming from the logs of the *Capacitance*.

A constant stream of cataloged news plays. Shot from the site of the launch, the camera work's shaky as dust kicks up, thick and blocks most of the view. Rockets flare. "*Capacitance* Launches This Morning" scrolls across the bottom of the screen as the news anchors are heard over the footage.

"While the world is in the grips of Rabid Neural Stasis, a team of scientists are going out of orbit to find the cure for the ugly virus. They've been met with criticism ever since the mission was announced, and the complaints continue while the team hasn't even left Earth yet."

The dust finally separates and the *Capacitance* is revealed, its thrusters boosting taking it up. The camera zooms out, still shaky, and the ship is off, rocketing through the blue sky.

"And you can see it now, the *Capacitance* has started its journey. We wish them the best."

The screen cuts.

//

Destination Discovered

DocLab 7-Cam:
The table has even more microscopes, extras brought from the other labs. With all of the chrome microorganisms separated in different casings, the med team decides to chip off pieces of the stones they have to get a better look at them. With caveman-like utensils in a hammer and chisel, they break down the asteroids. Assorted pieces are grabbed, and they all look at fragments of the debris recovered under the microscopes.

"All right, guys, let me know if you see something I don't," Angelique tells them. "I'm seeing a lot of little metallic fibers coming from the inside."

"Same here," Chloe adds. "Little metal pieces coming from within and through the rock."

"I wonder what the attraction is. Is it simply a magnetic draw or do they feed off it in some way?" Toni asks. "Maybe they eat these little fibers like metallic termites, but they can't eat at the exterior of the ship because of its smooth, polished texture."

"They don't appear to have an opening for feeding but with these things, who knows?" Chloe responds. "These little guys seem more mysterious than our surroundings."

"Maybe they don't take in energy by eating or taking in. Maybe they draw the energy from the metal with the coating," Miguel suggests. "It might not be just for protection after all."

"It's a good point. Perhaps when we've fused them together, they feed off one another, which sustains them, or their coating becomes stronger, allowing them to absorb even more." Angelique thinks. "I wonder, if one was separated for a long period of time, if it would lose energy and die."

She gets up, squinting hard into the bin as she reaches in with her pincers and pulls one of the tiny creatures out, separating it from the others and places it in a small jar by its lonesome before heading back to her microscope.

"How long do you think it would take for one to lose its energy, its life force?" Chloe asks.

"I have no clue. I never really thought about them losing it," she answers. "I know it sounds dumb and irresponsible, but it's something I haven't seen happen yet. I really do think if anything, they feed off of each other—the opposites anyway."

"Well, we know these things live in subzero temperatures so cold doesn't affect them, but what does heat do to them?" Miguel wonders.

"Not sure. You can't really count the laser-cutter as a heat source as I'm sure it was the actual cutting through it that killed it," Dr. Puck responds.

They continue working when they hear Harper over the intercom. "Ladies and gentlemen, this is your Captain speaking. All hands on deck. I repeat, all hands on deck."

The four of them look at each other wide-eyed and exit the lab in a hurry.

Security Feed—Corridor:
The med team rushes through the lit tube. Their boots clank and stick to the floor beneath them however briefly.

Bridge-Cam:
Entering the bridge, Stanton and Harper look back at them with hopeful looks. Past the two, through the window, and in the distance of the otherwise desolate universe is a large speck shimmering from the beaming lights of the *Capacitance*. The team's view zeroes in on the object as they walk in slowly. Lou Ann arrives, ready to get notes for her report. It's not long after when Saxon comes sauntering in. They both step forward, looking at the mass beyond the glass, gleaming in the ship's lights.

"Is...is that what I think it is?" Angelique asks calmly, barely getting it out.

"We believe so," Harper replies, looking back at the team.

Stanton pushes them forward. The *Capacitance* gets closer while the rock gets bigger in view. They all wait and watch, excited with galloping hearts.

In the silent excitement, Angelique feels Chloe's hand reach over and clasp hers tightly. Her hand squeezes back. She was right, something is actually out here, and it's amazing to see. They'd worked with a small stone not much bigger than a couple of footballs, and now they're approaching one of massive size. Angelique moves to the scope, pulling it down and extending the view.

Viewing Scope:
The large mass looks to have the exact same exterior as the stone they were examining in the lab: a mix of rock and metal with assorted colors throughout. Pieces of debris break off and fall away from it. Had they not found it when they did, it more than likely would have completely dissipated down to nothing.

Bridge-Cam:
The closer they get to it, the more they can see the glittery reflection from the ship's lights. The large mass shines and shimmers from the lights, not something they'd see with an average asteroid.

"You guys gotta see this," Angelique tells her team, gesturing at the scope.

"Pretty soon you won't need it, Doctor," Stanton says over his shoulder.

"Ever see anything like this, Captain?" Dr. Puck asks Harper.

"To be honest, I've never been out this far, but I certainly didn't expect to find anything like this. It's completely barren out here with the exception of this." He shakes his head.

"Buddy, I'm not sure if *anybody's* been out this far. We're pushing it," Stanton tells his old friend.

The *Capacitance* stays a steady course with the large meteorite directly in their sights. They're getting closer, and the rock that is their destination appears to grow along with the crew's excitement. They're approaching the solid mass looking to be somewhere between an asteroid and a moon. It's too large to tow or store aboard the ship and too small and jagged to securely land on. Stanton moves the *Capacitance* closer as they all stand on the bridge, watching this odd stone they've found.

Chloe looks up at Angelique. "Well, it's not the size we'd hoped, bigger *or* smaller."

"Yeah." Angelique smiles. "But it's here, and we *found* it."

They both smile.

Saxon looks at the asteroid-like rock with leery, peering eyes and then leaves the bridge while Lou Ann continues to take notes. Miguel and Toni are done looking through the scope and join them all at the window. They feel as though they have found a new world. Its oblong shape is covered with the gray and brown exterior, but as broken as it is, its brassy-like shimmer is apparent. It's clear it used to be much larger in size before it began breaking apart. It's covered in broken, jagged edges, shards spiking out.

"I wonder how big it used to be," Chloe thinks aloud. "And how long it's been falling apart."

"I'm guessing it was close to the size of our moon. I'm curious as to how long it was whole before it started to break," Angelique says.

"Makes you wonder what Earth will look like when it finally starts to give out," Miguel states. "Like *this* is what's at the core of our planet..."

"If *this* is out here, imagine what else is," Angelique says.

Ship Journal Log:

Being in such deep space, after seeing nothing but black for so long, it was comforting to see something else out here for a change. Maybe this is what happens to planets and moons not anchored by the sun. Like Miguel had proposed, I wonder how much this planetary corpse used to look like any of the planets in the Milky Way.

Without the sun, would Earth and its neighbors become what this had: a cold shell with its only life being germ size lifeforms scavenging for sustenance? If the sun happened to strangely and unexpectedly burn out, would the planets in said solar system begin to wither like the flames in the system's power source? And, if such a thing would happen, which planet's devolution would progress furthest first: those closest to the now-powerless sun or those farthest away?

I wondered if the galactic currents I periodically think about had anything to do with the disintegration of this mass, or perhaps there's something else, maybe inside of it. All of these thoughts and then some ran through my mind.

We gazed at what we'd found, stark in its background, a culmination of metal and rock shimmering beneath heavy lights while drifting amidst a thick black void. We set out to find a cure, not undiscovered lands, but it didn't make it any less exciting. The universe is a wondrous place. Despite all of our assorted training put together, nothing had prepared us for what we'd find at our destination.

//

NEWS REPORT - PRESIDENTIAL VISIT
Streaming from the logs of the *Capacitance*.

The screen's image reveals itself with the presidential march playing. A pair of anchors, man and woman, sit behind the nightly news desk while a video of the President of the United States shaking hands in passing is in a square between them.

"Later this week, the President will be visiting the city of St. Louis, Missouri, addressing the rise of Rabid Neural Stasis and the mourning families," the male anchor states.

His female cohort adds, "That's right. As it stands, St. Louis has the highest RNS rate of any city in the country, and the President is heading there to show his support."

The news fades as does the screen showing it.

//

Walkabout

Top-Cam:
Angelique walks atop the exterior of the *Capacitance*.

"I'm on a walkabout. Once, a strange and marvelous feeling, and now, it's so routine and casual that I may as well be walking out on my front porch. When I'm done, I'll check on my blood samples infused with the dearly departed micro beings."

She stops, briefly looking around the ship, the lights coming from it, and the blackness around her.

"At the moment, I couldn't be more thankful for the lights coming from the ship, as dark as it is out here. I *would* reflect on whether or not the darkness of the universe is simply a reflection of the depths of our souls and that in coming out here, we're really just going deeper within, but I have work to do."

She walks to the back of the ship, toward the large magnetic panels she had set up. With big steps and jumps, she makes it to the rear.

Angelique Cam:
She gets to the panels at the end of the ship, and as she suspected, they've frosted over. She sweeps away the excess frost settled on both the panels and the apparatus with her hands and it drifts, faintly, as snow in space. Some won't come off with an easy brushing so she has to punch it in order to break some of it up. Not too hard, Angelique hits it, breaking it up. *Now* it's coming off. She tears as much of it off as she can, and the pieces drift off into the void.

"I'm not sure of the power lifespan on magnets, especially ones like these, so I've brought a small piece of metal out with me, actually the same type Miguel had used to come up with his magnetic metal detector. I want to see if I can give them a charge, so to speak."

Angelique holds the metal firmly while she moves her hand in between the two panels to see if it will kick-start the propulsion in some way. She briefly moves it from one side to the other but not close enough to where either side will pull it from her hand, as they are quite strong. She moves it back to the center, holding it there, and waits. Like a fisherman who feels a tug on his line, in her hands she feels a pull from both sides. She retracts her "lure" and waits some more.

Movement.

Her magnetic propulsion has proved successful yet again. "Whew. I'll probably have to come out here every so often and do this again. Time to go back in."

Control Panel-Cam:
She's inside, out of her spacesuit, and down to her regular uniform, sitting in one of her usual seats.

"Come in. Come in. This is Dr. Angelique Puck of the *Capacitance* sending out a distress call. Come in. SOS." She turns off the communicator and looks into the camera built into the control panel. "Yet another distress call sent out. I'm gonna head back to my lab. At this point, I might as well move my bed in here." Dr. Puck scoffs with an eye roll before vacating the seat and the bridge.

DocLab 7-Cam:
Angelique enters her lab, shutting the door behind her, and gets right to work, stepping up to the table loaded with everything needed, with the exception of the blood samples. She moves to the fridge to remove the rack of vials before placing them on the table with the rest of her goodies.

"Time to check the blood. First up is the uninfected blood. I'm checking the positives, the DNA mixed with what we labeled the positive magnetic mites."

Angelique places droplets of blood on the glass beneath her lens and takes a peek. She looks, adjusting her view before releasing a sigh while shaking her head. "Well, the positives are a no-go. There's no change to this blood at all. Time to test the negatives."

She does so, removing the glass tray and replacing it with a fresh one.

Her hand drops the blood down featuring the negative magnetic mites, and her eye returns to the lens. "No change here as well. Now the combination of the opposites, the positive and negative microorganisms."

Angelique goes through the same routine. She checks it and her head cocks back, surprised.

"While it doesn't appear to have a radical change, nothing along the lines of a vast metamorphosis, the blood appears rich with vitamins, more so than what it was prior to the experiment. It's strengthened, boosted by quite a bit."

She continues to check her other uninfected blood samples, and it all appears to be healthier and charged with extra nutrients.

"I wasn't exactly looking for this, but it is an *amazing* find." Angelique looks up at the security camera, eyes and lens locked into a stare. "Welcome to the world of experimental medical science. You go in search of one thing, and amidst your stumbling in the unknown, you happen upon others that astound and amaze you."

She shrugs and gets back to work: a job even more tiring without a team. Checking all the uninfected blood is met with the same results, while the positives and negatives on their own offer nothing to normal blood, the two combined reveal average human blood to be loaded with an abundance of vitamins and nutrients it normally wouldn't have otherwise. She's excited beyond words but not really for the amazement of the new evolution of healthier human DNA but because if it's done wonders for *this* blood, what may lie in store for the RNS+ samples. Angelique clears out the tray and replaces it and prepares her next inspection.

"Now the moment of truth. I'm checking the samples of infected blood."

Her fingers and feet tap with a nervous excitement. Her heart's beating so hard it's practically stopping her breath. The drops are on the glass. She takes a deep breath and goes in for a view.

Her shoulders slump down, and her head hangs.

"The positives aren't strong enough for the blood with Rabid Neural Stasis. As with the others, I'll check the negatives and then the opposites." Another tray cleaned up, replaced with another tray and more blood. Another look through the microscope, and she groans. The negative magnetic microorganisms apparently aren't strong enough for RNS either.

"All right, next up..." Same routine: tedious, monotonous, taxing. The blood is placed on the glass beneath the lens. Her eyes shut tightly. "God, please...please...*please*..."

Angelique opens her eyes and leans forward to take in the view.

"Like the sample before featuring magnetically opposite nano-creatures, the blood is rich with vitamins and the disease is...*gone?*"

She sits up from the microscope baffled. Her heart pounds in excitement all over again, and her breathing picks back up before taking another look.

"Oh my, I—I—I...*I don't believe it!* THE VIRUS IS GONE!" Angelique screams, clenching her fists and shaking her head as her long hair whips around. She takes another droplet of blood from the vial and checks it to not get ahead of herself. "Not only is it clean but advanced. The DNA that was either dying or susceptible to further diseases is now RNS free and *enhanced*," she says, looking through the lens.

She stands, screaming in excitement. "Woo! Yes!" She looks around, instantly reminded of her being absolutely alone.

"I really wish I had someone here to share this with" She sighs. From one hundred to one, her excitement plummets. She is hit with waves of various emotions at a rapid fire pace as she gazes around her, imagining her crew here with her working alongside her. Angelique can see their smiles and their pride in her along with their excitement of the mission accomplished, and she succumbs to the overwhelming joy of her first love—*science*.

She nods, looking down at the table and the cure for the disease ravaging Earth. Now the thought in mind is simple—she surely doesn't have enough to make this work for the millions of infected people throughout the world. A new test is in order, so she brings out some of the other blood bags infected with the virus. "I mix some of *that* blood with some of the new *cured* blood and now, like *always*, I wait."

Angelique's Room-Cam:
Angelique enters her quarters and picks up her parents photo before sitting on the bed. Holding the picture brings tears to her eyes. She tries to find the words while choking up and outlining her mom and dad with her fingers.

"I know you'd be so proud of me. You *are* proud of me, I can *feel* it," she says, looking up. Of all the people in the world, of all the doctors and scientists trying to cure this disease that happened to take their lives, it was their daughter who found the cure. She cradles their photo, crying.

Control Panel-Cam:
She enters the bridge with confidence, however backed by sadness, and turns on the communicator upon sitting down.

"This is Dr. Angelique Puck, and I have defeated the RNS virus. We can stop Rabid Neural Stasis. It doesn't have to take our family and friends." She pauses. "Though I've done what couldn't have been done before, I'm still left all alone in the cold far reaches of space, and the realization is hitting me that I may never make it home, and worse, the *cure* may never make it home either. I need to make a full report of everything down to the very detail. If I don't make it, I at least want my work to live on." She exhales deeply, shutting her eyes. "Dear God, please let someone find the *Capacitance*. Please let someone find me."

Chloe's Room-Cam:
Angelique does her routine room checks but charged and energetic. She feels the urge to do a more thorough examination. She stops to look through Chloe's photo album again.

"I really wish she was here. I've found myself no longer thinking about Serena but of *Chloe*, her beauty and innocence. I miss you, Chloe," Angelique says, swiping through the pictures.

Saxon's Room-Cam:
Looking through the rooms and their bathrooms, she finds some as blank as before but others catch her eye. Saxon's bathroom, for

instance, has blood splattered in the sink.

"I don't recall seeing any cuts on his face, and I highly doubt this was from a cut while shaving." Angelique looks around the bathroom to find more blood smeared, some on the walls and some on the door. "I think Captain Harper was right when he spoke of Saxon going bananas. With the amount of blood in the room combined with his instability, I wouldn't be surprised if this was from an intentional, self-inflicted wound. Lord only knows what he was doing in here while we worked and slept."

Careful to not touch any of the blood, she exits the room.

Toni's & Miguel's Room-Cam:
Some of the other restrooms, as stated, are as blank as the quarters themselves, but one stands out as particularly devastating, more so than the blood-painted bathroom of their security officer. Every time there's a positive to a day, there's always a negative, and Angelique finds this to be true all too often. In Toni's and Miguel's bathroom waste basket, sitting atop miscellaneous trash, she finds a pregnancy test, and it's *positive*. She is sucker punched by the sight.

"Well, Miguel got his wish, and Toni was indeed pregnant, making their untimely demise all the more depressing." She sighs. "I wonder if he or she would've been the first child conceived in space. Toni and Miguel were good people and would've made great parents."

Stanton's Room-Cam:
Angelique enters with Chloe's photo-tablet in hand and goes right for the calendar.

"Everyone's drawers are full of the same issued clothing we were all given. Along with Chloe's photo-tablet, I'm grabbing Stanton's calendar of girls and ships. *Why not?* Since I have so many books downloaded, I figured I might as well get to reading at some point. Lord knows how long I'll be up here."

With her items of pleasure, she's ready to take a much needed break.

Top-Cam:

Another walkabout. She's back outside but not for scientific purposes. Angelique sits at the front of the ship where Chloe and she sat. Now she lies on her back, her boots securely planted to the vessel's exterior. She can feel the *Capacitance* moving beneath her and lets her arms float freely in antigravity. White suited, lying down on gray metal, floating in the dense black—a monochrome spectrum devoid of any lively color seen back home in the solar system.

Angelique-Cam:
Black, darkness and stars.

"Looking up into the black, I can't help but wonder if Toni's last thought was about her future child. Given this newfound information, it takes the wind out of my sails of finding the cure. Well, guys, if you're up there listening, we did it. After years of chasing the end on Earth, we finally found it in a place once only God could reach. The stars I see now, I don't imagine crawling toward me with their spider-like limbs or chomping jaws but as the stars I grew up watching. Far above me they twinkle, bringing a smile to my face. Yeah...we *did it*."

//

NEWS REPORT - RNS CARE
Streaming from the logs of the *Capacitance*.

The screen lights up with a news anchor behind his desk. "We've just gotten word that tragedy has hit an RNS Care Center in Arizona. Please be advised, this footage is graphic."

The news station cuts to the scene of the tragedy spoken of. The clip is brief but graphic. Like all RNS Care Centers, all patients are spread out in a grid pattern and, like all RNS Care Centers, nurses try to keep their distance.

This particular nurse did not, and the footage reveals her in the middle of the grid, caught between two RNS patients. Both of her arms are being viciously chewed on by a man and a woman on either side bound to chairs as her blood spills from both arms. They chew as she screams and tries to flail away from them, and they bite harder, not letting her go. Security rushes in, shooting the rabid biters with tranquilizer darts and pulling the woman out of there.

The footage cuts back to the anchorman, who shivers. "It's a hard watch. Ladies and gentleman, RNS is nothing to mess around with. Please be careful if anyone close to you is bitten."

News feed over.

//

Ship Journal
Dr. Angelique Puck: Login: 7575
Subject: **The Horror of the Stars**

We were getting close to our destination, this odd rock formation floating out in the middle of the star-studded desert: an oasis of sorts that we hoped wasn't a mirage. Pieces broke off of it at random as it hovered, seemingly stationary, almost as if it was waiting for us. While it was quite large, it wasn't at all flat enough to land on securely. Its edges were as mountainous as the rest of its shape: jagged and broken. We were all excited and couldn't wait to check it out.

Bridge-Cam:
The med team stands with the Captain, looking at the near-distant floating mountain while Stanton pulls them closer as their destination gets larger. It shimmers in the ship's lights like a version of the mite-covered stones they've inspected, larger than some starships.

"All right, gang, we're just about there," Stanton informs them, looking over his shoulder.

"Well guys, if we're gonna suit up, I'd say we better get to it," Harper says, walking in their direction. They turn to follow as he stops Angelique. "Doctor, I don't mean to tell you what to do. However, since we don't know what's out there, I suggest we let the dog out of his cage on this one."

She knows exactly what he means.

Security Feed; Lab Hall:
Harper and the rest of the med team are getting suited up to board the rocky mass as Angelique passes them, heading toward the sleep hall. They look at her questionably.
She nods to them.

"I'll be back," she says with her hand out and heads to the end of the hall, opening the door at the end.

Security Feed—Sleep Hall:
She approaches Saxon's door and presses the buzzer to its side as she awaits an answer. It isn't long before the large door slides open, and Saxon stands before her, smiling his disgusting grin. He stands in the doorway, leaning against the side with his arms crossed, eyeing her up and down.

"I knew you'd come around eventually." He chuckles.

She sighs and rolls her eyes.

"Not on your life. Grab your gear and suit up," Angelique tells him, with a jerking nod as he smiles legitimately for the first time on the mission. He turns back into his room, looking at his assortment. It seems the mere thought of the chance at getting to use his weaponry excites him.

She exits to go back to join the others.

Saxon's Room-Cam:
Angelique's gone, and Saxon hurries to the door, peeking out of the room.

"I'll be there in a minute!" He shuts the door and comes back in the room in search of something.

Saxon moves one bag to the side, not finding it before digging around in another one of his duffle bags. After a brief moment of searching, he finds a small camera, black and wire-like in appearance. He holds it up, looking at it in inspection, bending back and forth, figuring out how to wear and conceal it.

Security Feed—Lab Hall:

The crew is about embark on a journey to a new world and most of them are now dressed for the occasion. While suiting up, Chloe and Angelique share seductive looks at one another; their eyes gaze over each other's bodies while helping each other get into their suits.

The way Chloe smiles and licks her lips while fluttering her eyebrows will forever be burned into Angelique's mind. No one notices, but these two wouldn't care even if they did. The peepshow is over when they zip up. Angelique's helmet goes on first. Chloe grabs the sides of Angelique's head and kisses the glass dome, leaving beautiful lip prints of red lipstick about where the Angelique's mouth is.

They all head up and out.

Stem-Cam:

The *Capacitance* edges closer to the rock, slowly, to not pass it or run into it. From far away, it's only an asteroid, but under the ship's lights, something strange. Edges of metallic fibers are seen like on the smaller pieces collected. The mites they've been working with are seen clearly, racing all over its exterior.

Top-Cam:

Seeing this large mass from outside the ship without the framed glass divide is amazing, like a massive golden nugget teeming with alien life. The *Capacitance's* bright lights shine on it as they get closer, illuminating it more. Stanton and Lou Ann stay onboard while the rest of them are set to board the rock. With the light hitting its surface, Angelique notices the shimmering all over it, the same shimmer on the original, smaller rock they'd recovered. At first she thinks it's the metallic insides exposed from it breaking away over time, but then the glittery reflections move and scurry about.

Saxon emerges from the ship and joins the rest of the crew.

"Captain, do you think our boots will hold on that?" Angelique asks him.

"If it's metallic, they'll hold," he answers.

The crew is nervous and anxious as the ship beneath them moves closer to the large cluster.

"You doing okay, babe?" Miguel asks his wife.

She takes a deep breath. "I'm good. You?"

"Good." He nods. "This'll be a hell of a story when we get back."

They laugh.

"All right, guys, I think I got you to a drop point," Stanton informs them, hovering right over the flattest part of their destination found. Any farther and the team would surely rip their suits on the small spiked mountains beyond the area.

Captain Harper-Cam:
He views the rest of his crew as he explains the game plan. Everyone's gathered together awaiting orders.

"Okay, listen up, we're going to try to drop down. To do so you'll have to push or swim your way down," Harper tells the crew. "Try not to go past the drop point."

"I'll go first," Saxon says, stepping up, passing the others.

The group moves closer to the edge. He bends down, pressing the magnetic release on his boots. Harper and the others watch their security make the jump. To their surprise, he doesn't have to try to make his way down as partway the magnetic force from the metal and stone mass pulls him down. One would think the universe gave them gravity if only for a moment.

Saxon-Cam:
As soon as his boots lock down on the mass, his flash rifle is poised, and he inspects the area. Had Nelson not supplied him with updated equipment, Saxon would surely still be using bullets, but his latest weaponry shoots concentrated and compressed light. He looks around with his hands holding his gun out in front of him.

It's exactly as they suspected, identical to the rock in the lab only on a massive scale. Brown and gray stone covering a brassy and platinum mix of metal. What the normal camera on his suit's helmet catches so does the secret camera supplied by Nelson personally. Where he looks, his gun looks. The soldier's surroundings appear benign, so he looks up and signals for the rest of them. Harper gives him a thumb up and turns back to the team.

Captain Harper-Cam:
Harper turns around and waves on the crew to come closer.

"Okay, he's secure," the Captain tells them. "Who's going next?"

Toni and Miguel step up, look at each other and leap hand in hand. "Here we go!"

The magnetic pull anchors them down to the asteroid as Captain Harper watches to make sure they make it okay. The forceful gravitational like pull is something he's never seen in space. They're fine, secure. They look at each other and then the rock.

Harper waves on the next person to go. Chloe makes the jump next with her arms tucked in closely, letting out a scared whimper on the way down as if going down the largest slide at the pool. She's locked on as well, looking up and waving. Only him and Angelique.

Angelique's about to go when she looks to Harper. "This a new one for you?"

"I think this is would be a new one for *anyone*," he replies with a shrug and chuckle.

She jumps down.

Harper looks at the mass, and the space around it. "This...is ridiculous," he admits to himself before following right behind her. The pull is more forceful than either Angelique or Harper had anticipated, and they're down fast. The magnetic lock is stronger on this mystery island than it is on the ship's body.

Angelique-Cam:

Their boots lock onto the surface. They're still tethered to the ship with their safety cables. Angelique looks at her crew as they all get acclimated to the new environment before checking out the mass itself. The brown and gray rock exterior has apparently broken away over time for the most part as its metal underside is more than apparent. The little fibers Angelique was looking at beneath her lens not long ago are now all around her in great quantity, only these fibers are bigger, sharper.

Angelique gets a closer look at them: jagged rock and torn metal looking sharper than broken glass, an asteroid with serrated edges.

"Everybody watch out for these edges. They tear your suit, and you're done," she says, looking them over. She backs up, seeing it all and then the crew. It's fantastical. She and her team look around and at each other, excited. They brought their retrieval bags along to collect more of their little friends, which they instantly see scaling the walls of this decrepit would-be moon.

Captain Harper-Cam:
The Captain of the *Capacitance* inspects the mass they're currently held down to as well. It looks like they've discovered one enormous mineral, tattered by meteorites over time.

"I don't know what it is, but it's *strong*," he says, kneeling down, knocking on the ground beneath him. "Steps are harder to take on this thing than on the ship."

They're learning how strong the metal is in this mass and, thus, how strong the magnetic force is.

Saxon-Cam:
Their security officer isn't interested in this strange new finding. His gun is drawn, keeping his eyes out for anything sinister. His gun points where his view does, looking the mass over and aiming his weapon with each direction.

Angelique-Cam:
She doesn't start collecting yet and neither does her team as they all spend the time taking in their surroundings. Angelique looks at Chloe, Toni, and Miguel, who are sharing the same awe she has.

The rock they stand on is a golden, brassy hue for the most part, and though it is illuminated by the ship's light, they all still have their lights on them.

The med team, the Captain, and the soldier investigate their destination, splitting up for the most part in their small available area. It looks too jagged to attempt to climb and not get their air supplies torn. The surface's crust crunches beneath Angelique's boots with every step. Whatever rock there is, it is smashed between the metal and her boots. She can feel it, though it's not audible. The magnetic microorganisms are all around them, crawling all over this thing.

"Well, let's go ahead and start grabbing all we can," Angelique tells her team, looking them all over. While Harper continues to look around and Saxon has his gun drawn, awaiting anything to jump off, she and the scientists scoop up their little medical miracles and bag up all they can, and there's a lot. Pieces of debris are still breaking off and floating about. Nothing at too high of a velocity so they're able to dodge some and brush off the rest with ease. However, they still make sure none of it hits their helmets.

Captain Harper-Cam:
Harper's gloved hands check out one of the walls in front of him. He brushes off excess crust before pressing and holding his hand against the surface. The wall shimmers with movement. But there's something else.

"Doctor, you may wanna take a look at this," Harper says. He looks over as she makes her way over, stepping the best she can. Together, they look at this wall covered in the little space mites. "Do you see it?"

She looks closer. It seems as if something underneath the potential cells is *pulsating*. Angelique brushes her hand against it, attempting to clear off whatever they're crawling on. Whatever it is, it's large, much larger than what they've been looking at beneath a lens. Harper and Angelique look deeper. The object of their attention moves as the mites leave it and small pieces of debris break away.

Angelique steps back wide-eyed but can't find the words to say at the moment. Harper steps back. They both look at each other while everyone else continues to work in Angelique's background.

Angelique-Cam:
Angelique keeps backing up, with the Captain at her side, while keeping her view on the moving wall of the rocky mass. The pulsating continues, mites scurry, and bigger pieces of this thing's encasing break away.

All she can get out is, "Uh...guys..."

The thing beneath separates itself from the stone slowly as rock particles break away, floating past. She looks to Harper, whose vision is glued to it as well, before her view returns to whatever is moving beneath the crust. It looks to have five limbs and appears star-shaped. It continues to pulsate and moves as if it has just awakened. This shell covering it, this planetoid object, seems to have grown around it over lengthy periods of time and looks to be comprised of metal and stone.

Angelique looks around at her colleagues, who've now joined her and the Captain, before whipping back to the new discovery. Its husk is breaking away, and they're seeing it for what it is. It's large; its body is metallic, the same sleek chrome exterior the space mite-cells have. In between bits of shiny chrome are what look like ink-black muscle strands and in the dead center of its body, is a yellow light starting dim and blinking but soon becomes a bright light—the power of a spotlight from a circle the size of an average ashtray.

The crew steps back, not knowing what the being will do. It removes itself from the star-like imprint it has left as the debris breaks off and drifts. The thing steps out, seemingly as its first time walking in probably centuries. Its limbs, sharp and dagger-like at the ends, bend at the center as the creature sticks them into the mass, crawling up the wall. They all watch this thing, about half the size of an adult human but wider, moves about, not really paying attention to anything. Like the humans on its terrain, the creature simply explores, and much like them with their lights, its own light shines as it spider-walks its way along, inspecting.

Security Feed—Nelson's Office:

Nelson enters his office and sits at his desk, which is beeping accompanied by a blinking light on the desktop's smooth surface. He presses the flashing button and a screen emerges from the center. A red box stating "Incoming Feed" blinks along with the incessant beeping. He presses it and sees what Saxon is seeing, the discovered creature crawling around this metallic asteroid. His eyes widen, and he sits up straight.

"Oh shit."

A secretary enters, putting forms on his desk, not seeing the screen.

"Here are the files you requested," she says. "Also, your seafood club will be ready by lunchtime." Another day at the office for her but not so much for Nelson.

"That—that's fine. Just give me some time alone," he says, shooing her out. "And hold all my calls."

He can't look away from this alien being or its surroundings.

Angelique-Cam:
Angelique doesn't move. The only one of her crew in her view is Harper to her left.
The spotlight-like eye scans the ground, coated with the magnetic mites as they gleam brightly while scurrying about. Still separated, the crew tries not to make any sudden movements but slyly look over at each other. Chloe, Toni, and Miguel stare wide-eyed while Saxon waits.

"Stanton, I sure hope you're getting this," Angelique says quietly.

The creature whips its view over and catches her directly in its light. Startled and scared at first, she's shocked it isn't at all blinding, not nearly as forceful as its brightness would indicate. Its legs bend as though it's about to pounce. She backs up, holding her hands up, trying to emote that she's indeed no threat to it but keeps quiet. It pulls back as if it won't jump after all, but then comes Saxon.

"Everybody get back!" Saxon yells, stepping up to the alien, aiming his cannon.

Security Feed—Nelson's Office:
Nelson sits in his seat, alone in his office, as he watches the computer monitor extended from within the desk. His eyes are glued, intrigued, as the screen reveals what Saxon is currently seeing: a large, metallic, star-shaped creature and his cannon pointed directly at it. The yellow light shines outward.

"My Lord," Nelson says to himself through stilted breathing, seeing a more clear view of the monster of the stars.

Chloe-Cam:
Chloe's in the back of the group, seeing everyone completely. She and the rest of crew back away as the metallic creature seems startled by the man and his gun addressing it. While the Captain and the med team pulls back, the soldier steps forward with his weapon aimed, not backing down.

"Saxon, don't!" Angelique shouts, but it's too late.

He's already started firing. His gun kicks with bright energy blasts, noiseless. Most of the shots reflect off of its metal exterior. The team shouts, jumping back. The creature leaps for Saxon as he continues to fire, hitting it dead center in its bright yellow eye. The star beast's light shatters as it collapses to the stony surface with its body becoming nearly gelatinous.

Seconds later, a second being, appearing of the same make, comes from the same wall beside the imprint this one has left. This creature rises quicker, defensive as if disturbed, bursting from the crust. The pieces come off at a higher velocity and float out. They all back away but stay frozen for the most part.

Toni holds out her hand, and Miguel takes it in his.

Captain Harper-Cam:
The Captain's view stays primarily on the terrifying sight of the alien from within this meteor while his hand reaches out, patting Angelique's arm.

"Doctor, I think we should go now," Harper says.

The second creature shines its yellow spotlight eye around as the crew freezes. The light lands on Saxon.

Saxon-Cam:
With the creature in his sights, his weapon is at the bottom of his view before it pulls up. The soldier shoots at it like he did the previous alien, but he isn't fast enough.

Security Feed—Nelson's Office:
The creature leaps directly at Saxon, swallowing his view as he screams before choking and dying. Nelson attempts to vocalize but nothing comes out. He sits up in his chair and looks around. The screams of the crew are heard on Saxon's camera through his headset. Nelson exits out of the video, goes into the incoming files, and deletes it.

The progress bar edges across the screen: *File Permanently Deleted.* Pressing the switch on the desktop, the monitor descends down into the desk. Nelson taps his fingers on the desk, shifty-eyed and in thought before he stands and exits as if he saw nothing at all.

Chloe-Cam:
The thing stands on a frozen Saxon with all five of its razor-like limbs plunged into him and *through* him. Chloe screams as the others panic.

"C'mon!" Angelique says, as she kneels down to press the magnetic release on her boots. The others do the same and all attempt to jump from the rock only to be *sucked* back down to the surface.

"It's too strong for the release!" Toni yells.

Toni-Cam:
Miguel gets in front of his wife, pulling her behind him, shielding her.

"Miguel..." she says worried.

"Baby, just stay back," he says with his hand out. She backs up beside Chloe.

Captain Harper-Cam:
With his boots locked on to the surface beneath him, Saxon stays still, dead, while this monster digs its ends deeper into him.

"Guys, we gotta get outta here!" Harper looks at his crew, too stunned by what they're seeing to make conscious moves. "Stanton, pull us up! PULL US UP!" Harper yells.

The creature, whose home they'd unknowingly invaded, turns its sights past Miguel. He looks behind him to see it set on Toni distinctly. Toni backs up, terrified. It pulls its bloody, sharp points out of Saxon who, with the help of antigravity, stands up straight while still magnetically locked down, completely dead.

The bladed limbs of the monstrous being are bloodied, but the trigger happy man's blood freezes soon after as the drops come out of his body, passing the crew alongside assorted debris from the island's body. The creature crawls down Saxon's standing corpse and moves toward Toni and Miguel. With its light still focused, it walks with scurrying insect-like steps, and the microorganisms continue to scatter at its feet.

Toni screams and backs up, shaking her head repeating, "No! No!"

Miguel pushes her back farther before looking over to Saxon. Though it's a gamble leaving his wife's side at this time, Miguel immediately moves for the soldier's gun, still hanging from him. He grips the gun and turns to shoot. The first shots get its attention, and it turns toward Miguel as he continues to fire at it repeatedly.

Captain shouts, "Stanton, get us *out of here!*"

"I'm trying! I'm trying!" the pilot replies.

Chloe and Angelique move as swiftly as they can to pull Toni out of dodge while *it* focuses on Miguel.

Toni keeps screaming, "Miguel! Miguel! No!"

He keeps firing at it as it gets closer to him. Shots hitting its metal exterior ricochet as they did with Saxon and the beast before it. A few shots hit its visible black muscle, slowing it down a bit but not for long.

"Stanton, any time now!" Harper continues before reaching over and breaking off a piece of the miniature planet, taking the debris and throwing it at the creature, only to have it float to it with little speed. Harper grunts with frustration before he moves to Miguel the best he can to get out of the way, but the scientist isn't budging.

"Get back!" Miguel tells the Captain with a shove. He's determined, firing the weapon as if it's second nature. It's made it to Miguel as he fires into its yellow eye, apparently its life source.

"Miguel, get out of the way!" Harper yells to the man still shooting.

The monster from within the asteroid dies and shuts down. As it collapses, its top limb comes down, and its spiked end drives right into the glass of Miguel's helmet, breaking it.
Miguel succumbs to the cold vacuum of space.

Toni-Cam:
Toni trembles with stuttering breaths. The oxygen is sucked out of Miguel's suit and *him* instantly as every one of his crew members hears the hissing of the vacating air, briefly, from his headset.

Angelique-Cam:
Toni lunges forward as Angelique and Chloe hold her while the three see their husband, longtime friend, and colleague, respectively, die before their eyes.

"NO!" Toni cries out as Chloe and Angelique continue to hold her back. Like Saxon, Miguel stands lifeless with his body swaying in antigravity while his feet stay planted to this mass. The body of the large creature causing such a death slides off the man, as dead as its brethren before it. Miguel's face in the glass dome is cold and devoid of life.

Seeing as the star-shaped, metallic monster is dead, the women let her go, and Toni rushes to her husband with the magnetic force slowing her steps. She holds him tightly, crying and sobbing indistinctly. Angelique watches, unable to help her friend, all too heartbreaking and surreal. The planetoid beneath them rumbles. Angelique grabs Chloe's hand and looks over at her before they both look down. The ground quakes and breaks apart.

Captain Harper-Cam:
Harper tries to move closer to the rest of the group and waves for them to come in.

"Everybody get together!" Harper orders.

The girls move over to get Toni, who has an understandably strong grip on Miguel. The surface cracks open, and what pours out cannot be unseen. Dozens of miniature star-shaped creatures scurry with ease despite their atmosphere. Smaller versions of the two monstrous things that have killed two of the crew members: chrome in appearance, with the same sharp ends, except the bright yellow eye is not there. They are smaller than the last two but bigger than the microscopic mites. They scurry like a swarming infestation of angry spiders.

Angelique stomps at them and kicks them away. There are more and more of them coming from within the team's destination. Harper charges through, kicking more away.
Toni's frozen in her state of grief with her late husband and pays no attention to the critters running around with speedy ease.

Angelique-Cam:
One crawls up Chloe's back, and Angelique snatches it from her and sees what they hadn't seen prior—its underside, complete with a mouth with razor-sharp teeth, snapping as fast as their legs carry them. It's chomping and chomping at Angelique as she holds its little limb and throws it off to the side. She watches to make sure it's actually away while Harper continues kicking at others.

"Angelique! Look out!" Chloe yells.

Angelique turns to see one fast approaching.

Chloe jumps in front of her and attempts to kick it away with the strongest swing of her leg the surroundings will allow. As her leg makes contact, it jumps and bites her.

"Chloe!" Angelique screams.

Chloe cries in pain, grabbing at her leg with the creature still attached. Harper comes over to remove the five-legged spider-like thing from her when Angelique stops him. "No! Don't! With it on her, it has her air sealed. If you remove it, she'll die like Miguel!"

Flustered, Harper nods.

"Finally!" Stanton's voice echoes, and the crew is pulled up by their cables in a rush, breaking away from the surface. They look to make sure the only one of those things with them is the one technically still keeping Chloe alive.

"You're okay," Angelique tells her, holding her on the way up.

Top-Cam:
The crew makes it on top of the *Capacitance*. Angelique helps Chloe while Toni carries her husband and Harper carries Saxon. They make it to the hatch and pile in.

"Okay, Stanton, we're in," Harper informs the pilot.

Stem-Cam:
The *Capacitance* thrusts forward at high speed, jetting well beyond the asteroid. The stars at the side and in the distance become a snowy visage as the ship flies through space at a high velocity.

Stern-Cam:
The rockets flare and thrusters boost as the island of metal and rock gets smaller in the distance until it's no longer visible, leaving its monstrous inhabitants behind with it.

Top-Cam:
Stanton knocks the speed back down.

DocLab 7-Cam:
Angelique brings Chloe into the lab. The young woman limps as Angelique cleans off the table. The little beast on her leg strongly

vibrates with a rumbling noise.

"Okay. Don't worry." She helps Chloe, wincing in pain, up on the table.

Cargo Bay-Cam:
Captain Harper drags Saxon's lifeless body into the cargo bay and leaves him. He hangs his head with a large exhale, rubbing his eyes, before he leaves to get to the bridge. The former soldier lies still in his death with wounds—massive holes—throughout.

Security Feed—Lab Hall:
While the others have left to tend to the bodies they'd brought in, Toni's still where they entered, now widowed, holding her husband. She sits on the floor, holding him up. She rocks back and forth with him in her arms, crying uncontrollably.

DocLab 7-Cam:
The thing on Chloe's leg pulsates, and no matter how hard Angelique tries, isn't letting go of its grip. Tears stream down Chloe's face. Every time Angelique touches the intergalactic critter, it hurts Chloe more. Angelique stops and moves across the lab to get to the laser-cutter and removes it from the microscope. She brings it back over.

"Hold still," Angelique says as she turns the laser on.

She runs the blue beam over its chrome body, and it vibrates violently before finally falling off her, hitting the floor. Dead. Chloe hugs her hard before Angelique gets her out of her space suit to tend to her wound. She rolls up the pant leg of Chloe's uniform to see the rather nasty bite. She does the best she can, giving her a shot for infection, applying ointment to the wound, and dressing it followed by giving her something to help her relax.

Chloe's Room-Cam:
Angelique enters, carrying Chloe along. She's out of it as Angelique lays her down in her bed and covers her up. She watches Chloe briefly. She's asleep. Angelique sighs and exits.

Bridge-Cam:

Angelique, down to her uniform, arrives at the bridge to find Harper and Stanton having a heated discussion while Lou Ann stays quiet, taking notes off to the side. Harper is finishing getting out of his space suit.

"What the hell was that!?" Harper asks the pilot, kicking off the rest of his suit.

"I knew Taggart had messed with my settings! Everything was ass-backwards up here!" Stanton replies.

The men are standing, facing one another.

"Why the hell didn't you just *take off* then!?" Harper continues.

"It wouldn't have mattered! The amount of cable stored, it would've kept feeding and you all would've been killed before I'd gotten you outta there!" Stanton says.

Harper lets out an aggravated yell with clenched fists while Stanton, taking off his hat to rub his head, paces before the two men calm down. Harper rubs the back of his neck, trying to think.

"Well, we're out of dodge *now*," Harper says.

Angelique speaks up. "Yeah, but we have two crew members *dead* and one injured."

"Look, I'm—I'm sorry, I really am," Stanton tells her. "Is she going to be okay?"

"I did the best I could and gave her something to relax. I think she'll be fine eventually, but we need to abort the mission and get home as soon as possible," Angelique says.

"Well, I'll try to get us back on course, but as far out as we are, it might take us awhile," Stanton says.

The tension and unease is thick in the room.

"All right." Angelique exhales and hangs her head.

"I went ahead and stored Saxon in the cargo bay. I'll have to take Miguel down soon, but I wanted to give Toni a moment. I actually have body bags for these types of situations, but I was hoping I'd never have to use them," Harper says, shaking his head.

"Angelique..."

That soft angelic voice.

They all turn to find Chloe entering past the door at a snail's pace.

"Angelique, I don't feel so good." Her eyes look completely silver; they can't see her irises or pupils, any of it, only shiny chrome.

The others watch, baffled.

Lou Ann's almost too shocked to write anything.

Harper and Stanton share a wide-eyed look.

Angelique gasps.

"Uh, Chloe, why don't you come lay down," she suggests, moving closer to her. Chloe grabs her stomach in pain. Before Angelique can make it to her, Chloe bends over, groaning. Angelique puts her hand on Chloe's back. Her stomach pulls and jumps as she releases several stifled coughs. Angelique pats and rubs her.

Chloe vomits but not the average waste and stomach bile. Flowing freely from her throat are hundreds of chrome-tinted star-creatures, a bit smaller than the one that had bitten her. Her neck, her eyes, and her face, every bit of her, strains at the painful vomiting.

Angelique holds her, feeling the stress as the flow of insect-comprised vomit continues. The others watch in horror and disgust. A thick silver waterfall forcefully exits Chloe's throat and mouth into a wet, metallic pile. Strained veins bulge all over Chloe's pale neck and face. After the aliens vacate her body, she continues to vomit straight water. As she coughs heavily, another interstellar bug falls to the floor with the rest of them.

Completely drained and lifeless, Chloe drops to the floor, gone. Angelique collapses with her, holding her. The little monsters appear lifeless upon hitting the floor as well, but they grow larger, and their flat five pointy legs bend up at a jagged angle. The lifeforms scatter and everyone reacts, jumping back.

A beeping tone. The door to the bridge opens as Toni, down to her uniform, enters in a tear-soaked frustrated frenzy and before the others can warn her, she speaks, "Angelique, I'm *done*! I—AHHHH!"

She's swarmed in chrome creatures. She tries smacking and brushing them off. Angelique can't help her as they're too fast and too large in numbers. Stanton attempts to move over to help when Harper grabs his arm. The pilot looks back at him as the Captain shakes his head with a stern look.

The star-creatures devour Toni, stabbing, biting, cutting, anything they can do whilst crawling all over her. The horde of nano-beasts leave Toni, revealing nothing left but a wet skeleton that falls to the bloody floor beneath it.

Angelique rushes to the door, shutting it. "We can't let them get to the rest of the ship! Try to keep them contained!"

Stanton, Harper, and Angelique try their best fending the things off. Stanton looks over to Lou Ann, clutching her tablet, and pries it from her grasp, only to turn around and smack a few of the star beasts, bludgeoning them. Lou Ann looks more devastated by the loss of her device than the situation of these alien creatures destroying the ship and trying to kill them all.

"Doctor, this isn't going to work! We have nothing up here!" Stanton yells, throwing what useless bit of the tablet is left to the side, while Harper continues to stomp on them the best he can. The amount of the alien insects is growing at an alarming rate.

"I'll be right back! Try to keep them together and don't let them bite you!" Angelique knows what she has to do. She leaves the bridge, shutting the door directly behind her.

Security Feed—Lab Hall:
Angelique runs, heading to the lab when she sees Miguel's body lying where he was left. She winces, pulling her view away and throwing her hand up to block the sight, too painful to see.

DocLab 7-Cam:
Angelique enters the lab in a hurry to grab the laser-cutter. While there, she grabs the hammer and the spike still on the counter. With the items in hand, she exits.

Bridge-Cam:
Angelique returns to the shock of the growth of the creatures, not only in their numbers but in their size. The bridge is thick with alien life, so much so it's hard for her to see her other crew members. Many of the creatures make a move for her upon her entering. She turns on the laser-cutter, turning it out, hitting as many of them as she can. She moves the laser back and forth in a waving motion, but because the blue hair-sized beam isn't concentrated on one spot for very long, it moves more of them back than kills them.

Stanton and Harper continue stomping and kicking at the creatures. Lou Ann's replaced her broken tablet with a small notebook and pen she's kept on her. She stays back, not joining in the fray.

Stanton looks at Lou Ann. "Do something, girl!" He takes off his hat, using it to swat them away.

She stays back, scared, shaking her head, using her work as a barrier between her and the harsh reality she faces.

"Stanton! Harper!" Angelique throws them the hammer and spike. Stanton swings big, knocking around as many as he can with the hammer. Harper pokes and stabs at any one of them coming near him. Lou Ann stays back with her notebook, trying to get everything she can while *not* trying to help.

Angelique moves around to the guys with the laser.

"Try to get them all together! If we get them all in one spot the laser will have more time to burn through them!" she yells.

They do so and move them back, cornering them, but then they do something a bit familiar to Angelique. While being pressured together, they graft with one another before the crew's eyes, producing a much larger creature. It resembles a metallic starfish, chrome-plated with the stark black muscle shown in between. It doesn't crawl like a spider but walks like a hulking behemoth.

Angelique's heart sinks as her jaw drops. Then it happens. A small opening becomes a big opening and a bright yellow light shines from it, reflecting off of the metal insides of the bridge.

Bigger than the two on the big asteroid-like planetoid they'd left behind, its light goes directly to Stanton. In an uncharacteristically primal yell, Stanton throws the hammer at the beast, which bounces off. Its light continues to illuminate its prey as it towers over Stanton, who freezes, shivering in fear.

"Damn it, Taggart." Are his last words as the star creature lunges its sharp limb and stabs Stanton through his chest, picking him up and throwing him into the control console, causing a great commotion of sparks and electrical pops and a lot of damage to the system. Angelique keeps the laser on it, but it keeps moving out of focal range.

"NO! You bastard!" Harper yells at the sight of seeing his longtime friend killed and lunges at the beast, stabbing at it with the spike. He stabs at the exposed black muscle strands in between the silver to see a mix of stark black and bright chrome ooze from it. It turns, revealing its underside of razor-sharp teeth, before grabbing the Captain, picking him up. Harper screams and fights on his way up, punching and kicking the beast before the monster's jaws snap, biting Harper's head off in a crunch. Blood gushes down the creature to the floor. His body, like his colleague's, is thrown into power panels, causing the same catastrophic damage. Harper's blood is sprayed around with the rest of him.

Lou Ann screams as the yellow light hits her.

Angelique hits the laser to the creature, but it seems to reflect off its chrome-plated body.

She remembers the *eye*; she needs to hit that eye.

"Hey! Hey! Over here!" Angelique tries yelling at it to get its attention, to no avail. She looks around it in time to see a fifth of its sharp limbs stabbing through Lou Ann's notebook and through her. Too stunned and too scared to move out of the way of its plunging dagger-like end, Lou Ann's speechless as it pulls its limb out of her. Her bloody pen and paper drops to the floor, and soon the rest of her joins them. The creature then stomps its sharp end down into the reporter's skull with a thick splatting noise of stomping through mud.

It spins around like she wanted. Angelique finally gets at a good angle and shoots the blue beam directly into its mouth, between its razor-sharp teeth. She raises the laser-cutter aiming for the bright yellow eye of the murderous alien being. It lunges toward her, but she keeps the cutter on target. She backs up, opens the door behind her, and backs down the corridor as it follows with big lumbering steps on two of its five pointy limbs.

Security Feed—Corridor:
The lights of the well-lit tube reflect off of the creature's metallic body as it stomps toward Angelique. She keeps the laser focused on it, trying to keep it on the big yellow eye but also trying to keep her distance.

Angelique reaches the end of the corridor when the being's power source finally gives. The yellow spotlight cracks and shatters as its sturdy strong structure falls to the floor, now looking to have the texture of a jellyfish.

It's done.

Angelique, clearly running on adrenaline, keeps the laser-cutter on it for a moment before turning it off. She doesn't blink, and her breathing is erratic. She watches the alien corpse for a solid minute before she collapses, passing out from sheer exhaustion.

Her body, almost as lifeless as her fellow crew members who weren't so fortunate, twitches in her sleep as she rests down the bright corridor from the collapsed gelatinous, metallic creature. For roughly an hour she sleeps in an exhausted slumber.

Her eyelids flutter and open, seeing the bright florescent lights around her. Her head looks over to see the corpse of the star beast, whose short but potent reign of terror was halted by her, lying at the opposite end of the corridor. She slowly gets up and eyes it before jumping over it to the bridge.

Bridge-Cam:
Angelique looks over the damaged cockpit of the *Capacitance*, scanning her head from side-to-side. An about-face to the strong, sturdy, and sterile bridge of this ship she'd known prior, bodies lie and sparks fly with blood beneath it all. Her heart can't sink any lower, and the tears won't seem to come, though they're surely requested at this time. She's devastated but can't bring herself to cry. In a zombie-like state, emotionless, Angelique realizes she's *it*, and it's time to get to work, no time to be emotional. She turns back, looking at the beast lying in its death beyond the door.

Security Feed—Lab Hall:
Angelique, *survivor*, suits up alone for the first time, still wearing her emotionless stare.

Security Feed—Corridor:
The door opens, and she enters the corridor with a couple of the retrieval bags used for the mites. Using the laser cutter, she cuts the beast into pieces and puts the pieces in the bags. With its body no longer solid, the laser doesn't reflect off its armor-like exterior. It oozes out when cut but still remains a tangible pulpy substance.

Top-Cam:
Angelique emerges from a top hatch and looks at her surroundings, alert. She reaches into the bags, grabbing the alien pulp, releasing the monstrous pieces out to drift into the universe. She watches to make sure the drifting is away from the ship before returning inside.

Security Feed—Corridor:
She continues to cut the creature up, bagging up its pieces to take them up and out, repeating this several times until the beast is gone. When finished, there's nothing left but black and chrome fluids from the monster.

Security Feed—Lab Hall:
Disrobed of her space suit, Angelique looks down at Miguel's corpse, taking a deep breath. A longtime friend, confidant, and colleague, one of the smartest men she knew, bright, funny, and loving. She bends down and hooks her hands under his arms and drags him.

Cargo Bay-Cam:
The door slides open, and Angelique walks through, lugging a loved one's lifeless body. She lays him down beside Saxon before standing up straight and stretching her back. Dr. Puck looks down at their security officer before taking a breath and shaking her head as something off to the side grabs her attention. She walks over to find a cart, a dolly, and nods.

Bridge-Cam:
The door beeps and slides open as Angelique walks in pushing the cart into the chaotically decorated room. She stops it in the center of the bridge before looking around wondering where to start, who to start with. Captain Harper is the biggest; however, headless, so she starts with him. She pulls latex gloves from her back pocket, snapping them on before reaching down to Harper's stocky body. The blood has coagulated around the bitten stump of his neck while the rest of his matter lies in a pool on the floor as well as slung around.

Angelique's face carries expressions of disgust along with sadness as she lifts him up. She can't fully lift him, so she drags him across the steel platform, resting his headless and lifeless body on the dolly.

"Whew," she says, wiping the sweat from her brow with her wrist. Looking over to Stanton, who lies on the floor with a hole through his chest large enough to reach in without touching any of the edges, she nods. "I guess you're next, buddy."

Stanton, "Pilot Extraordinaire" as he joked upon meeting Angelique, is lighter than his friend. She is able to lift him a little better, but the struggle is still there as she's used to lifting vials and samples, *not* bodies. She places Stanton beside Harper on the dolly: longtime friends, they worked together and died together, now at each other's side one last time.

Lou Ann's body is lying on the floor with a similar hole in her chest, along with one in her skull, splitting her head wide open and exposing her mangled brain and broken eye sockets. The same look of disgust stays on Angelique's face as she lifts the much lighter Lou Ann and places her on the two men.

She kneels down to her brief lover, turning her over. She holds Chloe, looking down. Her eyes well up but still no tears stream as she wipes her eyes before they can emerge. The silver appearance once coating Chloe's eyes is gone.

"If I could kiss you, I would, but I still don't think it's safe. I trust you'd understand," Angelique says, running her hand through Chloe's messy hair. She picks the young woman up and walks to lay her down gently across the pile of the deceased.

Angelique sighs before looking over the puddle of mess and the skeleton within it, what's left of Toni, her friend and colleague of many years. It's hard to believe that this is even her. Hours ago, she was flesh and blood and now she's no more than a skeleton with even bits of her bones bitten away. She picks up her friend's skeletal structure carefully, to not drop any of her pieces. The skeleton goes on top of the stack, softly.

One more look at the room blanketed with interstellar atrocity, and she's off, pushing the cart, so heavy now it's giving her resistance.

Cargo Bay-Cam:
The door opens, and she continues to struggle pushing the cart as she and the rest of her crew enter the cargo bay. Though crew members normally take the small set of steps to get down here, she uses the elevator-like lift for transferring things via dolly. She looks for the body bags Harper spoke of. She finds them and returns. One by one, she bags them up, not removing their clothing as they might be contaminated. Other than Toni and Miguel, Angelique doesn't put them in any specific order; she places them in the bags as carefully and respectfully as possible.

Saxon and Miguel are put in their black body bags first. Toni's skeleton is put in gently. She puts Stanton's hat on him before closing his. Angelique's look of disgust and horror doesn't change between placing Harper and Lou Ann in theirs. The last in this grouping and, hopefully the last time she'll ever have to do this, Chloe is placed in hers. Angelique looks down at her, the last time she'll ever actually see her, before zipping up the bag. Still kneeling, she lines them up. Seven corpses, seven black bags. Of the many uses this ship has and the many things it was to everyone, none of them would've imagined "hearse" to join the list.

Angelique prays over them. "Dearly departed, you were all taken too soon. We weren't trained for this, but all of you did the best you could do in the situation we found ourselves in. You're with the Lord now. I wish I could give you all a proper service and burial, but I'm not in any position to do so. I trust you'd understand." She sniffles. "Heavenly Father, please look over these seven, *your children*. Toni, Miguel, Chloe, Harper, Stanton, Lou Ann, and Saxon are all in your kingdom. Please have mercy on any of their past wrong doings. Our Father, who art in Heaven, hallowed be thy name, thy kingdom come, thy will be done, on Earth...and in space...as it is in Heaven. *Amen.*"

Control Panel-Cam:
Angelique sits down in Stanton's seat and flips on the communicator. Upon hitting the switch, sparks fly briefly with electrical pops, and she jumps back.

"Great. I don't even know if this is going to work." She tries anyway. "This is Dr. Angelique Puck of the *Capacitance* to base on a distress call. My crew—*they're all dead. SOS.*"

She grabs the manual controls and turns them every way possible only to have the ship remain stationary.

"Shit! You're kidding me. Don't do this to me now." She looks everything over, flipping every switch for any kind of controls. *Nothing.* "Piloting Controls... Navigation... Steering Controls..."

She tries any kind of voice command she can think of and is met with the same silence as outside the ship.

"Shit..." Her head slings back with closed eyes.

Angelique looks up and around her. "Well, I guess I better clean this up..."

Her eyes dart around, and her breathing goes from shallow to deep and back to shallow, matching her erratic heartbeat. Terrified, she'll try to distract herself the best she can.

Ship Journal Continued:

With a bucket of scrubbers, towels, and cans of disinfectant, I began cleaning the mess the beast's corpse left in the lit tube of a hallway. On my hands and knees, I scrubbed without a single thought of testing the liquid for any reason. I just wanted it gone, clean. The creature's fluids were thick and gelatinous like its body became upon dying.

I looked around the bridge, still in disbelief. I sighed and got to work, starting with the pool of blood from our decapitated Captain. The room was full of different blood as well as the bodies of the little critters we'd managed to kill in the heavy scuffle. When I was done with the floor and the walls, I cleaned off the control panel the best I could. Moving from one pool of blood to another, I scrubbed until the bridge looked somewhat like it used to before terror had found us.

Holding my parents' picture once again, I prayed silently, long and hard. Staying so strong throughout that time without breaking down, it was time for a much needed breakdown. Everything poured out. My sobs, tears of sadness, loneliness, and fear projected from me much like Chloe's vomiting of tiny alien lifeforms. In my violent sobs, my hands nearly crumpled up the photograph before dropping it.

I slumped over as it hit me what had taken place, not just the creatures and the horror and death, but the fact that I was *it* and the ship was, for lack of a better term, broken down. My friends, my new lover, my pilot and captain, my colleagues: all dead with their passing forever branded in my mind. Survivor's remorse kicked in as much as the fear of the creatures' return. After letting out scream upon scream, and coughing from the strain, I fell back into my bed and cried myself to sleep while, even in slumber, the crying continued.

//

Simulation

I wake up to the sight of the dark, nothingness, wondering if I am awake, or even alive. Above me, a top opens. The light is blinding at first, but my eyes adjust. I'm in a sleep pod of some kind laden with padding.

Groggy, I sit up to see the rest of my crew doing the same as we're looking around this stark white room and at each other. I can't believe what I'm seeing. In the pod next to me is Chloe, alive and well like the rest of them. I want to shout "You're alive!", but I don't want to sound like a lunatic. Some of the crew are shaking their heads, trying to catch their bearings. Toni and Miguel, perfectly fine, look at each other with a chuckle. I can't take my eyes off of Chloe, Toni, and Miguel; I'm so happy they're alive. We all look at each other.

Could it all have been a dream? Are we still on the *Capacitance?* Where are we? I have a medical bracelet on, containing a barcode. The others seem to have them as well.

"One hell of a sleep. I don't know about you all, but I could use some coffee," Stanton says, rubbing his eyes and stretching, looking to the rest of us.

"Well, *that* was a trip, Doctor," Captain Harper says to me.

I nod, confused, noticing there are only six of us: Harper, Stanton, Toni, Miguel, Chloe, and myself. Where are the other two?

A door opens, breaking the solid white of our surroundings and men in lab coats enter.

"I see you all are up," one of them says, checking the monitors beside each of our pods.

I raise my hand. "I'm sorry, I don't understand. Were we *dreaming?*"

"You all have been in a simulation for forty-eight hours. Though, I'm sure it felt like more, months even. Each of you experienced different situations, encounters, emotions, and feelings," the scientist says as he and his team continue to work.

I look down and around the room; my crew and I are in white hospital gowns. One of them, apparently a nurse, is checking vitals of some of the others. It's *Lou Ann.*

"Lou Ann?" I ask, staring right at the woman. She and the doctor stop what they're doing and look at me and each other intermittently.

"This is Luanna. She's our resident nurse who's been checking in on you all throughout the process," the scientist replies.

I'm still lost. "I'm sorry. *Who* are you, again?"

"I'm Dr. Nelson," he says before lightly chuckling. "Don't worry, the fuzzy memory is only temporary. It looks like you all did well with our little simulation trial. You'll be set to leave momentarily. I'm going to go and make sure to get you all checked out."

Come to think of it, he *does* look a lot like Nelson.

He opens the door and there's an armed guard standing outside the room. It's *Saxon.*

"What's with the guard, doctor?" Stanton asks.

The doctor turns around. "Oh, that's Sexton. We thought it best to have someone watching the door while you all were in here, liabilities and all," he says, exiting.

I appear to be the only one noticing the three. We get up to leave as Chloe looks at me and smiles. Could she remember something?

My crew and I stand up, exiting our pods on shaky legs. We all take a stretch before we leave the room. I notice the door, and its sign

"SimLab 7". I think hard and exhale, trying to make sense of it all. We walk down long, stark white corridors.

Down the hall, Miguel speaks up, "I don't know about you all, but I am starving."

Stanton says, "I could definitely use some grub."

A few hallways more and we find ourselves at the cafeteria in this building, appearing as blank as the rest of it. We move through the line, filling up our trays with food, but I'm still feeling off. I feel like I'm the only one with this strange paranoia as everyone else looks fine. We're still in our gowns and medical bracelets. We sit at one of the many empty tables and eat.

"Man, I don't remember a thing. What about you all?" Stanton asks.

"I remember my wife and me talking, and I remember some system failures, but it all gets blurry after that." Harper's the first to actually answer.

I keep thinking about how in my "dream" Harper's wife became a widow. Harper was a good man, and he died screaming, which apparently was only in my version of the simulation.

Miguel points to his wife. "We were in space, and you were pregnant. We were going to have a baby in space, at least *conceived* there." He shrugs before taking a bite.

"Oh, wow," Toni says. "I think I remember something like that. I remember you being really cold, like ice, but I can't think of why. What about you, 'Lique?"

"There were these creatures that looked like metal starfish, only their legs moved like spiders, and they were pointy like knives." Of course I remember a lot more clearly, but I don't really want to go into it all at this point.

They all stare at me.

"Damn, Angelique, they gave you the good stuff." Miguel and the others laugh.

I chuckle and shake my head.

Stanton rubs his chest at a *particular* spot.

"You okay?" I ask.

"Aw yeah, eating too fast I think," he answers in his nonchalant tone.

I look to the beautiful girl sitting beside me. "What about you, Chloe?"

"I...I don't remember anything," Chloe says.

We all continue to eat while, under the table, she slides her hand over my thigh giving it a strong caressing squeeze. My heart skips a beat, and I look over to her as she's smiling and winking at me.

We finish our food and head back to our rooms to get our stuff. I don't even remember having rooms for this, same as I don't remember signing up to take part in any kind of simulation, but Stanton reminded us about the rooms when he pulled out his keycard at lunch. We all had them on us, unbeknownst to me. Down yet another white hallway, our rooms are all right beside each other. The hallway of doors looks almost like a sterile hotel, rooms in this medical complex of sorts.

My crew and I look down at the numbers on our cards, matching them up with the room numbers. Mine says 7575–my crew login number, odd. The keycards are swiped complete with beeping.

"Well, gang, this has been fun. We should do it again sometime," Stanton jokes.

"Hey, best sleep I've had in a while." Toni chuckles.

I'm about to head into my room when my neighbor, Chloe, looks to me, biting her lip. She waves at me with her fingers lightly, and I smile back before heading into this room I have no memory of ever being in to get dressed and, I suppose, go home.

Inside this room, I grab my jacket out of the closet, my clothes out of the dresser, and my bag off of the bed, and I turn around finding, to my surprise, Chloe standing in front of me.

"Angelique," she says to me.

I drop my things, and we grab each other, engaging in a kiss heavier than our supposed slumber in simulation. I can't believe she's alive, and she remembers what we had; she still wants me as I do her. She tastes incredible. Her hands run down my back, grabbing my ass, while I run my fingers through her soft hair, grabbing handfuls and kissing her harder.

Then it stops.

I wake up, still in the *Capacitance*. Another dream. I'm lying in Chloe's bed with my hair in my hands, wishing it was still hers. A dream that makes me miss her even more. I miss them all.

//

NEWS REPORT - A PLEA
Streaming from the logs of the *Capacitance*.

The news keeps feeding: a woman, sad and homely, speaks directly to a camera in her living room.

"Dr. Angelique Puck, you may not remember me, but you helped me once when I was given the Nu-Myelin Cell. My Multiple Sclerosis was getting aggressively worse, and you and your team helped me, *saved* me. But I come to you now, pleading, begging you to help my son like you once helped me."

The woman steps over as the camera follows her to see a young man, chair bound with his head tilted, staring out. "As you can see, my son has contracted Rabid Neural Stasis and I...I don't know what else to do. Please, save him like you did me. My son deserves to be healthy. He used to be such a vibrant young man."

She becomes too choked up speaking of her lifeless son, who stares with nothing in his eyes. She waves her hand for them to cut camera.

//

Ship Journal
Dr. Angelique Puck: Login: 7575
Subject: **Recovery**

My team assembled, and we set sail into the dark sea above us, the great black yonder. It was to be a standard medical mission in hopes to find more cures. One in particular, Rabid Neural Stasis, a disease practically turning Earth into a world of zombies bite by bite with no cure or treatment. That is where we came in. I was often questioned why we weren't looking for alien life or planets we could inhabit instead; I suppose curing diseases plaguing countless people isn't good enough to satisfy the curiosities of the universe. People who grew up on science fiction stories had set the bar so high in their minds, putting galactic travel on a pedestal so when great things come of our quests, they aren't looked at so much as revolutionary but disappointing as they aren't as big and tangible as expected.

The marvels we had found before this mission were indeed grand but on a personal scale. People could grow up healthier, with options for their ailments they hadn't had prior; however, there are those who'd prefer we'd find giant robots and monstrous creatures. Their wants for such finds *could* be said to be in the hopes they'd have the answers we'd always sought out or even technology to further our status as efficient war lords.

I, on the other hand, feel their wants for such fantastical things lie in their constant desire for entertainment. Entertainment is the biggest drug in the galaxy. One starts small, enjoying something, and then they need more, bigger, and better. They could send one group up into space to find medical answers and another up to find individuals they'd hoped to be the "Rulers of the Galaxy" and more civilian support would be found for the latter. Sad but true.

Advancements in medical science are life-changing, large, and frequent, but it doesn't get the desired love from the public as it's not physically a big find. It's all in the eye of the beholder, and people need something of a substantial physical size to consider it an epic, world-altering phenomenon. However, if those very people were to find themselves met with the terror we found, their positions and opinions would, without a doubt, change.

Things have been tough since the demise of my crew. I can't get it all out of my head and I don't think I ever will. It still strikes me ironic that the security Nelson had forced us to take on, a former soldier itching to fight, was the first to die. That, then, could've been a sign of what was about to take place. At the time of everything going down, I was at a loss for thought, a loss for words, and a loss for all logic and emotion.

I periodically check on them to make sure there's no creepy crawlies in there with them or using their bodies as hosts or even husks. I didn't know what I was going to do. It was like living this horrible nightmare, losing everyone, deadly creatures, left all alone in the far reaches of space without communication, cut off from any and everyone, I just wanted to wake up.

I still go on walks to gather the little magnetic mites, but I won't lie, regardless of how far away from the metal and stone mass I am, I still keep an eye out for those aliens, monsters, *whatever they are*. Thinking back on it all, I suppose *we* were the aliens invading *its* territory. The way the smaller creatures fused and grafted together, forming the Goliath makes me ponder: if they were all encased in the mass over time, did they form together in their forced proximity or are there simply different sizes and breeds within the species? Whatever the answer, I don't wish to see anything larger than the mite-sized beings anytime soon, if not ever again.

While the magnetic propulsion seems to be pushing me along, I still have no drive in the ship. My communicators are still down, and I can't tell if any of my distress calls have gone out at all. All I can do is hope and pray at least one distress call has made it through. Lonely isn't a strong enough word for how I feel at the moment. I have me, these pictures, memories, this journal, and some amazing medical finds to keep me company, and while at one point in time that would've been enough to keep me content, it doesn't do anything for me now. Not sure what any of it means anymore.

What good are a cure and a blood enhancement if they never make it back home to actually be put to work? What good is a piece of art if it's never seen? What good is life if it isn't lived?

I always grew up feeling different, searching for something and trying to make a difference. I had always felt I was supposed to go on to do great things. It was a yearning in me. Of course, I never thought about the sacrifice of myself and loved ones that would have to take place. So often, the world doesn't see what we're fighting for...and just how hard we fight for it.

I have helped eradicate complications with Multiple Sclerosis and have received much love from the MS community. My team helped bring an end to certain cancers and various forms of lupus. While I've always considered myself a strong, black, gay woman, I can now say that *this* scientist has defeated one of the worst diseases to ever hit the human race, and I find joy in that pride, regardless of its downsides. If I ever get to sleep in my own bed again, I'll find solace in a peaceful, relaxing sleep without the worry of what to fix next along with no worry of whether or not alien creatures might somehow find their way in while I rest.

I'm in the lab again, checking on my last test, whether one strand of cured blood can be passed on to the next with the same effect. I check my tubes and drip the fluid beneath my lens to have a look and...Success! If one person is cured, *that* person's blood can be given to the next and so forth—a cure distributed throughout the human race. This is a bigger find than what I could've ever hoped for. My colleagues did not die in vain, and to say it makes me happy and warms my heart is an understatement. It doesn't bring them back or change what had happened, but it is something of a positive among the list of negatives. At this point, a thought like this certainly helps me keep going. While I'm in the lab, I look over to the lone particle I placed in a jar to see if they'd lose power eventually, and while it appears lethargic, it's far from dead. Their longevity is a good sign, a little miracle of science.

I look at the other medical find, placing the uninfected blood, injected with the liquid chrome molecular corpses, on the glass under my microscope. It hasn't diminished. Wonderful. I still can't believe how enhanced the nutrients are in it. I wonder how much longer the average human being could live with this kind of addition to their system. I don't know how long I'm going to be out here, and since it's *my* discovery, I'm taking it upon myself to be the first living subject.

I find a thin rubber hose as well as a sterilized syringe. I'm filling it now, and it looks like liquid metal swirling about. I tie my tourniquet on and attempt to find the right vein.
Got it. The needle's in. I pull the plunger back a little drawing some of my blood out as it mixes with the chrome fluid. Even before I push it down, I see how it mixes. I push the plunger down, injecting myself with the blood enhancing particles, the corpses of microorganisms, and feel it course through my body. I take off the rubber hose tourniquet and put the needle to the side. It's instantly chilly, a cold metallic feeling but then warms up to match the rest of my blood's temperature. It runs throughout my bloodstream fast. Energy pumps through me along with my blood. It feels like getting a jump and my battery is recharged. I can't remember the last time I've felt this healthy. It works fast, this serum. My body's engine works with a nitrous oxide boost.

I'm my own guinea pig. With my newfound energy and the abundance of time, I decide to take this time to write down every detail of both discoveries: how I found them, what they are, and how to apply them to patients. With my mind and hands moving at almost inhuman speeds, I fill out the paperwork, listing everything needed to know along with any added thoughts or suggestions.

I knew the Nu-Myelin Cell had more to offer than what we were getting out of it, but I didn't know the extent of the richness held within the very same species. We would've never found it or had nearly enough had we not made this trip. We would've never found the positive and negative magnetic activity had I not had such a good crew here to point it out.

The blood-vitamin improvement seems as it could be as important as the RNS cure itself. With the exact same dosage of the same treatment we can have a better tomorrow. Military factions could be advancing their soldiers' health. Professional athletes could greatly benefit from it as well. I can only imagine what this would do giving it to newborn babies, how much healthier they'd grow up. The next generation will last longer and live happier, more fulfilled lives. Though I'm currently surrounded by the cold black of deep space, the sun is coming over the horizon for a brighter tomorrow.

Done with my report, I make two copies so I have one to keep in the lab, one to put up on the bridge, and one to keep on me. I've got no drive or communication, but thank God my copier still works. I've dubbed the cure "*The Capacitance Gene.*" Sometime after our attack, I took our bags, which were completely full of the little space mites collected from the planetoid we'd found, and separated the positives and negatives. It was a bit awkward and complicated to do alone, but given that I didn't have any other pressing engagements, I was able to get it done.

Now that both of the casings are full, I've made extra sure they're sealed tight. If by chance I am rescued, then I'll have everything set to go. I spent my life trying to help people and trying to get to the stars, and while I've certainly helped some people, I'm ready to leave the open universe for the safe confines of my home on Earth.

I'm back on the bridge, along with my file and my two cases of little, chrome, interstellar microorganisms, sending out yet another distress call. I'm curious if these calls are actually getting out, but because of the damage to the system, I can't see or hear on my end. I can only hope. I check the scope and extend the three levels of magnification: black, black, and more black only with stars in the distance.

When and if I get back, the first thing I'll have to do is hold a press conference for the lives lost, something I'm not looking forward to doing—more necessary evils. I know danger is in the nature of experimental science and we did reach our goal; however, I still feel guilty about surviving. It was my mission with my choices, yet I'm still here while seven innocent people tragically lost their lives. It'll always be with me. They'll always be with me.

//

Last Rites

Stem-Cam:
Deep space: as lifeless as it is colorless. At the moment, the stars in the distance seem disinterested in twinkling or even showing themselves for that matter. This camera at the nose of the ship shakes and vibrates as large asteroids hit and ricochet off the *Capacitance*. More of them are revealed as they hurl through the black, clashing into each other in their movement. The camera shakes more, along with its sight of a suddenly asteroid-filled space. Up close and incredibly fast, a cluster of rocks collide and break apart as pieces ricochet toward the camera, growing larger in their proximity.

Stern-Cam:
The magnetic propulsion apparatus is destroyed, smashed to pieces to drift out like the stones at fault. This camera shakes with more oncoming asteroids. The growing field is thick and hurling fast—too fast. Multiple meteors come at the backend of the ship, demolishing the frost covered rockets and soon the camera among them.

Top-Cam:
Asteroids of different sizes and shapes cover this stretch of space the *Capacitance* has currently found itself drifting. Despite not being home to alien lifeforms and being only rocks, the ship is pelted, bombarded with them. Various lights on the ship's exterior are broken upon the random collisions as the vision of the *Capacitance* is joining the darkness around it.

The camera's knocked inches to the side during its oscillation. Amidst the free flowing stones, one comes *right* for the camera: growing larger, getting closer, contact.

DocLab 7-Cam:
Angelique stands, barely, on shaky legs in her lab where everything is thrown around and jolted from its placing, even worse than their trip through the satellite debris. The *Capacitance* is being pummeled, taking quite a beating. Angelique, now in her space suit, can barely stand it's shaking so badly.

"I've run into an asteroid field or meteor shower of sorts, and I fear

I don't have long, s—so this will be my last entry." She gathers the cure and the paperwork. "If Stanton were here, he'd take us right out of this with no problem."

She suits up as fast as possible and grabs her valuables, awaiting anything that might happen and puts on her helmet with Chloe's lip prints still barely visible on the glass. The ship's being hit harder. She falls into the wall with the next hit.

"I can only hope somebody discovers this ship one day to find my notes and help save the world."

She's thrown again. The lab's camera shakes and vibrates violently.

Security Feed—Lab Hall:
Angelique rushes out, and her head whips back to the end of the hall as a loud smash and clatter is far too audible back toward the Sleep Hall. Angelique turns and runs as fast as she can to the front of the ship as the vicious pelting continues.

Break Room-Cam:
Angelique enters the break room before stopping, barely dodging the fridge as it's hurled to the floor, smashing upon impact. She scurries across the room as more items are thrown in the ship's turbulence.

Security Feed—Corridor:
She runs through the tube which used to be lit but now, due to the blows from oncoming asteroids, a good deal of the lights have broken. She steps on the broken glass, crushing it on her trek.

"I wish this ship had an escape pod of some kind, but Harper said he never had a reason for them. Allow me and my current predicament to be the reason all starships should come with escape pods."

She stumbles with the next quake. More lights break and the corridor becomes darker, almost black. She can practically feel sections of the ship behind her being torn and her heart's racing. The lump in her throat is so large she's almost choking on it. The last light goes out as she finds her way to the door through the darkness. She opens the door to the bridge, trying not to cry and to stay focused.

Bridge-Cam:
Angelique rushes in, holding her items tightly in her bag, to see from the window the storm of stones being hurled at various speeds smashing into the ship and each other.

"Oh my God," she says through panting. The *Capacitance* is tattered and bombarded as the universe shows no mercy. "Currents..." a thought to herself comes out quietly. Alerts and sirens are sounding off along with the distant sounds of the ship's destruction.

Control Panel-Cam:
Angelique sits down, turns on the communicator, and looks into the camera.

"This is Dr. Angelique Puck. I am the sole survivor of the *Capacitance*. I—I never meant to lead us to *this*. I've lost good people, and I'm...I'm *so sorry*. Toni, Miguel, Chloe, Stanton, Harper, Lou Ann, Saxon, I'll never forget you, and I'm so sorry for your loss and your families' loss."

She tears up, and her heavy breathing fogs up the glass of her helmet. The smashing and clashing against the *Capacitance* continues. She nods and bucks up as if the rocks bludgeoning her and her crew's temporary home are hurrying her along.

"Toni and Miguel, you are two of the kindest people as well as two of the best friends and colleagues a woman could have. You were brave for coming along on such a crazy journey. Stanton, pilot extraordinaire, my friend, you're piloting the heavens now."

Her speech picks up, blurting out everything she feels.

"Harper, easily the nicest and most easygoing captain I've had the courtesy of working with, your wife should be proud of you. Lou Ann and Saxon, we didn't get along and being a part of this mission surely wasn't your choice, but I would never wish your death on anyone. You're in a better place now."

The ship is bludgeoned once more, almost shaking Angelique out of her seat, but she holds on tight and takes a deep breath before exhaling while continuing her last rites.

"Chloe, sweet Chloe...you were so kind and so gorgeous. You mended my broken heart and warmed a place in me that had gone cold. You'll always hold a place in my heart. Mom and Dad, I know you're proud of me, and I know you love me. I love you, and I miss you, and I wish you were here. You'll always be the foundation of the woman I am today." Angelique continues, "Serena, I'm sorry things didn't work out between us, and I know you'll find someone more suited for you. To all those who could've been saved by the cure we'd found, I apologize from the bottom of my heart. I tried my best, I really did."

Bridge-Cam:
A small meteor amidst the storm hits the window, cracking its outer layer, as Angelique jumps up and back with a scream. She backs up, heart pounding and lungs inflating and deflating at an erratic pace.

"I'm so sorry for everything," she says through the lump in her throat while shaking her head. "If I hadn't have pushed to find that horrid place, everyone would still be *alive*. I've tried to get past it for the sake of survival, but it'll always be with me." She continues to back up while speaking in a stream of conscious. "While I found what I was looking for, I'm not so sure we belong this far out anymore. This deep into the vast universe is for deadly creatures and stars we'll never reach. Maybe we were never meant to reach them, I don't know."

Break Room-Cam:
Their dining area is still seen, albeit very little and completely trashed. The screen displaying a constant feed of news dangles from the wall with flickering images. Smash and quake—more blows delivered to the *Capacitance* from the universe.

Security Feed—Corridor:
Completely dark. Glass is heard shaking, breaking more, and there is a constant rumbling.

Bridge-Cam:

Angelique stands, alert and terrified, watching the craziness from her window.

"I don't know how much longer I have left." With her items in her bag hanging at her side, her hands comes together. "God, *thank you*. Thank you for making this ongoing, beautiful, and scary universe. I've had the chance to witness what most people only dream of, and I am eternally grateful for it. To the world, I'm *sorry*. I can only hope you find what we did before the entire world is infected."

It feels and sounds like the meteors are getting closer to this end of this ship, and they're hitting harder and more frequent. Another loud clash, closer. The Stargazer is smashed above. From the window, which used to hold the most gorgeous, picturesque views, the asteroid field is only getting thicker and more are coming in this direction. Angelique is struck in her movement, stopped where she stands. She looks at her hands and down at her body.

"Some—something is happening to me. I can feel it in my blood. It feels like the energy boost again, but it's different. My lungs are inflating, but they feel full, coated. I feel strong, confident. My skin is taut, solid like steel. Like the mites, it feels like I'm protected by some unseen sheath—an invisible bumper both encasing and surrounding me. I think it's *preparing* me. I—I—I don't know what it's doing. My whole body's tingling. I feel lifted, something's holding me."

She holds close her bag containing 'The Capacitance Gene' and her parents' photograph, among other items, awaiting the end in her newfound strength. The *Capacitance* is pummeled harder with strong solidity at harsh velocities. The alerts and sirens still ring loudly but not as loud as the onslaught from outside. She takes a deep breath with closed eyes and nods. Her eyes open. She's steady in the violently shaky ship.

"This is Dr. Angelique Puck signing off."

//

NEWS REPORT - WHAT'S YOUR GOAL?
Streaming from the logs of the *Capacitance*.

The lone monitor still plays its stream of cataloged news footage; however, the screen is cracked and barely held together while sparks pop in its darkened surroundings. The current news hardly able to be seen on such a tattered and fractured screen: Dr. Angelique Puck stands behind a paper covered table with microphones. "RNS Press Conference" scrolls across the bottom of the screen. She's painted with the flashes of various cameras.

"Thank you all for coming," she says, sitting down at the table.

"Dr. Puck...Dr. Puck..." A reporter fights to get her question in before the barrage of others.

"Yes," Angelique says, selecting this eager woman.

"What do you hope to accomplish with this expedition?" she asks.

Sparks fly with electrical pops as the screen's image is beginning to give out like the rest of the ship's power, flickering as the monitor is starting to fall apart.

Angelique thinks briefly before answering with a smile. "A brighter future *for all of us.*"

"So often, the world doesn't see what we're fighting for...and just how hard we fight for it."

ABOUT THE AUTHOR

Christopher Michael Carter was born on May 3rd, 1984 in St. Louis, Missouri. His previous poetry includes *Gun Control for Polar Bears* and *Reflections at Various Speeds*. Christopher and his family currently reside in Bevier, Missouri.

www.ingramcontent.com/pod-product-compliance
Lightning Source LLC
Chambersburg PA
CBHW070918190726
48292CB00004B/1020